ENTANGLED WITH THE DUKE

Historical Regency Romance

THE DUKES' LADIES
BOOK 1

ABBY AYLES

This is a work of fiction.

Names, characters, organizations, places, events, and incidents are either products of the author's imagination or are used fictitiously. Any resemblance to actual person, living or dead, or actual events is purely coincidental.

PRAISE FOR ABBY AYLES

Abby Ayles has been such an inspiration for me! I haven't missed any of her novels and she has never failed my expectations!

-Edith Byrd

The characters in this novel have surely touched my heart.

Linda C - "Melting a Duke's Winter Heart" 5.0 out of 5 stars Reviewed in the United States on December 21, 2019

This book kept me on the edge of my seat and I could not put it down.

Wendy Ferreira - "The Odd Mystery of the Cursed

Duke" 5.0 out of 5 stars Reviewed in the United States on April 13, 2019

Oh this was a wonderful story and Abby has done it again! This storyline was perfect and the characters were developed and just had you reading to see if they get their happily ever after!

- Marilyn Smith - "Inconveniently Betrothed to an Earl" 5.0 out of 5 stars Reviewed in the United States on April 8, 2020

The sweetest story, with we rest abounding! I especially liked the bonus scene - totally unexpected engagements. Well written with realistic characters. Thank you!

Janet Tonole - "The Lady Of the Lighthouse" 5.0 out of 5 stars Reviewed in the United States on December 27, 2022

I just finished reading Abby Ayles' The Lady's Gamble and its bonus scene, and I wanted to tell other readers about this great story. I love regency romances and I believe Abby is one of the best regency writers out there!

Carolynn Padgett - "The Lady's Gamble" 5.0 out of 5 stars Reviewed in the United States on March 16, 2018

Such a great Book! So enjoyed the characters....they felt so " real"....and loved the " deleted" scene. Thanks Abby, for your gift of writing the best stories!

Marcia Reckard - "Entangled with the Duke" 5.0 out of 5 stars Reviewed in the United States on May 22, 2021

I loved this story. It took you through all of the exciting ups and downs. The characters were so honest. I could read it again and again.

Peggy Murphy - "The Duke's Rebellious Daughter" 5.0 out of 5 starsReviewed in the United States on December 3, 2022

I am never disappointed when reading one of Ms. Ayles stories. They have strong characters, engaging storylines, and all-around wonderful stories.

Donna L - "A Loving Duke for the Shy Duchess" 5.0 out of 5 stars Reviewed in the United States on December 23, 2019

A thoroughly enjoyable read! Love the complexity of the intelligent characters! They have the ability to feel emotions deeply! Their backstories help to explain why they behave as they do! The subplots and various interactions between characters add to the wonderful richness of the story! Well done!

Terry Rose Bailey - "A Cinderella for the Duke" 5.0 out of 5 stars Reviewed in the United States on October 8, 2022

ALSO BY ABBY AYLES

The Keys to a Lockridge Heart

Melting a Duke's Winter Heart

A Loving Duke for the Shy Duchess

Freed by the Love of an Earl

The Earl's Wager for a Lady's Heart

The Lady in the Gilded Cage

A Reluctant Bride for the Baron

A Christmas Worth Remembering

A Guiding Light for the Lost Earl

The Earl Behind the Mask

Tales of Magnificent Ladies

The Odd Mystery of the Cursed Duke

A Second Chance for the Tormented Lady
Capturing the Viscount's Heart
The Lady's Patient
A Broken Heart's Redemption
The Lady The Duke And the Gentleman
Desire and Fear
A Tale of Two Sisters
What the Governess is Hiding

Betrayal and Redemption

Inconveniently Betrothed to an Earl
A Muse for the Lonely Marquess
Reforming the Rigid Duke
Stealing Away the Governess
A Healer for the Marquess's Heart
How to Train a Duke in the Ways of Love
Betrayal and Redemption
The Secret of a Lady's Heart
The Lady's Right Option

Forbidden Loves and Dashing Lords

The Lady of the Lighthouse
A Forbidden Gamble for the Duke's Heart

A Forbidden Bid for a Lady's Heart

A Forbidden Love for the Rebellious Baron

Saving His Lady from Scandal

A Lady's Forgiveness

Viscount's Hidden Truths

A Poisonous Flower for the Lady

Marriages by Mistake

The Lady's Gamble

Engaging Love

Caught in the Storm of a Duke's Heart

Marriage by Mistake

The Language of a Lady's Heart

The Governess and the Duke

Saving the Imprisoned Earl

Portrait of Love

From Denial to Desire

The Duke's Christmas Ball

The Dukes' Ladies

Entangled with the Duke

A Mysterious Governess for the Reluctant Earl

A Cinderella for the Duke

Falling for the Governess
Saving Lady Abigail
Secret Dreams of a Fearless Governess
A Daring Captain for Her Loyal Heart
Loving A Lady
Unlocking the Secrets of a Duke's Heart
The Duke's Rebellious Daughter
The Duke's Juliet

SCANDALS AND SEDUCTION IN REGENCY ENGLAND

Also in this series

Last Chance for the Charming Ladies

Redeeming Love for the Haunted Ladies

Broken Hearts and Doting Earls

The Keys to a Lockridge Heart

Regency Tales of Love and Mystery

Chronicles of Regency Love

Broken Dukes and Charming Ladies

The Ladies, The Dukes and Their Secrets

Regency Tales of Graceful Roses

The Secret to the Ladies' Hearts

The Return of the Courageous Ladies

Falling for the Hartfield Ladies

Extraordinary Tales of Regency Love

Dukes' Burning Hearts

Escaping a Scandal

Regency Loves of Secrecy and Redemption
Forbidden Loves and Dashing Lords
Fateful Romances in the Most Unexpected Places
The Mysteries of a Lady's Heart
Regency Widows Redemption
The Secrets of Their Heart
Lovely Dreams of Regency Ladies
Second Chances for Broken Hearts
Trapped Ladies
Light to the Marquesses' Hearts
Falling for the Mysterious Ladies
Tales of Secrecy and Enduring Love
Fateful Twists and Unexpected Loves
Regency Wallflowers
Regency Confessions
Ladies Laced with Grace
Journals of Regency Love
A Lady's Scarred Pride
How to Survive Love
Destined Hearts in Troubled Times
Ladies Loyal to their Hearts
The Mysteries of a Lady's Heart
Secrets and Scandals
A Lady's Secret Love
Falling for the Wrong Duke

GET ABBY'S EXCLUSIVE MATERIAL

Building a relationship with my readers is the very best thing about writing.

Join my newsletter for information on new books and deals plus a few free books!

You can get your books by clicking or visiting the link below

https://BookHip.com/JBWAHR

PS. Come join our Facebook Group if you want to interact with me and other authors from Starfall Publication on a daily basis, win FREE Giveaways and find out when new content is being released.

Join our Facebook Group

abbyayles.com/Facebook-Group

ENTANGLED WITH THE DUKE

She had long resigned from a life of love. He had long resigned from a life of settlement. But destiny never resigns when love is at stake.

Alexandra Woodley, daughter to the Earl of Grebs, has taken on the task of raising her three younger sisters and running the family's household. Her own future is long forgotten, she has to ensure that her sisters don't share her fate.

. . .

Theodore Hendricks, the Duke of Raven is a handsome and eligible bachelor who has no single care in the world. Adventure is all he seeks and the world is full of it.

A mere misunderstanding brings them to each other's acquaintance and nothing will ever be the same. Raven makes Alexandra an offer she cannot resist. This may be Alexandra's only chance to save her family...or ruin it once and for all.

1

Lady Alexandra Woodley searched feverishly through the basket of freshly washed clothes. She knew she was rumpling the soft cotton fabrics but had little time to care about it.

She made a note to apologize later to Polly, the maid, for making her ironing twice as difficult this week, despite her frantic rush.

If her sister's white evening gloves were not amongst the rest of the white fabric freshly removed from the line this morning, Lady Alexandra was sure she had no idea where else to look.

In frustration, she sifted through nightgowns, handkerchiefs, and cream-colored petticoats only to come up empty-handed.

She huffed, sitting back on her heels. The puff of air sent up a chestnut lock that had fallen in her face.

“I found them, miss!” Polly said bursting into the drawing room.

“Oh thank heaven, Polly. You’re an angel,” Lady Alexandra said taking the long evening gloves out of the young maid's hands.

“Where ever did you find them?” Lady Alexandra continued, coming off the freshly polished wooden floors to stand before the girl.

“They were under young Lady Sophia’s pillow,” Polly said with a cocked brow. “Going out of her way to make such trouble ain’t right if you ask me.”

Alexandra couldn’t have agreed with the maid more at that moment. Sophia Woodley was the youngest of the Woodley sisters, totaling four in all, and by far the most challenging one.

“I will make sure to speak with her and father sternly over the matter later tonight,” Alexandra informed Polly.

She was all too aware that Sophia’s little attempt to delay the three older girls from their departure this night had not only caused more work for Alexandra but for the entire house on the whole.

The Earl of Grebs had little to his name besides his four daughters. It made hired help a limited commodity, causing their two maids, one butler, and one cook to take on the task of several jobs throughout the day. Sophia’s stunt had robbed Polly of precious time that would have been used on other tasks.

Alexandra made a note to do her best to express that fact to her youngest and most carefree sister. Perhaps even make the child write a letter of apology to the maid.

It indeed wasn't a proper act for a lady to write a note of remorse to one's servant, but Alexandra also knew how much Sophia despised her schoolwork and the added labor seemed a fitting punishment for the crime.

"Josephine," Alexandra called down the hall as she made her way out of the one and only sitting room and up the stairs to the main bedrooms of the house.

She found her next eldest sister still sitting in front of the small vanity in the room the four girls shared.

"Josephine," Alexandra said, a little winded for the second time from the hurried walk to her sister's side. "Polly has found the missing gloves."

Alexandra threw them on one of the two large beds that served as sleeping quarters for the four sisters. She sat down next to them feeling her body sink down in the freshly turned bed.

"Where were they?" Lady Josephine Woodley asked as she tried to delicately place one of her dark brown curls into its proper place.

Alexandra shifted in her spot, uncomfortable with the restriction of a corset before standing to help her sister with her hair.

"Sophia had them under her pillow," Alexandra said going to work.

"That girl is rotten to the core," Josephine said, scratching her nose.

"Nonsense, she is just upset that we are all going to the ball tonight and she cannot."

Alexandra was used to playing the peacemaker between these two sisters. Josephine was only a year younger than Alexandra, and the two of them were by far the closest of all the Woodley girls.

Williamina was three years younger than Josephine, and Sophia rounded out the end of the line being four years under Williamina.

"We all had to wait to come of age. Sophia thinks just because she is the youngest she should get some sort of special treatment," Josephine continued.

"She is fifteen. It is only a year away from when the rest of us came out. Perhaps it wouldn't be too much to allow her to join us tonight," Williamina said, stepping into the room and joining the conversation.

Honestly, the estate couldn't afford all four sisters spending the season out with the ton. Alexandra knew this well, as she saw to all the estate finances by herself. It wasn't something she had shared with her younger sisters as of yet.

She sincerely hoped she wouldn't have to. She had two sisters already having spent a few seasons in society and well into their marrying age. If she could find a good match for either Williamina or Josephine, she wouldn't have to consider having all four sisters out next year.

It wasn't the first time that Alexandra had to carry a secret burden of the Earl Grebs' estate. After her mother's death bringing Sophia into the world, her father, the Earl Grebs John Woodley, had all but removed himself from reality. That left her at the mere age of eight with the weighted responsibility of seeing that the house was managed and her family taken care of.

At first, it had just been little things such as making sure her sisters had their Sunday best on for service when her father didn't seem to notice otherwise. Over time she learned to take over more and more, and he never stopped her, happy to find more secluded time in his library with his precious books and specimens.

Alexandra never had a proper coming out as she made sure her three younger sisters did. Instead, she attended social events much as the other matronly members of the ton, seeing to the needs of the youthful and single relations.

It was true that Sophia was partly babied, only because her father did little to engage with his daughters, and Alexandra had no knowledge of how to be a good mother when still a child herself.

Sophia had been at a significant disadvantage compared to her sisters from the moment she was born;

she had been without a memory of their dear mother, Lady Grebs. All had changed with their lady mother's death. It left all of the Woodley girls needing to grow up faster than their peers and even a little resentful.

Sophia was the most rebellious and resentful of them all. In response, Josephine was always at odds with what she considered special treatment for the youngest of the sisters.

"It is certainly something I would be happy to bring to Father," Alexandra said finishing placing the last piece of baby's breath in Josephine's hair, "But far too late for tonight. The carriage should be here in an hour."

"Sir Hamilton's spring ball is the first event of the season," Sophia said, stomping into the room still in her soft blue morning dress. "Everyone is going to be there for it, and if I'm not, then I might as well stay locked up all year long."

Sophia finished her rant by crossing her arms and sitting on the bed that Josephine and Alexandra shared.

"You are still too young," Alexandra said trying to cool down the heat between her sisters before a full verbal fight began between them. "I don't even know if I could convince Father to let you attend events this season," she continued.

"It's just not fair," Sophia said tears pooling in her big brown eyes before she stomped back out of the room.

Alexandra sighed in disappointment.

"Don't give in to her tantrum," Josephine said noticing

her elder sister crack in resolve. "Remember it was your gloves she hid. Now you have little time to get yourself ready."

"Oh, I wasn't planning to do much to get ready anyway."

Alexandra had not only been mothering her three younger sisters her whole life; she had entirely taken on the mother role. That included shaving any personal time she might have for herself for the betterment of the younger Woodley girls.

"Alexandra, you could shine in that room tonight. Let us help you a bit," Williamina said in encouragement.

"Oh, yes," Josephine added. "It would be so much fun. We could make you sparkle like a diamond if you let us. Then perhaps you could finally find your beau."

"I haven't any time for beaus or diamonds, and I promise you nothing you could do would hide the fact that I am an old maid already," Alexandra chastened her sisters. "Neither do you. It's nearly time. Hurry up and finish getting ready. I must see that Polly gets Father his dinner," she added hurrying out of the room.

"Twenty-three is not nearly that old," Josephine said to Alexandra's fading figure. "If anything it shows your maturity in waiting to find a good match."

She held her head up high as she studied her image in the looking glass. Of all the Woodley sisters Josephine was by far the vainest. The defense of Alexandra's age had little to do with her older sister and much more with their proximity in age.

Alexandra paid no heed to her sister's enticements as she made a final walk of the house. The hired carriage that would take them to Sir Hamilton's London house was to arrive at any minute.

She would need to see that her youngest sister was put to the task of apologizing for the night, that Polly was not too far behind in her evening chores to assist the cook, and above all to make sure her father got some food in him.

More often than not, John Woodley would get into fancies of fantasy and forget all about the necessities of life like eating or paying the servants their monthly wages.

He was currently in such an altered world. Last week a new specimen had been gifted to him from the new world across the sea. It looked nothing more than a giant pincushion to Alexandra and therefore, far too dangerous to be kept in a fine home, but her father was never one to see reason when it came to his hobby.

Earl Grebs had little assets when he took his father's title, and very little by way of increase when he married the countess. They had cared dearly for each other, and money had mattered little.

The Earl did, however, have a very guilty habit of purchases and donations to a lifelong passion of his. He was an obsessive naturalist. He loved to collect every volume of books on anything from zoology to botany. Lady

Grebs had rounded him out some and tempered his passion.

With her death, Lord Grebs had forgotten the world he lived in and chose to shut himself inside the make-believe natural world of his library.

For all his love of the outside world, he had a terribly fragile constitution. This left him to explore and discover the world from the confines of his sole property, 62 Garden Place, London which was dangerously close to the undesirable west end neighborhood of Covent Gardens.

The pincushion would keep him locked away for at least another fortnight as he studied his new stuffed specimen. Next, it would be donated to his one and only love outside of his wife, the London Museum of Natural Wonders.

After a quick stop to the kitchen to procure a tray from the cook, Alexandra found herself standing in front of the library door.

Outside of the sitting room, the breakfast room, and kitchen, this was the only space on the first level of the London townhome.

It was a tight squeeze to fit four girls and their father into such a small house for the season, let alone all year round as was the case for the Woodley's.

"Father," Alexandra called with a soft knock before entering with the tray of mutton stew with boiled potato in her hand.

She set the tray down on the desk with the high back chair spun around from her. She didn't need to see the other side of the chair to know what was going on there. Her father was no doubt hunched over the small table against the wall that showed his latest in a string of stuffed prized possessions.

"I just can't seem to find anything similar anywhere else," Earl Grebs said softly to himself, and he stood from his chair, book in hand, to walk the small room.

"Father," Alexandra repeated.

He blinked looking up from his work, "Oh, Alexandra dear. I didn't hear you come in."

"I know," Alexandra said with a sigh.

As much as she wanted to be dissatisfied with her father, or even resentful towards him, she couldn't. He was a broken-hearted man, only half of the whole he once was.

His hair had greyed over the years to the white of a cloud tinged with yellow tips from the lack of regular bathing and the tobacco from his pipe that regularly filled the room.

His skin was so tight against his face it was almost as thin as the paper in the books he loved so dearly. There was a soft shine of silver prickling his chin in the glow of the fire that was nearly out.

Alexandra would have liked to blame her father for her hardship in life, and she certainly had a right to, but she didn't. Instead, she only wished she could do better to take care of him.

"I brought you your dinner, Father. Please do take a moment's pause to eat."

Lord Grebs looked down at the silver tray.

"Yes, of course, thank you, dear," he said setting his book to the side and turning his high back chair around.

"We will be leaving soon for Sir Hamilton's ball."

"Is it that time already? I feel as if we just celebrated the Yuletide. How can it possibly be April already?"

"The earth spins around the sun, days turn to weeks, and weeks to months," Alexandra said with a soft smile.

He gave her a twinkled look back through his grey eyes. It was the same speech he had given her as a child with the model solar system he had in his study. She loved that model.

Lord Grebs was fascinated with the world and that which grew on it. His eldest daughter, however, had taken her passion to the skies. He had been more than happy to encourage her.

Lord Grebs was blessed with four beautiful daughters and no sons. It was unlike him to keep a conversation about ribbons or dolls and thus had little to connect to the women of the house. His Alexandra however, was much like him. She was passionate about exploration and fearless in ways he could never be.

"What would I do without you, my dear?" he said with a glisten to his grey eyes.

His words extended beyond the simple silver tray before him.

She touched his hand softly as he sat to take up his meal.

2

The Duke of Raven's carriage pulled up to the front steps of his Aunt Rebecca's London townhouse just as the sun began to set behind the trees of Hyde Park.

He had been traveling as fast as possible to get to her side after his aunt's urgent plea to return home. Even still, with the first ship from the new world, the fastest horses money could buy and riding non-stop from Liverpool, it had still taken him several months to get to this place.

He was desperate to know what had made his beloved aunt, and the only family he had left to speak of, so worried to request his immediate presence.

Even with the urgency, he would have liked to arrive in London at a less ostentatious moment. The streets were filled with ladies strolling leisurely from their day of shopping or socializing and gentlemen returning from their clubs in preparation for the night's frivolities.

Theodore Hendricks, the Duke of Raven, was never truly fond of the seasons in London. Though it was still early in spring, he could already tell from looking out the carriage window that lords, ladies, and fine people from all over the country had already flocked to the city for the start of this year's focal months of the season.

He took a steadying breath before opening the door to his carriage that had come to a screeching halt in front of the lavish townhome. It didn't help that it was also right on the corner of Park Lane where anyone who was of importance was walking at this very moment.

Though he walked the short distance through the garden and up the steps in large quick steps, he still caught many eyes and whispers from passing groups.

Raven couldn't decide if the discussions were because he was a reclusive duke who rarely stood on England shores, or of his recent state of attire.

He had stayed in the same traveling clothes the last three days as he reached the end of his journey. He hadn't stopped once to freshen up or even shave the dark shadow that was most assuredly growing along his jawline.

He had one great fear welling inside him. Aunt Rebecca Sinclair was his mother's sister and very much a mother to him after his own parents died out at sea. Being an elder sister to his mother, she was much more on in years than most maternal caretakers might be.

His greatest fear was that his aunt had taken ill or received bad news on her health from a physician and had little time left to live, or even worse, no time at all.

He had scolded himself the whole time he was on the boat across the Atlantic willing the wind to push him faster towards home.

From the moment he was eighteen and allowed to determine his own fate by his aunt's admonition, he had left the comfort of his country seat to see the world as his parents did.

Aunt Rebecca hadn't been happy with his choice, as it was the way she lost her dear sister, but she would not stop him. He was technically the owner and proprietor of all the estates she used, and the benefactor for all that she needed.

Raven had thought he had done right enough by his aunt and the woman who helped raise and shape him by giving her whatever material thing her heart desired.

As he returned home, he realized he had done his dear aunt a grave disservice by leaving her so lonely. Aunt Rebecca would never travel with him; in fact, she refused to even ride ferryboats after her sister's death, and Raven had just chosen to go without her.

It pained him so to know that he had abandoned his aunt, possibly condemning her to a lonely death, all for his unnatural desires to see every speck of this beautiful world.

He would rectify the matter now. He would stay at his aunt's side, give her whatever she bid of him, and make sure the end of her days were the happiest of her life.

"Aunt Rebecca?" Raven called bursting through the door.

He knew he should have knocked, even though it was technically his house, and wait for the butler to let him in. He didn't have time for that, nor did he care if he would be walking in on the household in a less than perfect state. He needed to put eyes on his aunt that very moment, lest his guilt eat him alive.

"What is all the commotion-" he heard her shaky voice call out from the evening sitting room.

He couldn't help but sigh relief. At least she was still on the earth. Raven removed his hat and gloves, handing his jacket and cane over to a butler who had rushed to his aid.

"Good evening, Your Grace. Please allow me to welcome you home," the stoic man said, taking the articles of outer clothing.

"Aunt Rebecca, it's me," Raven called out to his aunt who had risen from her place. He could hear the sound of her freshly pressed petticoats rustling as she got closer.

"Oh, Theodore, my sweet child. You have come home at last," she said reaching out her arms to her nephew.

Raven happily embraced her before holding her at arm's length to study the old lady.

She did look much more in age since last he saw her.

Her cheeks had drooped down into jowls much like the little bull-fighter dogs she liked to keep as company. Her hair had gone completely grey now, set back in its tight bun with a small lace cap over it.

Though she looked weathered from the years, she was only a few months shy of seventy and one; she otherwise looked in perfect health. Her eyes had a beautiful light under their honey brown color, her cheeks were slightly rosy with good health, and her grip seemed firm enough.

In fact, if Raven was to guess, she didn't look ill of health at all.

"I knew you would come, but still I am relieved to see you did," she said, touching his face lovingly.

She had to reach up to do so as Raven was unusually tall even for a man. Not to mention the fact that his aunt must have also shrunk some in the three years since he saw her last. Now the tip of her head barely reached to his broad shoulders.

"I must say though, you look quite a fright," Aunt Rebecca said taking his arm and leading him into the drawing room. "It is Providence alone that brought you here this night. I do hope you will not be too weary for the task."

"What task, dear aunt? I feared the worst when I got your letter. Please don't make me wait a moment longer and tell me what the matter is," Raven said, irritated that his aunt seemed quite at ease.

"Feared the worse? Whatever do you mean, child?"

"Your health," Raven explained.

Aunt Rebecca took a seat on one of the sofas near the hearth. Though it was still early spring, it was unusually warm, and a fire was not needed.

Aunt Rebecca rang the bell and asked for some refreshments for the duke.

"I am in perfect health, why would you have thought otherwise," Aunt Rebecca said with startled confusion.

"In your letter," Raven tried to explain though he refused to sit. He pulled it from his pocket where he had read it over and over these last few months. "You said, 'Please hurry home. Before the spring would be best. Time is of the essence.' What else am I to make of that statement?"

Aunt Rebecca thought her own words over, and her eyes widened with the realization that he had taken her emergency to be a life-threatening one.

"Oh my child, please do forgive me. I never meant for you to read my letter in such a way. I only wished to impress upon you the time urgency."

"Urgency for what?" Raven attempted to ask again.

"For the season, my dear."

Raven stood stock still in his place. He calmly put the letter back in his breast pocket and took a seat on the couch opposite his aunt. He rarely got angry, and certainly never with his aunt, until this moment. He took a long deep breath to settle his nerves.

"Are you telling me, Aunt Rebecca, that you rushed me here from halfway around the world so that I could be in London for the season?"

"It isn't just a season, it is THE season," Aunt Rebecca corrected.

"And why is that, my dear aunt?" Raven said as kindly as he could though he could not help but grit his teeth.

He was sure that over the last few months he had gained some gray hairs of his own worrying over his aunt and her health. He had rushed home like the wind to be at her side, only to find that she had made a false emergency over a socialite season.

"Why only your future happiness of course. I have secured the most prestigious match for you. It was not easy to do as you might well know since you haven't chosen to be present for a single season since you were eighteen."

"Yes, well I didn't enjoy it much then, and I dare say I won't now. What gave you the notion that I was in want of a wife in the first place?"

"My dear you are thirty, and one years of age it is high time that you found a wife and started your own family. I understand you enjoy the exciting life that your parents were mesmerized by, but you have responsibilities to consider. Even your late father saw the importance of marriage as he married my sister in his twenty-fifth year."

Raven rubbed his eyes, not sure if he was willing himself to stay awake or hoping that he could rub this from his memory.

"You have no idea what lengths I went to so as to be at your side as soon as possible."

"I am dreadfully sorry for that," Aunt Rebecca said, batting her eyelashes at him. "I never meant to worry you so, but had I told you my reasoning you wouldn't have come."

"No, I wouldn't have come," Raven agreed.

"Please, dear, I may be in good health now, but you never know," she said, drawing out her words and looking more sunken than she had in a long time.

"Yes, and having me marry a complete stranger of your choosing will be just the youthful elixir you need to live on many more decades?" Raven scoffed.

"Perhaps, perhaps not. But it would do my heart good to see you happily married. Oh, and just think if I could have little great nieces and nephews to hold before I leave this world?"

"I can be happy without a wife, and I am certain you will leave this world with a smile on your face even if there is no babe to hold in your arms," Raven retorted.

At that moment the serving girl came in with a tray of tea, wine, and some cold pies from the earlier supper. Raven didn't speak for some time as he made quick work of the food.

He had scarcely stopped to change horses and in that time only took the small amount of food he could eat quickly in the carriage. He was ravenous, to say the least.

"I know you can be happy without a wife," Aunt Rebecca said once her nephew had begun to slow on his eating,

"But I assure you, you will be much happier with one. Won't you do me this one favor? After all, you are here now," she encouraged.

"Marriage is not exactly a little favor to ask," Raven scoffed back.

"Then not marriage, just stay here for the season. Make an effort to interact with your peerage. Just meet the girl. That is all I ask of you."

Raven was already feeling his anger melt away. He had never denied his dear aunt anything. After all, had he not spent the last several months wishing he had done more for his aunt and spent more time with her? He had just sworn in his own heart he would do all to make the woman happy. Was he willing to go back on that promise already?

"Fine, I will stay for the season, if that will make you happy. You just tell me who it is you want me to meet, and I will be the charming duke, but only because you asked me to. I can't promise a marriage by autumn so don't be disappointed when it doesn't happen."

Aunt Rebecca clapped with glee.

"Oh, of course not, dear Theodore," she cleared her throat and said, coming back to her senses.

"So when shall I meet this wonderful lady of yours," Raven said slumping in his seat like an errant child that had been bested.

"Her name is Lady Charlotte Weiderhold. Her father is Earl Derber. It is rumored that her older sister, Lady Mary, is a favorite of Prince Fredrick. There may be a wedding in their future."

"I highly doubt the Duke of York and Albany would marry an aristocrat," Raven scoffed.

Rumors like these were common. Every member of the ton's life revolved around the royal society. It wasn't the first time one of King George the III's sons was rumored to be attached to an aristocrat, thereby elevating that member's social status. Nothing ever came of it, however.

"Even so," Aunt Rebecca waved off the notion. "Their family is already the talk of the season. They are a very sensible, stable family. It would be a perfect match for you."

"I believe what you are saying is they have money, so I don't have to worry about sharing mine," Raven corrected.

Aunt Rebecca puffed out her cheeks at his smart words before flicking open her fan and cooling herself.

"I must admit I was not entirely against you going away for a time to keep you from so-called ladies of society who were only so by name. You have to understand how the woman folk work. Mothers would do almost anything to secure a duke such as yourself to their daughter, and ergo their house. I was fine with you traveling the world if that meant you weren't going to jeopardize your living to a pretty face."

"I hope you are not saying this Lady Charlotte is not much to look at then," Raven said, trying to hold back the smile forming on his lips.

"You are being a tease now," Rebecca snapped her fan shut and promptly smacked his hand with it.

Raven pretended to be hurt by the action.

"She is very lovely to look at. I only mean that is not all of her qualities. She would be the perfect match for you in my opinion."

"And the fact that it would elevate your popularity with the other ladies if, say, your nephew married the talk of the ton has nothing to do with it?"

She narrowed her honey eyes on him and wrinkled her lips together.

"You are a wretched boy for teasing me so," she said with feeling, though a smile played on her lips as well, "Will you do it then, for me?"

"I will meet her," Raven agreed. "Yes, I will do that for you, my dear aunt."

"Good, then you must go and get ready right away, or we shall be late."

"You can't possibly mean right now?" Raven blurted out. "I have only got home, and I am beyond fatigued."

"Tonight is Sir Hamilton's opener ball. As I said it was Providence alone that brought you here in time, as I accepted Sir Hamilton's invitation on both of our behalves," she added quickening her last words. "Now go," she waved her fan at him in a shooing manner.

"I will have James bring the carriage around; we leave in an hour's time. It may be a tad late, but not unfashionably so," she added more of a thought to herself.

"What have I gotten myself into," Raven grumbled as he hoisted himself from the comfort of the chair.

3

By some miracle, Lady Alexandra Woodley managed to get her two younger sisters out of the house, her father to remember to have his supper, and her youngest sister at the task of apologizing to Polly for the extra work.

As they sat in the hired coach on their way down the cobbled streets of London she couldn't help but breathe a sigh of relief. She realized at that moment she hadn't even really taken the time to look herself over before the ball.

It didn't matter much to Alexandra how she looked, except for putting on a good face for her two younger sisters.

She looked across the carriage at Josephine and Williamina, who were discussing something between the two of them. Both looked radiant. Josephine was wearing a soft green pastel dress; between that and her dark hair wrapped in little white specks of baby's breath, she would be the Belle of the ball.

Alexandra was sure that it was Williamina's year to shine. She was the right age to settle down, and she had already turned a few heads over the last few years. If she could just get Williamina or Josephine a good match this year and see them settle she would have one less burden when it came to Sophia's coming out in twelve months' time.

Williamina looked just as ravishing as her older sister. She was wearing her only evening gown, a soft rose-colored satin. It worked well with her pale skin and the hint of red tint to her golden hair. Where three of the Woodley girls had taken after their mother's Spanish roots of olive skin and dark hair, Williamina had been fair and as beautiful as a porcelain doll just like the rest of the Woodley side of the family.

Williamina was still only nineteen however and a mite too young for marriage. Of course, it was still a possibility as many ladies married at her age. The disadvantage, however, was the undeniable lack of funds.

Williamina had beauty and a kind disposition on her side, but she was still far too young to see sense in using those traits to her advantage. She still had the hopeless thoughts of a romantic as many girls her age did.

Though Alexandra had regretted it, she had already

had to shoo one suitor away just last year. He was a fine gentleman to be sure but no title to his name and no more funds in his coffers than their own family.

He would in no way provide the life that Williamina was accustomed to. It was Alexandra's responsibility to see her sisters happily off in their adult life. She owed her mother at least the sense to protect the younger girls from a disastrous match. Williamina may have had eyes for him at that moment but time would pass, and infatuations wane and then she would be left in a dire situation. Alexandra couldn't allow that to happen, not on her watch.

She rummaged behind her own forest green cloak and into the petticoat pocket of her dress. It was not quite as fancy as the other girls though she still chose to wear pastel blue in symbolism of her virtue. She couldn't allow any rumors of her own standing jeopardize her sisters' chances.

For a single woman to wear anything beyond pastel in the season was to suggest that she no longer considered herself single. Natural reason would be spinsterhood, but then there was always the gossip of adulterous behavior if the girl was still at a young age. Alexandra couldn't risk such a thing no matter how silly she felt parading around in the soft blue silk.

She reached deep into her pocket and produced the offending white gloves. She hadn't had time to put them on and instead slipped them inside the folds of her dress. It was only now as she slid the first one onto her right hand and up the length of her arm that she realized the problem.

Two of the three buttons that secured the garment in place only a few centimeters below the sleeve of her dress was missing. Without them, not only would she look even more of a poor frump girl amongst the ton than her well out of season styled dress did, but it would also prevent it from staying in place.

She gave a long sigh. Had Sophia not taken upon herself to hide the things by way of punishment, the mending could have been easily seen to with time to spare. Now she would have to go the whole of the night tugging at her glove and praying that no one noticed the missing buttons.

"What's the matter, Alexandra?" Williamina asked, noticing the long sigh.

"Nothing, nothing at all," Alexandra said not wanting to inform her sisters.

It was probably a longer ride than most had that night to travel from the less than fashionable side of London to Sir Hamilton's townhouse that he rented out for the year. Not having a seat of his own with endowed estates, his address was ever revolving but still significantly more desirable than the earl's bestowed estate.

Alexandra had always wondered what it would be like to leave the confines and coal smoke of the city in the winter to retreat to a country seat. Unfortunately, her grandfather had fallen on hard times, lost the estate and much of their fortune. The only thing that kept Earl Grebs from just being a Lord by title alone was the small townhouse in London and a minimal yearly pension of investments.

Alexandra ached to see anything beyond the rows of houses and masses of people that populated London. Even to spend one year in the country on her own land would have been a dream come true to her.

The prospects of such were slim, however. Alexandra's sole goal in life was to find a better outcome for her younger sisters than the one she was facing. She never had time in her youth to enjoy the ton truly. She did little socialization beyond advancements for her sister's benefit. Between that and the fact that they all had almost no dowry to speak of, gentlemen didn't exactly seek her out.

She would live in her father's small townhouse all the days of his life. Upon his death, the title and house would then pass on to the next male heir: a cousin of her father's younger sister who was currently in India commissioned as an officer.

Then her life and existence would be a mystery to her. She would be at the mercy of her cousin to take her in out of the charity in his heart, or to leave her on the streets to fend for herself.

It was for this reason she had spent the whole of her

teenage years and young adulthood striving to find better situations for her younger sisters.

She couldn't bear the thought of letting her mother down and leaving them just as weak as she would be someday.

Tonight was very likely the first night of Josephine's last chance at finding a match. She could focus on nothing else except this fact. Even missing buttons would have to be pushed aside for such an important goal.

They arrived at Sir Hamilton's just as the bulk of the crowd arrived. It wasn't the most ideal as she didn't want her sister to get lost in a vast throng, but it was safe. Too early or too late could raise eyebrows in a negative light. If Alexandra had learned anything from her family history, erring on the side of safe was much better than trying the risk.

As soon as Alexandra and her sisters made their introductions at Sir Hamilton and Mrs. Hamilton's welcome procession line, she went straight to work to scout out any and all prospects that were present this night.

There were no wild cards to speak of, and part of Alexandra was relieved to the fact. The single gentlemen present this night were the same that attended almost every season. It meant her sisters had some connections to them.

There was always that worry for Josephine, however. With no new prospects as of yet, it would be hard for her to make a match. These gentlemen had seen, danced, and had conversations with Josephine for the last three years more or less and had either not found interest, or found their poverty too much of a deterrent.

After making her rounds of the room and seeing that both her sisters were settled into their own group of familiar friends, Lady Alexandra went to take her place with all the other motherly figures.

Though Josephine and Lady Alexandra were only a year apart, she had never felt in the right place when she joined Josephine and the other ladies of similar age. Lady Alexandra had so many problems and obstacles always in front of her; she often sought out the older ladies for advice.

It made all the frivolous talk of Josephine's friends seem so pointless compared to the worry that seemed to weigh her down.

"Lady Alexandra," a kind voice called out, waving a lace fan in the air to get her attention.

Lady Alexandra walked through the pressing crowd that still seemed to be flowing in to find Countess Eagleton. Lady Eagleton was probably the closest to her age of all the married ladies at the young age of thirty-four.

She married at the young age of seventeen to the Earl of Eagleton. Unlike most women who went straight to producing children early on in their marriage, and thereby excluding them from many seasons in town, Lady Eagleton had not received that blessing in her life.

It always made Lady Alexandra ache for her. She did love Regina so and hated the pain she felt over not producing an heir. Of course, the words were never spoken of her failure in that respect, but it was still clear to all of society that she was letting the earldom down.

Both ladies grasped hands warmly when they finally navigated the crowds to the other. Once she let go, Lady Eagleton immediately flicked open her fan and started to wave herself. Lady Eagleton came from a good family of well-established money. This along with her ravishing beauty had led her to an early marriage.

Lady Alexandra didn't have to wonder much about the relationship between what she would consider her best friend and the Earl that was twice her age. Their marriage had been one of family negotiations and not a matter of the heart. Though Eagleton was kind enough to his young wife, it was still safe to say there was little by way of passion or love between them.

Even Lady Eagleton's inability to produce a son had been little consequence to the Earl as he had already fathered two boys, now the same age of Regina with families of their own, with the late Lady Eagleton.

Still, the lack of an heir put Regina in a precarious place. Once her husband inevitably went the way of the earth she too would be at the mercy of a distant relation, if a stepson could even be called that, for support. A child of her own would warrant her a portion of the Earl's estate to help provide for the child and by consequence her as well.

"This place is ridiculously hot," Regina said fanning herself rapidly. "I dare say spring has come and gone in a blink and summer is already upon us."

"I hope it is not so," Lady Alexandra replied. "I fear with the heat starting sooner it will only lead to hotter times ahead. I do detest the heat."

She had heard of lords and ladies retiring to the Lake District or even to the oceanside along the Scotland border when summers were much hotter than usual. Such a thing would be a detriment to her sisters. Even if Josephine didn't find her match this season, she was desperate that one of them did if only so that she could afford Sophia's coming out in twelve months' time.

4

Aunt Rebecca did manage to get her grumbling nephew to the ball, though much later than she had anticipated. By the time they arrived all other guest had already entered the premises, the welcome line was disbanded, and finger foods and lemonade were brought around by servants to those that so desired it.

Aunt Rebecca couldn't help but hold her head up a little taller with pride as all eyes turned to her nephew upon their entrance. She was well aware of the rumors spreading of his impending arrival this season as well as his desires to choose a wife. After all, she had started most of them.

She needed to get people talking about her nephew and preparing to give him the attention he was due. After all, Aunt Rebecca was sure she would never be able to convince Theodore to spend a second season in London. This was her last-ditch effort to do her motherly duty to the memory of her dearly departed sister.

He had undoubtedly grown more into the dashing man his father had been in the few years he had been parted from her. Raven was turning out to be every bit as handsome as his father with the subtle touches of her sister that only Aunt Rebecca knew.

She would have never thought it possible for her nephew to grow more, but he had somehow managed that, or at least she hadn't remembered him towering over her so. Though he had taken his sweet time in preparing for tonight's pivotal event, she couldn't help but be glad for it.

Theodore had washed away the grime and exhaustion of traveling, freshly shaved and washed. His hair shown like ebony still wet and slicked back. He was wearing one of his finest sets of pantaloons and navy jacket that thankfully the groomsman had seen to the moment that Theodore arrived.

This was going to be a significant year for not just her dear nephew but also herself. She did love the boy greatly and desired to see him settled down to happiness. If anything, it would at least alleviate the worry of the dangerous perils of his travels. She was sure that she could not live through his demise as well as her sister's.

But it was more than that fact which drove Aunt Rebecca to beg her nephew home and implore him to give this season over to all the attention of finding a wife, more specifically Lady Charlotte; Lady Rebecca Sinclair's social standing depended on it.

If Aunt Rebecca was able to connect herself to one of the most spoken of families of the season, she too would increase her popularity. It was something not always manageable for a spinster. On top of her lack of husband, she had little by way of title beyond her curtesy Ladyship. Others had given her respect as the sole caretaker for the Duke of Raven, but now he was a grown man. She was beginning to fade into obscurity, something she greatly detested.

Her winning ticket to ensure her social standing for the remainder of her days would be to acquire a seat on the Woman's Relief Society for Orphaned Children board. She had been a shoo-in for quite some time. After all, had she not personally come to the aid of her orphaned nephew?

Unfortunately to receive a seat on the board a seat would need to become available. It was a long waiting process as these desirable seats were held for life, or as long as health would permit. Only now was one becoming available. Lady Derber, Lady Charlotte's mother, was falling on hard times as of late. It was rumored that she would soon be giving up her seat and focus the remainder of her days on her children's happiness and her own health.

If Raven was able to secure marriage with Lady Charlotte, not only would it possibly moving him a step closer to the royal families themselves, by marriage of course, but also help Lady Rebecca become a more appropriate option for Lady Derber's replacement.

Everything had already been moving along quite smoothly. In fact, even better so. Aunt Rebecca had never dreamed that the duke would have arrived home so swiftly. At best, Aunt Rebecca had suspected they would be playing catch up mid-season due to all the other suitors flocking to Lady Charlotte for the very same reason she wanted to press her nephew.

He had arrived at a most fortuitous time, and he looked more dashing and handsome than she even remembered. Best of all, he had a great title that few could rival. Her only concern was convincing Theodore that taking a wife and settling down was worthwhile.

He had his mother and father's adventurous spirit. Even their untimely death hadn't stopped him from taking right up where they left off. There were the lands that his father acquired in the new colonies that intrigued Theodore to no end and was the constant worry of Aunt Rebecca. But more than that he had managed to travel all over the British empire wishing to see everything.

Aunt Rebecca had the daunting task of now not just convincing him that he needed a wife but that it was high time he stopped crossing great bodies of water, if for nothing more than the sake of her constitution.

The Duke of Raven did his best to hide his grumble as he and his aunt entered Sir Hamilton's fine house. The party was in full swing by the time of their arrival, and many eyes turned to stare and whisper over them.

They were not looks of shock or surprise at his unexpected entrance which told him Aunt Rebecca had already announced his coming to a great many people. He did little to hide the scowl that now darkened his already black brows. He had no desire to socialize any night with the young misses of the ton, but even less so on this night.

Though he had done his best to look the dashing gentleman for his aunt's sake, he was certainly not feeling it on the inside. The fact that he was simply on his feet was a miracle in itself. In fact, he was sure if his aunt would only take her eyes off of him for a second, he would be able to find a quiet nook hopefully not already filled by couples desperate for just a second of privacy. There he could slip into a wonderfully blissful sleep until the night was over.

Sadly, he knew such schemes would not be possible until he made his rounds and said hello to the various fine gentlemen of the party. He may not have enjoyed socialization, but he still knew proper etiquette and didn't want to snub anyone.

Aunt Rebecca was all too happy to let him go as she hurriedly twittered with some of her older friends that seemed to seek her out the moment the two arrived. Raven found most of the men having a glass of brandy and snuff before the night's dancing would begin.

Before Raven could scarcely scan the room, a large hand clapped him on the back.

"I never expected to see you here tonight, Your Grace," a deep husky voice called over the cloud of tobacco smoke it produced.

Raven took the hand of the Earl of Eagleton happily.

"I hadn't thought it was so long since last I set foot in London, but looking at your face, I can see that much time has passed," Raven said back in jest.

"Yes, well, some of us can't stay dashingly handsome forever like you, Raven my boy," Lord Eagleton said back with a husky laugh.

For a man in his mid-sixties, he really didn't look that bad by way of health. His hair had gone complete grey now, whereas the last time Raven saw him, he did have some smattering of dark chestnut to it. The lines on his face were much deeper set, though he was sure they were always there.

Raven had grown up as close companions to the Earl's oldest son, who was the same age. They went to the same boarding school and often were caught causing the same mischief in cahoots with one another.

With the passing of his own father, Raven had looked up to Lord Eagleton much in a paternal way. Lord Eagleton had undoubtedly never spared him a reprimand when the two boys were caught in their mischief.

"Where is Charles? And Fredrick, of course? Are they both here tonight?" Raven said scanning the room.

For the first moment, Raven thought he might have found a bright silver lining to what was sure to be a long and cumbersome evening. He hadn't spoken to his dear boyhood friend, the Viscount of Bembury, since Charles' marriage several years back. If he remembered right, he even had quite a brood of his own.

"No, neither are here tonight. Charles is back at the estate with his wife. She is due any moment with child number four. Charles is sure this one will be a boy. I dare say he has gotten so used to ribbons and dolls with his three girls he wouldn't know what to do if he did have a boy," Lord Eagleton said with another hearty laugh.

"Fredrick, on the other hand, was stationed to the Indies only last year. He and his new bride are enjoying the warmer weather there much more than I expected. She was a frail thing, and I wondered if she would survive the trip at all. Fredrick says she has been thriving there, much to my surprise."

"The Indies are indeed a great place to rejuvenate the soul. I tell you the air continuously smells of spice and flora. It could lift the spirits of the rottenest man," Raven replied, not realizing that Fredricks commission had taken him to such a place. He made a mental note to look the young lord up when he next visited the area.

Raven had never been terribly close with Lord Fredrick, aside from the constant teasing that he engaged in along with Charles. None the less, he knew it would be enjoyable to both parties to set up a meeting, and perhaps Raven could find a way to put in a good word for Fredrick. Having a duke as a public friend was always a benefit to commissioned officers, not to mention the fact that Raven still felt a mite bad about that time they filled Fredrick's clothing cabinet with a beehive.

"And what of your lovely young wife?" Raven continued enjoying his conversation with the Earl.

"She is wonderful. A true kind-hearted lady. She is so kind to both boys and such a loving grandmother to Charles's little girls. I worried for a time that she might be lonely or feel empty, if you know what I mean, but that hasn't been the case at all. She loves the family and puts all her energy into making the house a happy home."

"She does sound like a wonderful woman," Raven concluded, having never actually met the new Lady Eagleton.

"Yes, she is," Lord Eagleton said with a satisfied sigh at his good fortune at two happy marriages. "And it is quite high time that you start the search for your own wonderful woman."

Raven did his best not to roll his eyes at Eagleton's tone

that was beginning to sound very reminiscent of his childhood.

"You may have been lucky enough to escape marriage thus far, but now with my own two son's set in life you can bet I will be narrowing my eyes on you, my boy."

"I am sure you will not have to trouble yourself," Raven replied. "My aunt already seems bent to the task."

"I am sure she is," Eagleton agreed. "Still, I will have Lady Eagleton put her feelers out for you. She is of a younger age than your aunt and sure to know the ladies in question better. I will be sure to introduce her to you later tonight."

"I am certain to be honored just to make the acquaintance of the woman who has brought you joy even in your old age," Raven said.

"I may be old, Your Grace, but I still have enough strength in me to give you a full tongue lashing on the importance of respecting your elders," Eagleton replied, though his face shone brightly with humor.

5

The night had gone as smoothly as Lady Alexandra could have hoped for. That was, of course, with the exception of the tiresome glove that continued to snake its way down her arm.

The days had been unseasonably warm for so early in spring, but now with the night fully upon them and all doors and windows in the ballroom open, a glorious breeze was finding its way through. It was a much-needed relief for the ladies draped in fine silks stuffed so closely in the dance hall.

Lady Alexandra had thus far spent much of her night in the company of Lady Eagleton and a few other ladies, but always with a watchful eye on her two sisters.

Josephine, in particular, was making what seemed to be

wonderful advancements. A certain lord by the name of Baron Mckenzie was never far from her side this year.

It was not his first season in London as he had come for several years with his father, Viscount Newton. He had always had some interest in Josephine but never seemed to be more than just a casual acquaintance brought on by mutual friends.

The way the baron was always seeming to put himself at Josephine's side tonight gave Lady Alexandra some hope for this season.

The Baron didn't have a significant footprint in the peerage, but he would inherit his father's title one day, and as far as Lady Alexandra knew, was a very kind and responsible man. It was all that she could hope for one of her sisters.

"I see you are watching Lord McKenzie circle around your sister like an annoying little fly," Lady Eagleton said noticing her gaze.

"I don't think she minds much," Lady Alexandra said, trying to discern her sister's temperament as Lord McKenzie engaged her in another conversation.

"Look, she is giving him her card," Lady Alexandra said pointing out the act. "She would not be so cheerful accepting to dance with the man if she was annoyed with him."

"Or perhaps she is just being polite about it," Lady Eagleton retorted.

Lady Alexandra exchanged a glance with her dear friend. The usual silent words of dear friends of the female sex were then spoken. They both knew if Josephine didn't like someone polite behavior was often far from her mind.

"Well, I hope he doesn't fill up the whole card," Lady Eagleton continued. "I just got word from Lady Cunningham that a very handsome young duke has just joined the party at a most unfashionably late hour."

"Have you now?" Lady Alexandra asked, though she put little stock in her friend's words.

Lady Eagleton was the foremost on any pertinent information, which also meant that some of it wasn't exactly proven true before she passed the news along.

"I know this one to be the truth," Lady Eagleton said putting her own gloved hand on Lady Alexandra's arm. "Lady Cunningham heard the news from Lady Rebecca Sinclair, the said duke's aunt."

Lady Alexandra was well aware of who Lady Rebecca was. Though they had never traveled in the same circles, she had seen the woman from time to time.

"I am vaguely aware that she had a nephew but not much beyond that."

"Theodore Hendricks, the Duke of Raven. He is a very close acquaintance of my husband's family though I have yet to meet him myself. Young Charles has spoken of him quite often. I believe they were good friends in their boyhood."

"But you have not met him yourself?" Lady Alexandra asked, still full of skepticism.

"No, you may remember that the Duke of Raven's parents were lost to sea?"

"I have some recollection of the fact in conjunction with his aunt. She was his caretaker after their unfortunate death."

"Yes, well," Lady Eagleton said wrapping her arm naturally in Lady Alexandra's so that they might take a turn about the ballroom before the dancing started. "It seems that their exit from this world didn't deter their only son from following on the same path. It seems he is quite a world traveler and owns vast tobacco plantations in the Colonies."

"The Duke of Raven is said to return to London this season to acquire himself a wife at his aunt's behest. It would be a fine match," she added with a nudge.

"I am sure it would be," Lady Alexandra said with a laugh. "However I am sure I am not the only one to set her hat on him. What could one of my sisters offer a Duke compared to all the other fine single, well-endowed ladies of the peerage."

"I wasn't talking about them, so much as you," Lady Eagleton said with a roll of her own eyes.

This made Lady Alexandra laugh out in full at the notion.

"Yes because an ancient spinster lady with no dowry to

speak of has a high chance with the Duke of Raven," she said between spurts of laughter.

"Perhaps you would if I had my husband put in a good word for you. As I said, the Duke has a very close connection to my step-son."

"That is very kind of you, Regina, but I fear you put yourself at risk enough by your kindness of friendship. I wouldn't want to tarnish you any further with our connection."

"Nonsense. You always think so low of yourself," Lady Eagleton scolded.

"I can't say I do in all honesty. I haven't the time to think of myself at all let alone in a negative way. Perhaps when my three sisters are settled, and that weight is lifted from me, I will have a moment to consider what light I consider myself in."

"It is a burden you shouldn't carry on your shoulders. You have already taken on the responsibility to raise them, not to mention the responsibilities that your father has forgotten. You have done enough. Shouldn't you also look for happiness?"

"Happiness will come when I can stand before my mother up in the clouds and tell her that I have taken care of her little girls," Lady Alexandra said with a solemn sigh.

It was something she had never said to a soul and was sure her own father didn't even know. It was a weight and a burden she was asked to carry for her whole life through.

On the day that Lady Alexandra's mother died, she had gone to the lady's side. Her mother was so pale and weak. She had only just delivered little Sophia a few days before. Unlike before, she had not recovered from the ordeal.

The doctor had just pronounced that there was little left that could be done for the Viscountess beyond prayer and divine intervention. How Lady Alexandra had prayed for her mother in those days.

Nothing had come of her words sent heavenward. Instead, her mother announced that her end was nigh. She called each of her daughters to her side one by one to give her final words.

To Lady Alexandra alone she had implored the child to look after her sisters. She had put the weight of the household mantle on the frail eight-year-old's shoulders and implored the little lady to see to her sisters' success in life.

Lady Alexandra had made that promise to her dying mother. She still remembered the look of peace and relief that shown in her dark-brown eyes before the life drifted out of them. It was that worry that had kept her lady mother hanging on for the last few days. Now that Lady Alexandra had been set to her lifelong task, her mother would rest in peace.

She wouldn't let her mother down. She hadn't so far. She had taken care of the house, raised her sisters, saw to their education, and prepared them for the roles life would give them in their future. It didn't matter the cost or sacrifice to do so.

Lady Eagleton didn't agree with her friend's determination to put her sisters before herself. In all honesty, her heart ached for Lady Alexandra.

She wouldn't have wished such a life upon someone such as Lady Alexandra, but if anyone had the tenacity to do so, it was Alexandra.

As much as she wished away her friend's circumstances, she also admired her bravery throughout it. Lady Alexandra was a dutiful daughter, a superb sister, and if anyone deserved a life of love and happiness, it was her.

Though love was undoubtedly a forgone ideal to Lady Eagleton, she had seen it enough in others. Of course, she did have great admiration for her own husband and considered herself to be lucky to have such a warmhearted companion. It wasn't love that she had for him.

That was something she had only seen and never felt. It wasn't an unusual circumstance for a lady of the ton to go through life without love, and she didn't consider it to be solely required for happiness. What she did see from various members of her family and society on a whole when they did find it, was that happiness was doubled over than one could even imagine.

Lady Eagleton had wished such emotions for herself as a young girl before her father and the Earl arranged her marriage. A part of her still hoped for it deep in the recesses of her heart, but she knew she would still live a happy, satisfied life if it never came her way.

She was sure, however, that unless Lady Alexandra found something so profound as love, she would never be shaken from her determination to put her family before her own needs. And certainly, if anyone was ever in need of doubled over happiness, it was the lady who had received so little in her life already.

"Oh look there he is," Lady Eagleton said coming from her thoughts and pointing her fan discreetly across the room.

"How can you be sure?" Lady Alexandra said taking a quick glance at the two men that Lady Eagleton had pointed at.

"Obviously it is he. A young, handsome duke laughing in such a friendly manner with my husband."

Lady Alexandra took a quick moment to study the gentleman. He did look much younger than she expected when told he was a close friend of Lord Eagleton, but then she had to remind herself that it was the Viscount he was friends with.

Though he did have a dashing smile of perfect white teeth as he spoke with the Earl, there was still something that made her consider him quite stoic.

Perhaps it was the fact that he towered over every other person in the room, including all the other men. He had large square features that reminded Lady Alexandra of the ancient marble statues from earlier civilizations.

He was most fashionably dressed in a dark navy coat with tan pantaloons and high rich brown leather boots. It was all the heights of fashion and perfectly placed on his body.

The thought of his perfection made Lady Alexandra unconsciously tug on the glove that had begun to slip again.

It was his face that made him look so solemn she finally decided. He had the same chiseled facial features to compliment his sturdy angular frame. His nose was slightly longer than usual and pointed at the tip. More than this, what caught Lady Alexandra's attention was his thick black hair brushed back and made to shine in the candlelight. She was sure he looked just as his title entailed. A raven.

She only knew the creatures due to her father's research endeavors. They were considered to be smart but cunning. Beautiful to look at but quite mischievous. She was sure that the Duke was exactly like his name stated.

"He does look quite friendly with Lord Eagleton, but there is something about him that unsettles me," Lady Alexandra said honestly to her friend.

"Perhaps it gives you a quiver in your belly, sends your face to flush red," Lady Eagleton egged on.

"Oh nonsense," Lady Alexandra said waving her friend off with a giggle. "I think you have been reading far too many of Mr. Wright's Circulating Library romances."

"I have, and I am not ashamed of it," Lady Eagleton said putting her chin just slightly higher into the air. "In fact, I have one that I am sure you will love."

"Oh, to have time to read," Lady Alexandra said with a sigh.

She loved to read just as much as her best friend, but always seemed to be lacking in the moments to do so. Because of this, she had as of yet to subscribe to a lending library despite her own family's poor selection of books.

"You must make time, my dear," Lady Eagleton said. "Now come and promise me that you will let me scheme on your behalf. It will make me so happy to do so this season."

"Fine, I will let you scheme, though only on my sisters' behalf. And I must warn you; it will do little good when the Duke learns of the family you are sponsoring. Our financial misfortune is widely known."

"Nonsense, he will have money enough. I am sure that instead, he will be on the hunt for a prospect of love," Lady Eagleton said emphasizing the last words causing Lady Alexandra to roll her eyes and both girls to giggle as if they were young again.

6

"My dear," Aunt Rebecca coming quickly to Raven's side as the band took its place on the small stage. "The dancing is about to begin. I must introduce you to Lady Charlotte."

She was all ruffles as she hurried over to him and again Raven groaned inwardly.

"So I see you have an eye for Lady Charlotte already," Eagleton said with merriment as they walked into the great dance hall together with many of the other gents.

He had insisted on following Raven so that he might introduce him to his wife. He also had promised the lady a set as she dearly loved to dance.

"I have not set my eye on anyone," Raven said narrowing his eyes at his aunt.

"Ah, I see. Well, if anyone is up to the task then it is this tenacious lady," Eagleton said bowing politely to Aunt Rebecca.

"If you will both excuse me I am sure my own wife will be most disappointed if we don't dance the very first set, and I dare say I would rather get it over with anyway."

He gave Raven a farewell wink and wished him luck before making his way through the ever-growing crowd to find his wife.

"I must introduce you to Lady Charlotte right away," Aunt Rebecca continued with the Earls departure.

She was tugging at Raven's arm like an errant child.

"I have spent half the night next to Lady Derber. She has gone on incessantly on how both her daughters have found infinite amounts of good fortune this year. I am sure Charlotte's card is almost full already. Do hurry," she added when Raven continued to take the trip through the crowd at a leisurely pace.

Aunt Rebecca continued to scan the room doing the best she could manage at her short stature.

"Oh dear, I can't seem to see a thing," she said with a huff as a group of gentleman flooded in the room from another door blocking her view.

"Perhaps you can tell me what she looks like and I can do the scouting for you, dear aunt," Raven said wishing to get this over with.

"Well," Aunt Rebecca said finding this to be a satisfactory compromise. "She is wearing a fine blue silk with long gloves. Her hair is the most beautiful golden brown with large angelic eyes and porcelain skin."

Raven narrowed his eyes into slits at his aunt.

"I only need a basic description not an entire tale of her most beautiful qualities."

"I am just trying to help, my dear," Rebecca said as if such a notion of making her nephew fall in love from the mere words had not crossed her mind.

"Oh, I believe I see her now. She is standing with a slightly older blonde lady."

"To be sure that must be her older sister," Aunt Rebecca responded. "Do you see a way we might get to her for an introduction?"

"Eagleton himself is not far from them. It will take some time for us to cross, Aunt Rebecca. I will go on my own and have the Earl make the introductions. He knows the lady and her family already. You just wait here, dear aunt, at these chairs," Raven said wishing to smother out his aunt's matchmaking vigor.

He set his aunt at some chairs along the wall and walked away quickly to get some refreshments for her. He hadn't been to London for some time, but it still seemed to him much hotter than he remembered despite the gentle breeze blowing through the windows from time to time.

"I think I will have a wonderful view of you dancing from just here," his aunt said settling down into her chair with a drink in hand.

Her cheeks were slightly rosied from the heat, and he could tell she wasn't entirely comfortable at the moment. He considered citing that as a reason they should leave right that moment.

He knew Aunt Rebecca would not have such a thing. She would not be moved from that ballroom until he at least danced with the lady in question.

Once he saw his aunt settled, he turned his attention back to the woman on the other side of the room. Much to his dismay Lord Eagleton was no longer there.

He found the backside of his parental figure and his new wife walking towards the open portion of the hall to prepare for the first set. It was only then that Raven saw that the lady speaking to Lady Charlotte wasn't at all her older sister but Lady Eagleton herself. He thought this matter was of little consequence as the girl in question hadn't moved from her spot even with her companion's departure.

Raven considered waiting till the earl was no longer engaged in the set to go and make the proper introductions for him. Much to his frustration that would mean waiting for the length of dance and then having to endure the second set with Lady Charlotte.

It was more time than he was willing to bargain with. If he simply went to the lady himself, asked for the first available dance she had, he could retire to a quick nap before his time would come.

If his aunt was right, it could be several sets before she had one that wasn't already promised to another.

The sooner he got his name on her little fan booklet and told his aunt of his place, the sooner he could find some moments of rest.

Raven continued to tell himself it was better to get the matter over with as he took his long, determined steps across the room. His tall frame and large stature had some great advantages. In this instance, others would move quickly to let him through.

He ignored several longing glances that came his way from other ladies of the room and kept his eyes on the one and only target he had for the night.

He was surprised to see that she wasn't in a group of young ladies as most of the other single girls did. So often they either stayed at their mother's side, timid and waiting for a chance, or ventured out with some of their friends hoping that the gents would mingle with them.

This lady did neither. Instead, she stood in her spot, just off of the main dance floor. Like her aunt, Lady Charlotte would have a good view of the floor but didn't seem to be moving to take up the first dance herself.

Raven wondered if his aunt had been wrong in thinking her card would be full already as it didn't seem any man was coming to collect her either.

As soon as Raven got within speaking distance of the

lady, her attention turned to him. He was so tall that he was used to such a fact.

However, when the lady looked up at him with her large brown eyes, he seemed to forget his words for just a moment. He was never one to be tongue-tied or unsure of himself, but for only the briefest of seconds, he feared that he had made an error barging before the lady so.

Swallowing hard, he took a deep bow before the lady.

"Forgive me for introducing myself," he said as he bowed. "I am the Duke of Raven. My aunt Lady Rebecca Sinclair tells me she is a great friend of your mother's."

The lady's delicate brown brows furrowed in misunderstanding.

"Perhaps I am mistaken?" Raven asked seeing she didn't either recognize the names given or the connection.

"No, I am sure you are not," the lady assured him with a soft smile. "I know your aunt, but by name only I must confess. I had no idea that she had a connection to my mother."

"Oh," Raven said straightening up and washing with relief. He had never feared embarrassment amongst the ton until this very moment.

"I wonder if you might indulge me with a set, if you still have one available," Raven continued motioning to her Programme du bal fan. "I know it would appease my aunt," he said by way of explanation.

The lady looked down at the fan in her hand, "Oh dear,

this isn't...I don't have," she took a slow breath. "I don't have any dances set aside at this time."

"Splendid," Raven said happy for his good fortune. He could dance with Lady Charlotte for the first set and convince Aunt Rebecca to return home having fulfilled her desires for the night.

"Would you do me the honor of dancing the first set of the evening with me?" Raven asked.

"Of course, Your Grace," the lady replied with a soft bow.

He seemed to watch time stand still for just that moment. He was sure he could see a soft blush rush up her cheeks.

He reached out an arm for her to take, which she did. Together they walked the length of the hall to the dance floor. Though she tried to do so discreetly, he watched as she tugged at her long glove. It was only then that he noticed that two of the buttons were missing.

It was a most curious thing to him, but he thought little of it. He made the walk in silence to then study more of her.

What lady that was coming to a ball would not bring a booklet to write her partners name in it? Especially a lady that was already creating such a stir if his aunt was correct.

He noticed too that though her dress was of fine blue silk, it was of a earlier fashion and even had some fraying to the cream ribbon around her waist and down her back.

Surprisingly he didn't find these facts to deter from her beauty to any degree. She was a delicate creature to look at but more than that she seemed to walk with a great air about her. He could tell, though he wasn't sure how, that she was not a frail miss of the ton as so many were.

Though he hated to admit so, he was finding that perhaps his aunt had done right in insisting he gives the season a try.

After all, if he could find a lady that shared in his mutual interests and love for travel, it might not be so bad to have a companion to go along with him.

The duke led the lady up close to where the earl and his wife were already standing. He knew from this point both his aunt and the Earl would see his efforts and perhaps not pressure him so to find a partner. Though the idea intrigued him, he would still have liked it to be of his own volition and not pressed upon him.

The Earl's silver brows rose in surprise as Raven took his place on the floor with the lady across from him.

"I believe you know Lord Eagleton," the lady said seeing the silent exchange between the two of them.

"Yes, he has been somewhat of a father figure in my life," Raven said as the dance began.

"I am good friends with Lady Eagleton," she said by way of explanation of her words.

"Though I believe she hasn't had the pleasure to meet

you herself, she has already spoken many high praises of you tonight," she continued.

"Then that must mean that the Earl has not divulged all the horrible trouble that his son and I always found ourselves in," Raven said with a soft smile.

She blushed and looked away. It was a shallow conversation to start, but it was undoubtedly what was proper of a dance.

"Lady Eagleton informed me this is your first season in town for some time, your grace."

"Yes, I tend to avoid London as much as I can," Raven replied.

"So you don't like the city?" the lady continued to keep up a steady conversation.

"I have never particularly enjoyed it. There is so much of the rest of the world to see. Why stay here when wonderful things are waiting to be discovered?"

"Hopefully you will discover something new of the city while you are here at present."

"Are you a protector of it, then?" he asked narrowing his hawk eyes on the lady.

"No, not really. Though it is the only home I know, so I suppose in that way I do have a fondness for it as well as its hidden gems of wonder."

"Never left the city? That's surprising to hear," Raven retorted.

Surely her family would return to their country estate

during colder months or at least go and visit other estates around the country. He didn't hold on to the thought as they did their turns on the floor, however.

"What gems might you find here?" Raven asked the lady, rather enjoying their conversation.

"Well, of course, there are the parks and theaters."

"Yes, but by the way you say that, I would guess you don't frequent those. Where would you say you spend most of your time?"

"Actually if I am not at home with my sisters I am at the Natural Museum of zoology and botany."

"Oh not that dreadful place," Raven blurted out without even realizing it.

"Dreadful?" The lady retorted.

"Forgive me," he said clearing his throat. "I went there as a child myself. I wanted to see and learn everything about the world around me, and that was sure to be the place to get close to real specimens. But it was just so..."

"Not to your taste?" She asked, though he could tell her words had visibly cooled.

He wondered if he had offended her. He hadn't meant to. As a boy, he had considered it to be amazing and perhaps a lady who never left London would too, but once seeing what the world had to offer, he learned how misguided the studies and conclusions drawn at that place were.

"Completely backward, in all honesty," Raven said gently but not willing to give up honesty.

"How so, Your Grace?" she said narrowing her own eyes at the gentleman.

"So often their classifications of animals are completely off base, the scientific assumptions they make only lead to the fact that they have no practical knowledge outside of the city themselves."

"Perhaps it is better now," Raven added quickly when she didn't meet his eyes or respond. "Forgive me, Lady Charlotte. I meant no offense. Perhaps we could go together to the museum, and you can prove me wrong."

Raven was suddenly desperate to get in this lady's good graces again. Somehow his offer and apology didn't do justice as her head snapped up to look at him in utter shock at the mere utterance.

"I am not Lady Charlotte, Your Grace. I am afraid you have mistaken me for another."

7

Lady Alexandra Woodley could not imagine being in a more embarrassing situation. At first, she had been delighted when the duke introduced himself to her, and even spouted a connection to her family through her late mother.

She had found it curious that Lady Rebecca had told the duke that she and her mother had been friends. It was news that had never been spoken to her from either Lady Rebecca or her father.

She had waved that warning away, however. It didn't matter how the duke was connected if it meant he might find favor with one of her sisters. Of course, the second warning was when the duke asked her to dance.

No one ever asked Lady Alexandra to dance. In fact, she was a little frightened that she might not remember the steps. Her whole focus at social events had been to make friends with the other matrons of the ton to find partners for her sister, never herself.

Even still, when the duke asked her to dance she merely thought he was being polite in dancing with the eldest sister first. She had learned of a miracle connection between a most prominent single duke and her family, and she would take advantage of that moment.

Even with fear of miss-stepping she had agreed to waltz the first set with him. It would give her the opportunity to introduce him to her sister's personalities beforehand.

She had done her best to begin some light conversation. Through the whole of it, however, she felt her stomach knot with nervousness. He was far more handsome and imposing up close than he was at a distance.

She had to tell her self several times that this man could very well be her future brother-in-law if she played her cards right.

He may have the charm and mannerisms of a duke, but she could not let that blind her from the course she was on. She was determined to see her sisters put to him before the night's end.

That determination changed, however, when he so blatantly criticized her father's life work. Every aspect of the Natural Museum of Zoology and Botany had been at her father's behest and sponsorship. To say that all he did was a laughing stock was more than insulting.

It had been more insulting, however, because over the last several years she had been the one predominantly overseeing the various curators and scientist as best she could.

Certainly, she was no expert in that field. It had all come out of necessity as her father soon refused to leave the house even to his once beloved sanctuary. He cited that the traffic on the streets had become more than his frail constitution could take.

From that moment on all information or specimens were brought to the house for approval just as he was doing at that moment. And then information was carried back to the Museum via letters or Lady Alexandra's personal inspections.

It wasn't a subject that Lady Alexandra had much interest in, and she did not do these errands and added work out of her own passion. Instead, it was the simple fact that her father had tied up the last of his inheritance as an investment of the place.

If the Museum were to fail, any chance of a dowry would be lost to the sisters. As it was, the pavilion was not as successful as she would hope and dowries were going to be meager at best.

If his distaste for her father's passion had not been off-putting enough, the duke then proceeded to call her by the wrong name.

It was as if she had raised up on top of a high tower only to come crashing down again.

She felt utterly ridiculous now that she had even thought the duke would have introduced himself to her of all people. She mentally kicked herself for thinking that a fine lady such as Rebecca Sinclair would go the whole of Lady Alexandra's life never speaking a word to her and then press her duke nephew to engage in a dance over a dear friendship.

They took several moments around the floor in utter silence. Both were lost in their own thoughts of the current revelations presented. Neither one could simply leave. They would have to stay until the set was completed.

Lady Alexandra felt all the more tortured as Lady Eagleton looked her way over and over again with an excited gleam in her eyes.

"Please do beg my pardon, miss. My aunt described a lady with brown hair, a blue silk dress, and high gloves. I made the misfortune of seeing you and making the assumption."

"That I was Lady Charlotte," Lady Alexandra finished for him.

"I didn't mean any offense, it was a simple mistake," he said defending himself.

"I should be honored I suppose," Lady Alexandra replied, not precisely enjoying the way he was now becoming defensive about the fact.

"Perhaps you would do me the courtesy of telling me your name," he said after a few more moments past.

She couldn't believe he even had the nerve to ask.

"I dare say I couldn't bear to own up to it at this point," Lady Alexandra said looking every direction except the partner in front of her.

She was relieved that the set was finally coming to an end.

"Perhaps though, Your Grace, as we part ways I can do you the service of pointing out the true target of your desires. She is just there," Lady Alexandra said nudging with her chin to another set of partners on the floor.

The Duke of Raven studied the girl she had motioned to. No surprise she too was wearing an elegant blue silk dress with high gloves and gleaming white pearls strung through light brown hair.

"And just in case you are wondering," Lady Alexandra said looking him in the eye finally as the dance ended.

She took her soft curtsy as was customary before finishing her sentence.

"My father is the patron of the Natural Museum of Zoology and Botany. If you truly think your vast knowledge of the world is far superior to those in the pavilion, you might consider putting it to good use."

Raven cocked a brow not understanding her words entirely.

"A candle loses nothing from lighting another. What is

the point of vast worldly experiences if you will not impart it on those not as fortunate as yourself to experience them, Your Grace."

With those final words, Lady Alexandra turned with her head held high and left the dance floor. She may not have been considered worthy to be in his elite circle and perhaps her father's museum was less than par compared to others. It made little difference to her. She had come too far and worked too hard to see her family name disgraced and made fun of.

Lady Alexandra strolled directly out of the room and to an adjoining one were a bowl of punch was still out to quench the thirst of tired dancers. She did the best she could to ladle a cup for herself without showing her shaking hands too much.

She had never spoken in such a manner to someone her superior, probably no one at all in honesty other than when she had to scold her sisters.

Perhaps the Duke had meant to be contrite in his apology and, to be honest, it was a simple mistake. Oh, how she wished he had made it with any other woman that night instead of her.

In her moment of embarrassment and anger, she had

lashed out. Lady Alexandra had soiled her image in the eyes of the duke permanently.

It would only be a matter of time before he learned her name, her relations. How long before he began to share his ill meeting with her to other gentlemen? Soon her whole family of eligible ladies would be considered undesirable for yet another reason. That was all her making.

"Oh, to be sure, that was straight from one of my romance books," Lady Eagleton said with a flurry coming to Lady Alexandra's side.

"I even asked the earl if he put the Duke of Raven up to it. He said he hadn't. Isn't it just so romantic?" She said with a whimsical gloss to her eyes. "He came right up to you and asked you to dance. It's like a fairytale, isn't it?"

"He thought I was someone else," Lady Alexandra said blatantly doing her best to sip her punch and calm the shaking of her body.

It was not for fear of the duke's repercussions. Instead, she could feel the adrenaline of fury still pulsing through her to have been embarrassed so.

"What? How could that even be possible?"

"He thought I was Lady Charlotte," Lady Alexandra said quickly. "Not to mention the fact that he had some rather pointed opinions on my father's life work."

"I can't image he would say anything offensive? The earl has had nothing but high regards for him, young Charles as well. Perhaps it was a misunderstanding."

"The only misunderstanding was with whom he thought he was dancing."

Lady Alexandra decided to leave out the fact that the duke's rude comments had not been with foreknowledge of who she was in relation to the words he spoke.

Even still, she was sure that a refined duke should know better than to speak down on any establishment that might have a connection to any person in any party. She was sure that was a bit extreme and ridiculous of a thought, but she didn't care in the least.

Lady Eagleton began to scan the room for her husband, determined to remedy the situation. Perhaps the Duke had mistaken Alexandra's identity for another, but they had seemed to genuinely enjoy the dance together, well at least the beginning part she had seen of it.

"Do not worry yourself over it," Lady Alexandra said putting a hand on her friend's arm. She knew Regina's desires without the words even being spoken.

"I am sure the earl will clear everything up, though," Lady Eagleton pressed on.

"I think I will instead find a hackney to take me home early."

"Oh, please don't go. There is still much fun to have."

"I would not want to risk tainting my sisters with the bad interaction," Lady Alexandra said, tears welling in her eyes.

She refused to cry, let alone cry in a public place. Never

in her life had she felt so unimportant and belittled as she had the moment the Duke revealed his true desired dance partner.

"I really think this is just a silly mistake. Perhaps we could all laugh about it later?" Lady Eagleton gave one last effort.

"I don't think I could bear to ever look on the Duke of Raven again, let alone have a humorous conversation with him."

Lady Alexandra only sniffed once. She tugged up her glove for the last time before squaring up her chin. Life was full of much harder trials than silly balls could produce. She would not let this moment define her.

"Please see that my sisters find a carriage home at an appropriate time."

"Of course," Lady Eagleton said embracing her friend. "We have plenty of room in our own. I will see to it that they return home safely."

"Thank you," Lady Alexandra said just above a whisper before setting her half-drunk cup down on a servants tray and exiting Sir Hamilton's home.

8

"What on earth possessed you to dance with Lady Alexandra Woodley?" Aunt Rebecca said as they rode in the carriage back to their house.

"It was a mistake I assure you, Aunt Rebecca," he said, just barely able to keep his eyes open in the soft light of dawn.

After his error with the mystery lady, whom he now had a name to, he had found an introduction to Lady Charlotte. They had danced the third and sixth set together.

She seemed a nice enough lady and said all the right things. There was also the constant commentary from his aunt at his side between dances speaking of her good fortunes. Apparently, his first mistaken dance had seemed to her an accusation against her own choice.

"I should hope it was a mistake. You do know who her family is?"

"I am afraid I am not entirely sure," Raven said, at least happy that this conversation keeping him awake long past his desire of it, would have the purpose of exposing the mystery girl to him.

"It isn't her fault, of course," Aunt Rebecca started, which told him there was some great misfortune to her tale. "Her father is Earl Grebs."

"I know that name," Raven said jogging his memory.

"I am sure you do. Lord Grebs' father had several great misfortunes in his lifetime. I am not entirely sure of all the details just that it may not have been in very moral means. They lost the family fortune. Then Lord Grebs and his wife had four girls before she too passed away. I am sure you can imagine a destitute Earl with four girls had little chance of finding a replacement."

Lady Rebecca gave a long sigh watching the light grow out the carriage window.

"So their misfortune is to have little funds to their title?" Raven asked, actually considering this not a very horrible circumstance and indeed not the first time that a lord found himself in such a state.

"Well, then there is her father. He is most reclusive. One could say he always was, but much more since his wife's passing. The last I heard was he holes himself up in their house — it's not in a desirable neighborhood at all and very near Seven Dials —and looks at dead creatures."

Lady Rebecca gave a shiver at the thought.

"I don't think they are dead creatures as much as specimens."

"Oh call them what you like, it is still strange to me," Lady Rebecca said with a wave of her hand. "Let us talk about happier things. Do tell me what you thought of Lady Charlotte."

"Perhaps we could discuss the matter tomorrow. I am quite done in for the night," Raven said with a long yawn though he was never one to not give into his aunt's wishes if she pressed.

To his good fortune, she didn't press this night. Instead, she held in her tongue and excitement over the matter until the following day.

"Oh, I can't stand the anticipation any longer," Aunt Rebecca said the following afternoon as the two sat to a very late breakfast. "Do tell me what you thought of her?"

Raven had to give it to his aunt for her self-restraint. They had made it almost halfway through the meal talking of almost any other aspect of London except for last night's ball.

"She seemed to be a very kind lady," Raven began slowly.

"Oh and isn't she so lovely to look at. You must act quickly, however," Aunt Rebecca continued, taking a currant roll off the plate as she spoke. "You are not the only gentleman to set his eye on her."

Raven sat back and continued to eat his food as his aunt went on. It seemed all she needed was a start to the subject and then she would happily carry on the conversation all on her own.

"You did dance with her twice which is more than anyone else I dare say last night," Aunt Rebecca finally finished. "Do tell me you will be seeing her again soon? You must call on her quickly before another can steal her attention away."

"I have already spoken to Lady Charlotte about taking a turn in the park together on the morrow," Raven said. "I plan to call on her after our meal to secure the time," he added much to the delight of his aunt.

Though she was a woman of age, she bounced up and down on her velvet seat as if she was a twelve-year-old school girl.

He couldn't help but delight in the happiness he had brought to his aunt as he watched her grey curls bobble to and fro under her flapping lace cap during her moment of glee.

He wasn't entirely honest with his aunt, however. Of

course, he did have plans to call at Lady Charlotte's residence. It also was true that they had made plans to take a stroll through Kensington Gardens.

She had pressed for Hyde Park, but Raven was not yet ready to make such a public statement. Instead, he had suggested he take her along the various fountains and beautiful flowers of Kensington's Gardens.

He had a passion not just for adventuring but also learning the lay of the land and things that inhabited it as he had expressed the night before to the now known mystery lady.

He had suggested he take Lady Charlotte and give her a sort of walking tour of the flora of the area. She had seemed intrigued to the idea though he wasn't entirely sure if it was just out of politeness.

There was another reason that he had picked Kensington Gardens. He would take her on the far side of the park that had a street running adjacent to the Museum spoken of the night before.

In truth, he hadn't gone there since boyhood and considered the long night if he had been hasty in his judgment of the place. Had Raven been given the opportunity he would have sought out Lady Alexandra again and tried to make amends.

Her lasting words had also seemed to haunt him: "A candle loses nothing from lighting another." Perhaps some good could come to his time in London. He would tour the

Museum and see if he could put his vast travels to good use.

In fact, from the moment that he finished the first dance at Sir Hamilton's opening ball, he could get little in his mind beyond the lady he had danced with.

Even before he had learned her name, Raven found himself distracted with the impression she had played on him. It took several mental reminders that he was only here at the request of his aunt, and not genuinely looking for a match.

If he happened upon a suitable pairing that was amiable to his aunt, he would, of course, see to it. It was clear after last night's carriage ride that Lady Alexandra didn't fit on that list of optional pairings.

There would be no point to peruse that avenue further with such knowledge. Still, the duke couldn't seem to get her out of his memory.

Despite the pressing memory on his mind, he filled his day with the necessities of life. He went and called of Lady Charlotte who was not at home. He left his card behind and had a relatively enjoyable conversation with her mother. Lady Derber assured the Duke that not only did her daughter remember their engagement on the morrow but was looking forward to it greatly.

After that, he spent the remainder of the evening at Brook's gentleman's club to take his dinner and complete some various business before turning to some of the gambling tables.

Raven didn't consider himself a gambling man though he knew enough to play the favorite card games of the time. In truth, he found little enjoyment from it. Perhaps if he had, London itself would have seemed more enjoyable to him as it was a widespread practice and almost the sole leisure activity for gentlemen.

He left the club rather early compared to most, though it was dark and the lanterns had all been lit. He walked the streets of London back to his home, still unable to get Lady Alexandra from his mind.

He did his best to look at the lanes and walks of London as she must. Lady Alexandra had confessed to never going anywhere outside the city.

It had been a curious revelation at the time when he thought she was someone else. Now knowing her parentage, it was entirely reasonable. Many impoverished lords only held on to a London house for all year residency. It was no surprise to him that she had never set foot in even the English countryside.

As he walked the streets, he considered this type of life. It was undoubtedly a polar opposite to his own. Raven had spent his childhood from country estate to retreats near the ocean. His adulthood considered the vast world his home.

As Raven considered a life never outside these streets and walks of London, he found himself feeling very claustrophobic. It didn't cause Raven to look down on her family as his aunt did, but instead pity her. Pity her to the point that he wanted to change that fact in her life.

She clearly must have also had a curious mind for things outside her city. Why else would she have claimed to visit her father's museum so often?

Raven remembered himself as that young boy walking the museum halls with his father. He had convinced the late duke to take him after much begging.

He had been so fascinated on that first trip into the museum. It wasn't until later when he began his own education of the world he had learned how erroneous much of it was.

Had Raven been like Lady Alexandra, seeing nothing outside of London, he too would have found the Museum to be a haven from this smoke-filled city.

Though Raven couldn't quite put his finger to it, he was sure there was something about Lady Alexandra that was most intriguing.

It was for this reason that he found himself standing before Lord Eagleton's house instead of his own so late at night. He was desperate to get some information about the lady.

"Unfortunately my husband is out for the night," Lady Eagleton informed him as they sat in her front drawing room.

Raven took a quick moment to study the young wife.

She was not so young as when the earl had first married her. At the time, Raven and young Charles had gone on incessantly over the fact that the earl had chosen a wife almost the same age as his oldest son.

Lady Eagleton did look quite mature for her young age. She still had the youth and beauty of her generation of course, but she did have something distinguishing about the way she carried herself.

"And you have decided to stay in for the night?" Raven said searching for conversation between the two of them. He would have liked to ask about the connection to a certain lady who didn't seem to want to leave his mind, but knew he couldn't just blurt such things out.

"The earl went to the opera. I wasn't ready for such a tiresome adventure after Sir Hamilton's ball," Lady Eagleton said delicately.

"I never cared much for operas myself," Raven said sensing her real meaning.

Lady Eagleton relaxed into a smile at his words. He watched as the fire played off the gold locks of her hair and lemon colored cotton dress as she poured out the tea.

"It is just the fact that it is all in another language," Lady Eagleton confessed after handing the Duke his tea. "It would be one thing if it was just French. It takes an effort to understand that language at all in my opinion. But then to make it overly dramatic with long drawn out words makes it near impossible. I have no taste for it."

"I couldn't agree more," Raven said, never really caring for the opera though he wasn't sure if they truly did share the same reason.

Raven just found it a complete bore to sit and watch someone sing on a stage for hours on end.

Raven spent another hour with the Lady of the house though there seemed to be little he could glean off of her regarding Lady Alexandra.

Though the duke tried to include their now mutual acquaintance in conversation casually, Lady Eagleton was always quick to change the subject.

The only information he received was the fact that Lady Alexandra was a wonderful dear friend to the countess and very beloved once people get to know her.

He couldn't help but feel any mention of the lady's name put the countess in the defensive. It was clear that she did care much for this friend of her's and seemed very much at odds over talking the matter over with Raven.

Still unsatisfied with the day's events, Raven finally retired from Eagleton's house to return back to his own. Aunt Rebecca tried her best to engage him for the night, but in all honesty, he still had had little time to recuperate since his long travels. Instead of joining his aunt for an evening of cards and socialization, he retired to bed with his apologies.

9

"Alexandra! Alexandra! Where are you, child?" Lord Grebs called out in a fit as he marched up and down the narrow hall outside his library.

"Father, I am here," Lady Alexandra said, hearing him as she came in the door.

Lady Alexandra had spent the morning out looking over fresh produce at the bi-weekly market. She handed her basket of fresh cheese, bread, and some dried apples to Polly before rushing to her father's aid.

Rarely was he removed from his library, but often as was the case these days, it was in a fit of discomfort.

She took her father's hands and eased him back into the room. Though the day was still warm, she lit the small hearth for comfort.

"It is just all a disaster," Lord Grebs was saying walking the small room.

"It can't be all that bad Father. Just tell me the problem, and I shall find a way to fix it."

"It is the dear animal," he said pointing down to the oversized pincushion still in its place of honor.

"Are you having trouble in your studies then?" Lady Alexandra asked, taking a seat.

She found that when her father was in such a state the best aid she could give him was a calm, relaxing atmosphere.

"John Lucas needs the specimen and my notes today," Lord Grebs said with finality only half noticing his daughter's presence. "Hellen in the kitchen is being so unreasonable," he added.

"I don't think Hellen is trying to be unduly difficult. What concern does she have with the creature? I can't imagine she would desire it on a dinner menu," Lady Alexandra said smiling at her own wit.

"It's not that, Alexandra," Lord Grebs said with a huff.

His hair was exceptionally unruly this morning. Lady Alexandra had a feeling that today was going to be an exceptionally difficult one.

"I called for Thomas to come and pick the creature up. The porcupine needs to be at the museum by tomorrow morning," Lord Grebs repeated.

"Thomas has the day off; you know that," Lady

Alexandra said though she was sure her father didn't know that nor did he know what day it was, save in relation to the museum's schedule.

"Well, then Hellen must hitch the cart and take it to the museum. It must be there before tomorrow morning, as well as my notes," he said, as if the thought just came to him.

Lord Grebs fisted a small notebook and waved it in the air.

"Hellen has her own duties to attend to. She hasn't the time to hitch the cart and run errands. After all, it is why I go to the markets for her every second Monday."

"Well, it doesn't matter what other duties there are, this is far more important."

Lady Alexandra took a long steady breath. Everything that had to do with that museum took far more precedence than anything else in her father's eyes.

"I'm sorry, Father but it just can't be done."

"Well then you take it," Lord Grebs said pointing his book at his daughter.

"I wouldn't know how to hitch the cart nor how to drive it."

"Then hire a hackney," Lord Grebs interjected.

Lady Alexandra looked down at the hands in her lap. They were ghostly white against the grey of her muslin morning dress.

"You know, Father, that we have limited funds for such a

thing each month. The last was used up not two days ago for Sir Hamilton's ball."

Lord Grebs made a sound that suggested that such a use was a shameful waste compared to his emergency.

"I'm sorry I can't be of more help, Father, but if Mr. Lucas does not come here himself to pick up the item, then it will just have to wait till Thomas can hitch the cart tomorrow," Lady Alexandra said standing to leave the room.

There would be no calming her father today. She was already doing her best to bridle her tongue against telling him what she really thought of his outlandish emergency.

Though she found his mind's workings to be beyond reasonable at this moment, he was still her father, and she would not dishonor the man by speaking harsh words to him.

Instead, she left the room, knowing there was little chance of him following. It didn't stop the long stream of explanation on why the distinguished scientist Mr. John Lucas could not leave his work for even a moment that day to collect the porcupine himself.

Lady Alexandra had finally thought the discussion was put to bed and the day could continue on until she heard her father calling again.

"Look! Look, Alexandra," he said as she left the drawing room where she was overseeing Sophia's painting lesson.

"I found this in the back garden shed," Lord Grebs said, wiggling a baby pram in the hall.

Bits of dust flew up from the black material head cover and wicker basket. Lady Alexandra had a moment of a coughing fit.

"Whatever is that old thing for," Lady Alexandra asked not even knowing how Lord Grebs had ventured into the back garden and shed and dug it out.

"Look, it fits just perfectly inside," Lord Grebs said wheeling the small baby carriage closer to her.

Much to Lady Alexandra's surprise, the stuffed porcupine was set in the wicker baby carriage with an old baby blanket covering its bulky size so that only its face stuck out looking directly at the driver.

"That is the most ridiculous thing I have ever seen. What do you expect me to do with that?" Lady Alexandra said forgetting her wishes to keep her father calm.

"You can take it now, obviously," Lord Grebs said motioning to the carriage. "I couldn't bring myself to ask you to carry it on account of the quills. There is no danger of it shooting them at you, but they are still very uncomfortable to touch."

"How very kind of you, Father," Lady Alexandra said with little feeling as she studied his suggestion. "Are you asking me to wheel your stuffed creature in a baby pram all the way to the museum?" She asked, attempting to wrap her mind around her father's crazy wishes.

"Well take Polly with you, of course. You can have her wheel the cart if it would make you feel better," Lord Grebs said not seeing anything wrong with the idea.

"The whole of the ton would think I was walking a baby around the streets of London. Me? I am an unmarried woman. I can't even begin to imagine the gossip such a thing would cause."

"Oh nonsense," Lord Grebs waved off. "It will be quite all right. It is imperative that this work reaches its destination today," he reiterated, returning to his manic tone.

As much as Lady Alexandra dreaded the idea, the only one she feared more was that he would call one of her other sisters to do it in her stead. She couldn't risk that happening to them.

"Alright, I'll take the thing to the museum," Lady Alexandra said.

She watched as her father's face washed over with relief and split into a smile. She couldn't help but feel some satisfaction in knowing that she at least calmed her father for today.

She highly doubted that such satisfaction would be enough as she made the long walk through London, past Hyde Park and Kensington Gardens to her father's favorite museum.

For the trip, Lady Alexandra did accept the company of the housemaid Polly. She put on her most unnoticeable brown walking dress, and a large matching hat that covered much of her face.

Her one and only hope was that she could get to the museum without anyone spotting her. There she would drop off the items and instruct the carriage be destroyed so that she would never be forced to such a degrading task again.

For the beginning of the journey, there was little worry. It wasn't until she got into view of Hyde Park that her nerves really set in. Of course, her father had insisted such a request to occur right at that moment causing her to arrive at the park at the height of the fashionable hour.

Though it was still early in the season, the park was already full of ladies and gentlemen riding in gigs or just walking along the park's pathways.

If she could but make it past the park, she would be relatively safe as not many continued on past its lanes and into Kensington Gardens.

Lady Alexandra decided to take the longer route going entirely around both parks instead of straight through as she usually did. It would cost more in time but also make it less likely she would be spotted by a member of the ton.

It was with relief that she saw the museum steps come into view. Lady Alexandra was sure that a moment in her life had never occurred where she was so happy to see the place.

Sadly, as they got closer, a new realization dawned on

her. The door leading into the museum was ushered in with a rather large row of stone steps. It would be impossible for her to get the baby carriage inside the building.

"Polly," Lady Alexandra said as they came up to the bottom of the steps. "You go inside and inform Mr. Lucas that I am here and that if he wants his specimen for tomorrow, he should come and collect it presently."

Polly nodded in understanding before turning to hurry up the steps. Lady Alexandra looked around, one hand resting on the carriage as she waited. She was sure the worst was over.

This part of the street was all but deserted with few venturing to the museum. The only landscape in front of her was the rear entrance of Kensington Gardens.

The chance of anyone coming upon her and her strange carriage contents was almost next to none.

She almost wholly relaxed at that moment until her heart stopped.

She was almost sure she could see the top of a hat coming around the bend of the garden wall towards the exit gate. She tightened her grip on the handle of the carriage, begging the person silently to go the other way.

The person didn't turn away, however, but instead turned to go through the gate. She saw the hesitation of recognition in the Duke of Raven's dark eyes as they went immediately to the museum and her at the bottom of the steps.

In a sheer moment of panic, Lady Alexandra could only think of one thing that would save her from the embarrassment of being confronted by the duke with Lady Charlotte currently on his arm and that was to get rid of the carriage and return home.

In the act of pure desperation, she looked between the front door and her place at least twelve steps apart. Mr. Lucas had still yet to appear, but that would not stop her.

Perhaps it was momentary insanity, but with her goal in mind, Lady Alexandra gripped the handlebar tight and proceeded to pull the carriage up the steps of the museum.

10

The Duke of Raven picked up his afternoon date right on time. Clearly, the lady had been anticipating the interaction as she was produced the instant his name was given to the butler. Though he was glad not to be made to wait, he also couldn't dismiss the gnawing question of what prompted the lady to be so excited.

Though they had danced two sets at Sir Hamilton's ball, they in truth had spoken very little to each other. Had Raven been slightly less exhausted he might have been keener to produce conversations to entice information out of the reserved lady. As it was, that night, and he dared say every night since, his mind had been occupied with images of Lady Alexandra. Little beyond intrigue over the lady had filled his mind that night.

Raven was determined that today's outing would be

much different. After all, he was here at his Aunt Rebecca's wishes. It would serve him little to honor his promise to her by actions without at least taking the time to truly get to know Lady Charlotte.

She certainly was a well-bred lady, and he scarcely could find a companion so adequately suited for the Duchess of Raven. When he greeted her within the foyer of her family townhouse, the exquisite and fashionable decor of the residence, as well as her dress, were not missed on him.

Lady Charlotte was wearing a well-tailored walking dress in cream with lace trimmings. Her waist was accentuated with a rose embroidered ribbon, and in her white-gloved hand, she carried a matching cream parasol with painted roses. He was sure it was of her own work as was the perfectly accented walking hat with silk ribbon roses tipped just to the side.

He studied her as they walked to the gig he had parked outside. She was beautiful indeed. Her golden-brown hair was pulled back into a tight twist with a pair of perfect ringlets cascading down the opposite side that her hat tilted to. Her skin was of a fine ivory texture with just a touch of rose at her cheeks to give her vibrancy. Even her very movements were that of a refined lady.

Though such things were undoubtedly taught to her from a young age, there was still an air about her of refinement that could never be taught, only bred. Raven was confident that if he did choose to make her his bride by season's end, she certainly would do the position justice.

"I thought you wouldn't mind if we went to Kensington Gardens today for a walk," Raven said after assisting the lady to her seat and taking his next to her.

He motioned for the chestnut stead before him to proceed forward and they moved with a slight jolt.

"Are we not to take a ride then?" she asked back in her delicate voice before popping open her parasol and holding it overhead to shade from the sun.

It was still early in the afternoon, but without a cloud in the sky the sun shone down bright on them. In truth, it was much hotter than most spring days Raven had experienced in London. In her fine dress, Lady Charlotte had probably hoped for a slow ride under the shade of the large trees within Hyde Park.

It was also beginning to roll into the most fashionable hour when anyone who wanted to be seen would also be riding a gig around the grounds of the park. He had considered all these facts before picking up Lady Charlotte this day. Though he wanted to do his promise to his aunt justice, he still wasn't sure he was ready for such a public showing of their acquaintances.

After all, Raven had danced two whole sets with the lady at the ball. That was a questionable action in itself. It had fulfilled its purpose to both his aunt and Lady Charlotte's mother that he was considering courting Lady Charlotte seriously this season.

To be seen only days later in a gig along the cobbled roads of Hyde Park was inevitably the next step in showing his serious bid for courtship. As much as he wanted to do so for his aunt's sake, he was not ready to make that step just yet.

"I know it is slightly on the warm side today, and perhaps too strenuous for a walk," Raven started as they made their way down the street. "But I am aware of some very beautiful flowers that have come to bloom recently in Kensington and thought you might enjoy them."

"That does sound very lovely," Lady Charlotte agreed. "Though I must confess I do worry some for the hem of my dress," she added with honesty.

Raven stole a look at the lady before returning it to the road before him. She had undoubtedly chosen a gown to be seen in not walk in. The paths of Kensington Gardens were clean and fine ones for the most part, but he couldn't in all honesty promise she wouldn't soil her hem if they did walk it.

Raven told himself that he should agree with the lady and just take her on a carriage ride around Hyde Park. Though he knew it was right, he did honestly have a desire to walk the flora of Kingston. It would be a great enjoyment to experience some greenery inside the confines of the city. He also had a desire to share this passion with Lady Charlotte. After all, if she were to be his wife in the future wouldn't they want to have shared interest, or at least the ability to discuss each other's likes and dislikes?

Though all of this was true, Raven couldn't help but confess to himself that the real reason for going to Kensington Gardens was so that the end of their walk would result at the natural museum. He would have liked to examine it again after his interaction with Lady Alexandra and found an outing with Lady Charlotte a perfect excuse for it.

"I am sure with this warm weather the path will be dry and not damage the hem of your fine gown too much. However, if you would rather not, I understand," Raven replied as they crept closer to the two neighboring parks.

"A walk does sound very fine," Lady Charlotte replied. "I am sure you are right that I will find the beautiful flowers most enjoyable. They are sure to be most inspiring."

Raven couldn't tell if she was telling the truth or just merely being polite, but either way, he accepted the offering and circled round Hyde to park next to the entrance of Kensington Gardens.

"What type of inspiration are you seeking?" Raven asked.

"I enjoy painting, though I don't profess to be very good at it. Landscapes are my current passion."

"If I may judge your work by your parasol, it looks wonderful to me already," Raven complimented.

"You are very kind, Your Grace. They are, in fact, my handiwork. I am honored to say I have had some excellent tutors who have guided me all my life."

Raven parked at the main entrance to the garden and walked around to help the lady down. He could hear the excitement and merriment coming from Hyde Park just across the way from them. He was sure that along with the conversations, cantering horses, and chirping birds he could already hear the start of a horse race. It was yet early in the day for such, but a necessity for young lords out to prove themselves to the ton.

Raven smiled affectionately at the thought. Both he and his good friend Charles Whitehall Jr., now Viscount Bembury, had taken their chances on the back of steeds along those dangerous rows. Though Raven had an affinity for riding and had almost never lost a race, he had little interest in the act of horse racing, or gambling on such. It was just as well as such action, though often done by young pups and watched by many of the ton, were not exactly a proper past time for a duke.

Kensington Gardens in stark contrast was more open without the rows of towering trees that lined the streets of Hyde Park. Instead were winding garden paths surrounded by well-manicured bushes. Fountains could be heard bubbling from within its gates, and Raven could only imagine the glorious natural sanctuary that must lay in wait within. To him, it was a heavenly paradise compared to the loud, smoky business of the city.

He took a long intake of breath as they paused before the gates. It was a slice of heaven that almost reminded him of the wilds of America that he wished so dearly to return to. Even the rolling hills of the English countryside would be satisfactory compared to the cramped living quarters, yelling hackneys, and constant action in London. He let out his elbow which Lady Charlotte took with the softest touch.

"It does look quite lovely here today," she said softly as they entered the gate. "I can already see many pops of color. You were right to guess this was a prime time of year to see the natural beauty."

There were very few couples in the garden, and many were simply passing through on their way to Hyde. Of course, Raven and Lady Charlotte greeted them all politely, but as they delved deeper into the waving paths of the Garden, they soon found themselves to be far away from any others.

"My mother tells me that you are a great adventurer," Lady Charlotte said after some time.

"That is very right of her to surmise," Raven agreed. "In fact, in honesty, I would have to say I rather detest London."

"Oh, I couldn't imagine not enjoying such a wonderful, enterprising city," Lady Charlotte countered.

He liked that though she was certainly polite, she also was willing to disagree with him. Raven often found that people simply said things to please him whether it was true or not.

"Well, perhaps you will take the time to point out some of its good qualities to me. Perhaps with your suggestions, I will change my mind," Raven said leading the conversation to something easily discussed at length.

"Well, there is the theater of course. I dare say there is no opera house, save Paris of course, that could come close to the Haymarket."

"Do you attend these often then?" Raven asked with a slight bristling remembering his conversation with Lady Eagleton only the day before.

"Oh yes. I dare say I am a very eager student of all the arts. Painting, music, and theater are very fond pastimes to me."

"I see," Raven said.

"I would guess by your words that you don't share in this opinion," Lady Charlotte said looking up at him with a soft smile playing on her lips.

"No, not my favorite past times. I can already tell that I would enjoy your artwork, however," Raven said nudging to the parasol. "Your roses are most exquisite."

She modestly looked away blushing.

"Roses are the easiest for me because we have so many in the garden behind our manor. I often sit out there for long periods just practicing sketches with my notebook. I do wish I had better skills at other arrangements of flowers, but as of yet I find I lack the skill."

Raven led Lady Charlotte to a particular portion of the garden at the back end that he knew would be presently filled with wild snowdrops along the path. He was sure she would enjoy their simple, delicate beauty.

"Oh, they are so wonderful," Lady Charlotte said releasing her hold on Raven to lean down and study the low hanging flowers better.

He took a moment to relax his arm. The day was turning out to be much hotter than even he had initially intended. Without the shade of trees, they were under the full exposure of the sun. It was probably improper of him to expect her to walk in such a climate.

To his great pleasure, however, they were very near the back entrance of the Garden that was directly across from the natural museum.

Though the bushes were quite tall in this portion of the Garden, he was still tall enough to make out the roof of the building. Surely it would be open and much cooler inside than their current situation. It would be a perfect excuse to lead her to venture inside with him.

"I fear that I have exposed you to this warm climate far too long," Raven said doing his best to act casual despite the growing anticipation to enter the museum again.

Though he knew it was a silly notion, he had the

deepest desire to enter the edifice as if it would somehow give him more information on the once mysterious lady of the ball.

"I know of a museum of wonders just yonder. Would you like to walk it with me? It will be much cooler inside, and they even have a butterfly terrarium where you might find inspiration for future works."

"That does sound lovely," Lady Charlotte said coming to stand and linking her arm within his again. "I only wish I had thought to bring my tracing pad."

"Well, if you find it as interesting as I hope you will, then I would be happy to escort you for a second trip."

Raven smiled down at the lady. Though his mind seemed filled continuously with another, there was no reason that he shouldn't have thought of Lady Charlotte. She was turning out to be a most enjoyable companion, and at the very least their union would be one of comfortable friendship, if it was determined by their experiences thus far.

As they came around the bend, Lady Charlotte gave a little giggle, "You can't mean that museum?"

"Yes, I did," Raven said looking down at her with an embarrassed chuckle of his own.

"It is so silly, everyone says so," she said though not forcing him to turn away from the Garden exit.

"I know. I must confess I am of the same opinion. As a child I was quite fond of the place, the safari room in particular," he added with a lopsided smile. "I suppose it is nostalgia that made me think of it. We don't have to go inside if you would rather not," he suggested though he hoped she wouldn't take the opportunity to turn around.

At that very moment, Raven looked out at the museum with much longing. It was then that he noticed the figure at its steps for the first time. It was a woman standing along with a child in a pram. If a fine lady without a maid on a London street wasn't strange enough, it was even more so when he realized it was Lady Alexandra.

For all his might he couldn't fathom why the lady would be standing thus with a child. Even more shocking was the fact that within the moment he recognized her, she began the impossible task of hauling the child up the steps of the museum alone.

11

Lady Alexandra should have known that her rash actions would have only drawn the Duke closer to her. But in the moment of great embarrassment, she had not stopped to think a single action through. Her only thought was to get the blasted beast in the building and run for the safety of her own home.

It was a stupid notion, to say the least. Before she even got the old carriage up the first step, she could already see the Duke hurrying closer. In fact, he had left his walking companion behind him in his haste to come to her aid.

Beyond him, Lady Alexandra could make out the figure of the very fine Lady Charlotte. If things couldn't have been more disastrous, it was she who was walking quickly to catch up to her companion. Lady Alexandra did not doubt by evening time the entire ton would hear of her walk with a porcupine in a carriage. Lady Charlotte may have been a fine lady, but she was not above gossip, and at the moment had the ear of every fashionable lady of the season.

Lady Alexandra had just struggled to get the back wheels up the first step, with the front wheels balancing precariously on the tip of the second when her next backward motion ended in stepping on her own walking dress hem.

Losing her balance, her eyes shot up just in time to see the Duke of Raven reach her in three bounding steps. The shock of it all made her let go of the pram to go careening towards him. Effortlessly he sidestepped the falling basket, twisted around, and grabbed the handle with his hands.

"Oh, my goodness," Lady Charlotte cried, fearing for a child inside no doubt.

She lifted her skirts just enough to walk faster and reach the pram herself.

Lady Alexandra found herself seated on the steps of her father's blasted museum staring up at the Duke of Raven.

Once Raven was sure that the basket wouldn't travel further, he turned to the lady's aid. Reaching down he quickly scooped her off the stone steps before releasing her. It was just a moment's connection but one that sent excitement surging through his body.

"Is the child alright," Lady Charlotte called out desperate to see into the carriage. It was no doubt most confusing to her that no cry had come from the tumble down the two steps.

"Please don't bother yourself, Your Grace, Lady Charlotte," Lady Alexandra said with two quick curtseys.

Lady Alexandra was desperately trying to get around the wall that the Duke of Raven was creating between her and the most embarrassing contents of the basket. He refused to move, however, grabbing her elbow instead to catch her attention.

"Are you quite alright, Lady Alexandra," he said staring at her with a most sincere gaze.

"I can assure you I am not injured," Lady Alexandra said again trying to sidestep the man.

"Where is your maid?" he said not releasing his hold despite her apparent wish to be removed from him. Raven looked around the street certain that no well-bred lady would ever be caught walking the streets of London alone with a baby.

"She is just inside, Your Grace. Polly went to get assistance for the pram."

"Well then why didn't you wait for such assistance? You could have seriously injured yourself and the child," he scolded down at her.

"My goodness," Lady Charlotte said again but now at a high squeak. "What on earth is that thing!"

She had a handkerchief in her hand as she took several steps back from the small carriage. Lady Alexandra would have liked to crumple to the ground right there on the spot. At the noise, the Duke of Raven turned to see what was wrong.

"Why on earth would you be pushing a hideous creature around in a baby's carriage," Lady Charlotte said weakly with shock.

Lady Alexandra prayed she didn't faint. That was sure to make this disaster worse. Raven reached out and pulled the carriage to him again. Removing the small blanket entirely, he exposed the whole of the creature. Lady Charlotte gave a little shriek at its fully exposed form, long yellow teeth and all.

"Please, I do beg both your pardons," Lady Alexandra said desperately trying to get between the Duke and the porcupine. "I don't mean to cause a scene."

"Well you certainly did that none the less," Lady Charlotte said in utter shock. "Why on earth would a single lady presume to push a pram? And then to put such a horrid creature inside. It is lucky I have a strong constitution. Were it my mother who took a moment to peer down at the basket's contents she would have swooned on the spot."

"I did not hope to be seen at all," Lady Alexandra tried to explain. "I promise you it was out of pure necessity that I am here on these steps in such a way," Lady Alexandra tried to explain.

She was desperate to make the lady see that this was not at all what Lady Alexandra had hoped to happen this day. Perhaps if she could make Lady Charlotte see that fact, she would keep this most horrible interaction to herself. Lady Alexandra could only imagine the sideshow her sisters would now become after an event such as this.

"Why, is that a northern porcupine?" Raven said turning back to Lady Alexandra.

The movement gave her the leverage she needed to cut between the Duke and the basket. She quickly went to work covering up the dreadful beast again. For now, she was sure that every moment she laid eyes on the thing, she would only remember how it was the ruin of her dear sisters' future.

"It is, Your Grace. I do beg your pardon again for the atrocious sight. I was unable to carry it on my own, and my cart was not accessible to me this day," Lady Alexandra tried to explain. "It was imperative to my father that it be delivered today for a showing in the morning."

"What strange things you do," Lady Charlotte said eyeing the basket as Lady Alexandra hurried to hide its contents. "Of all the preclude wonders in this museum, one never considered the wildest to be a lady on its steps," she said with a jolly laugh.

Lady Alexandra's eyes hit the floor as her face flushed red. For yet a second time she had been shamed in front of the Duke and his chosen companion. Tears burned her eyes, and she fought to keep them at bay.

"Why not take a hackney?" Raven asked.

Lady Alexandra couldn't bear to speak the truth of the matter to him. It was shameful enough as it was, to confess the lack of funds for such a thing would be too much to keep her emotions back.

"Could you imagine that, Your Grace," Lady Charlotte said with another giggle. Now having gained her composure from the shock, she was rather enjoying the comical scene before her. "The poor driver would have had heart palpitations at the sight. That thing would have no doubt punctured holes all throughout the hackney and cost a man his living."

"It isn't alive," Lady Alexandra mumbled under her breath.

Luckily Lady Charlotte didn't hear amid her giggles.

"Why did you not ask for assistance? I would have happily helped you transport the specimen," Raven said to Lady Alexandra.

This stopped Lady Charlotte's laughter. Lady Alexandra too looked up surprised at his bold declaration.

"Are you acquainted with this lady then?" Lady Charlotte ask.

It was a sweeping moment of relief for Lady Alexandra. If Lady Charlotte didn't know her name, perhaps her sisters were saved yet.

"It is only that, as I said," Raven stumbled turning back to his party, "I was very fond of this museum as a child.

Lord Grebs, Lady Alexandra's father, is the patron of the place."

Lady Alexandra deflated again. There went her chance at anonymity.

"Still that is little cause to offer assistance to one such as, well a practical stranger," Lady Charlotte amended quickly.

"It is for the specimen of course," Raven tried to play off. "The quills on the animal are most delicate."

"They don't look very delicate to me," Lady Charlotte retorted.

"They are hollow, in fact," he explained. "Making it very easy for them to break. It is understandable that Lady Alexandra would transport it in such a unique manner to preserve the specimen," he explained looking back at Lady Alexandra.

She couldn't believe that he was actually attempting to soften the blow of this disastrous encounter.

"I would be happy to carry it in for you," he added.

"Oh, please don't, Your Grace," Lady Alexandra started pulling the basket away from them and back to the side of the stairs.

"You certainly can't do it on your own," he pressed, motioning to the climb behind her. "I fear you will hurt yourself if you try again."

"I thank you for your concern, Your Grace, but I assure you I am quite capable. Help will be along any moment, besides. I bid you both a good afternoon," Lady Alexandra rambled out, desperate for them to go on their way.

Raven narrowed his dark eyes on the lady. Though he could see this was a terrible event for her, he couldn't help but feel the warmth of the comical situation bubble up within him. He couldn't help but let a smile slip at the clear stubborn will of the lady before him.

"I am afraid my honor would not allow me to turn my back on a lady clearly struggling. If you do not let me assist you in your endeavors, then I will wait right here till you have safely reached the top."

Raven was fully expecting the lady to give in to his demands and allow him to walk the item up the steps for her. Instead, she stood a little taller tilted her chin in a most becoming manner and took the tentative step up the first step on her own. He had never felt more admiration for an act of womanly bravery than in that moment.

"Lady Alexandra," a soft voice called up from inside the building.

A maid hurried down with a gentleman quickly in tow.

"Please, m'lady, wait till we reach you," the maid called out in panic.

Lady Alexandra gave out a long sigh of relief. She wouldn't have asked the duke to assist her if her life depended on it, but she also wasn't too fond of the idea of making an attempt a second time with an audience.

"Lady Alexandra, what on earth were you thinking

walking all the way here from your house," the gentleman's voice said as he reached the bottom of the steps.

"Forgive me, Mr. Lucas, from taking you from your work. My father insisted on its delivery today, and I saw no other way about it."

"Although I have made it quite clear that from now on you are to call on me if there is a need of transporting quilled creatures," Raven interjected catching the attention of the gentleman.

"Forgive me, Your Grace," Lady Alexandra said still flustered. "May I introduce Mr. Thomas Lucas. He is the head scientist of the zoology department. Mr. Lucas this is the Duke of Raven and Lady Charlotte Weiderhold."

Lucas bowed as was proper to the two members of the ton.

"Zoology you say," Raven said with sparked interest.

"Yes, Your Grace," Mr. Lucas said taking the carriage from Lady Alexandra.

"I am most fascinated by the subject myself. Pray, tell what is your emphasis on?"

"Honestly, Your Grace, I focus on whatever Lord Grebs can produce for me. We have minimal supplies, unfortunately. Thankfully with this creature, we will be having a lecture of curious native creatures of the new world."

"How very fascinating. I will have to be sure to attend."

"I would be most honored indeed if you did so, Your

Grace," Mr. Lucas said swelling with pride at the notion of a prominent Duke at his morning lecture.

"You must beg your pardon, however, as I must return to my work post haste," Mr. Lucas said by way of apology. "I would hate to be less than prepared for tomorrow's endeavors.

"Of course," Raven said waving the man off.

"Perhaps it is time we return to the gig as well," Lady Charlotte suggested at Raven's side. "The hour is getting late."

"Of course," Raven said remembering his companion. "Lady Alexandra, would you care to join us. I have plenty of room in the gig, and your job seems to be done here."

Lady Alexandra looked to Lady Charlotte, who barely fluctuated in facial expression but clearly didn't want the added company.

"I thank you for the kindness, Your Grace, but I think I will join Mr. Lucas to ensure he has all my father's notes along with the item."

Raven did his best to hide the disappointment. He wasn't surprised at her refusal. Lady Alexandra had been thoroughly embarrassed by the encounter though he had found it to be the highlight of his day. He hadn't wanted it to end just yet.

There was something quite enticing about Lady Alexandra that he just couldn't quite put a finger on. She was clearly unorthodox in many ways. Perhaps it was the surprise of her actions that seemed to befuddle and entice him all at the same time.

"Well, in that case, we will bid you good evening," Raven said to the lady with a bow, rather reluctantly.

For Lady Charlotte's part, she relaxed into a smile and took the duke's arm. Just before they departed out of earshot, Lady Alexandra could hear the hurried talk of the duke's companion in the strangeness of the encounter and all she could think her mother would make of it.

"Come along, Polly," Lady Alexandra said with a heavy heart to the maid who had waited a few steps above of the party.

"Let us go inside and see to the beast before our return home. We still yet have a long walk ahead of us," Lady Alexandra said as she turned, lifted her walking dress, and made her way into the museum of natural wonders that would forever be the curse in her life.

12

Lady Alexandra found the discarded carriage just inside the museum doors. She looked at it with pointed malice.

"Polly, see that this is removed to a storage closet at the back of the museum and never sees the light of day again," she said with satisfying thoughts of its demise.

"Yes, m'lady," Polly said with a quick curtsy before walking off with the offensive basket.

Lady Alexandra let her gaze travel around the room. It had only been a few days since she last saw the building and little had changed. She knew it well enough to pick out any misdeeds or misplacements.

Though the museum didn't hold the highest degree of honor among the ton, it was an enjoyable place for many of the common folk of London. The time of day didn't lead to much business, but still, a few guests paused around the building.

It was an old edifice very regal in design. The floors were of fine tile, and the main room had a roof reaching high above the second floor ending in a beautiful dome-like shape made from glass. It let in the most exquisite light so that candles or lamps were rarely used.

A large wooden walkway skirted around the main room giving a view into the various offices and labs of the second floor. She was sure that Mr. Lucas had already hurried up the wood staircase on the east wall and to his own office to inspect the creature.

She would venture there herself to see that his needs were met in a moment's time. Presently she was more decided on taking a turn about the exhibit portion of the museum. From this main entry, just as there were rooms detached from the main walk like spokes on a wheel, their image was also mirrored below. Instead of small offices and slightly larger laboratories of above, the rooms below spoke of grander spaces.

To the east was the staircase and just beyond the largest of all the indoor rooms. It was reserved for the wonders of Africa. Naturally one of the most popular exhibits was its lion pride and elephant with a baby calf.

Often, Lady Alexandra's father was determined also to house a giraffe inside. How he planned to manage that feat with the museum's ten-foot ceiling was beyond her. She was sure that such an attraction would bring the Londoners by the tons and perhaps bring the museum, and her family, out of ruin. Desperately she hoped the possibility would somehow come, though being a realist, she doubted it.

On the west side of the building, the area was only split into two rooms, one to hold the curiosities of the new world, the latter to show Asian wonders. They were not quite as popular, and truth be told less filled than the bigger safari room. It was her father's current project to bring popularity to this place with such specimens as his porcupine.

Directly behind the main building was a glass-encased wonder and truly Lady Alexandra's favorite exhibit of it all. This green dome, filled with beautiful tropical plants the year round and exotic insects, was by far the most enchanting to her, though rarely visited by the common folk when having to contend with lions and elephants.

It was no small feat to keep such tropical wonders, both insect and plant, living through the harsh London winters. Even with its protective dome to ward off the chill of such, it was still a constant battle to keep the temperature inside up to favorable conditions. It was one Lady Alexandra had taken a personal interest in. Before her complete takeover of the museum, the room had been little more than an indoor/outdoor garden for gentile folk and Londoners alike to meander through when the weather didn't cooperate outside.

Since then, Lady Alexandra had worked hard, with the help of Mr. Lucas, to integrate tropical fauna and living specimens to bring what she could only hope were the tropical wonders of other worlds to this little portion of London.

Having little faith in a giraffe, she was sure that this enclosed dome would be her ticket to getting society's approval of the museum. She had already invited several prominent members of the local Zoological Society to tour it and received excellent tips and pointers from them. Her dream was to make this place accessible to the lords and ladies for events year round. In so doing, she would bring popularity back to the museum of wonders.

Lady Alexandra hesitated in going straight to the second floor to see to Mr. Lucas's needs. She so wanted to stroll the garden paths inside her sanctuary and see that all the care they needed were being properly seen to. More than that, she was in desperate need of the calming effects of her tropical paradise after the ordeal she had just experienced.

However, before a step further could be taken, she heard her name called over the banister. Looking up, she found Mr. Lucas at the top and waving for her to meet him presently. For fear that something had gone terribly wrong in transporting the beast, Lady Alexandra lifted her walking dress and hurried to the stairs.

She found Mr. Lucas waiting for her along the walkway, and together they entered his humble office. It was humble in size, but also the largest of the second floor. At least a dozen local scientists visited the museum on a regular basis and used these offices to study and write reports on specimens of all sizes and shapes. Along with the offices were also four very well-kept labs where various tests and experiments were performed for medicinal and scientific purposes.

"I do hope the creature was in good condition," Lady Alexandra said, entering the room along with Mr. Lucas.

It may not have been the altogether proper thing for a lady to do with her maid still below disposing of the carriage, but it was not something Lady Alexandra had considered.

Mr. Lucas was very much like a brother to her. Even before she was forced to take over all the mundane business of the museum, she would still visit the museum oft with her father in her early teen years. It was then that she was introduced to Mr. Lucas. At the time, he was tutoring under another's skills.

Since that time, he had far surpassed in knowledge any other scientist that walked these halls. It had been only natural for her father to give him more and more responsibilities until he was the head of the zoology department here at the museum. All information, experimentation, and changes of the museum pertaining to the stuffed creatures always went through him first. More than this, Mr. Lucas also had the honor of presenting every new specimen to the small but proud zoological society that resided in the upstairs rooms of the museum.

It was this important task for the morrow's morning that had both her father and Mr. Lucas so flustered and pressed for time. As far as either of them understood, the beast sitting on his desk at the moment was the first to be examined within the walls of London intact. So often the creatures would be damaged from time on a ship, crammed into cases, and tossed about in travel.

Though the porcupine was fierce to look at, it was apparently quite fragile. Once discussed and presented at length in the morning, the gentleman would next extract small specimens for study, taking care to preserve the overall appearance of the creature. Within a week's time, he would add it to the exhibits of new world wonders.

Though the presence of the creature would relieve some pressure for Lady Alexandra at home, her father having nothing to occupy his mind as to forget all else, her responsibilities here would likewise increase.

She would be left in charge of the day-to-day necessities as the patron of the museum to make sure the horrid little creature got its proper debut. If it were up to her, Lady Alexandra would have happily put all the stuffed animals away in the recess of the basement like so many worn and no longer interesting specimens lived. Unfortunately, it was the closest most common Londoner folks would ever come to seeing such majestic creatures outside of paintings. That fact, and that fact alone, was the current sole income for the museum. Without it not only would the building cease to be, but all the scientific work and progress on the second floor would no longer have a home to call their own.

This place was the one and only love for Lady Alexandra's father, and she was sure if she were to close it down it would be the death of him. It was why her endeavors in the flower atrium were so vital. If she could make the tropical living room appeal to the ton, then she could rent it out for events and thereby ease her finical burdens.

"Very fine condition, thank you Lady Alexandra for your care in bringing it to me," Mr. Lucas said circling around his desk and studying it.

"It is just so fascinating. I never dreamed of seeing one intact and in person. Just look at the beautiful shape of its tail," he said brushing it softly with the tips of his fingers.

Lady Alexandra smiled at her good friend. He was looking at the animal with the loving affection that her father also showed to it.

Though she didn't necessarily share in the same passion, she had to appreciate the man for his dedication and persistence in a field he loved so dearly.

"I have so much to do tonight," Mr. Lucas said more to himself.

He was a rather thin man with a scarecrow-like frame, and thick glasses to help him see better. Beyond that, he was rather handsome not to mention of almost the exact same age as Lady Alexandra herself.

"Perhaps I can assist in some way?" Lady Alexandra asked politely.

She honestly didn't want to as she still had the walk home, but also knew instinctively that was what the man had hoped for by his quiet mumbles.

"That is so kind of you, Lady Alexandra. If it wouldn't be too much trouble, and if I shan't be taking you away from other duties, I would love some assistance in going over your father's notes."

Lady Alexandra removed her gloves and set them delicately on the desk before unpinning her hat as he spoke.

"I fear that sometimes, in his excitement, Lord Grebs' writing is so fast and my eyesight so poor that I can scarce read it. Perhaps you could help me by dictating while I transcribe the areas still needed in my own lecture," he said, holding up several sheets of paper that had its own scribbled and crossed out information all over it.

Lady Alexandra never understood this. Almost all of the scientists that she encountered, her father included, always wrote so quick as if the specimen might run before they finished the examination. It would only result in illegible writing leaving the scientist to squint at his own writing and trying to remember the thought that had come to him at that particular moment.

She had often jested her father that his writing was not simply hurried but also coded so no scientist with espionage intent from a rival institution could decipher its meanings and steal his brilliant observations.

"I would be more than happy to help you, Mr. Lucas," Lady Alexandra said plastering a smile onto her face.

She was sure that this would be a task that would take the remainder of the evening but saw no way out of it. She wasn't entirely sure that Mr. Lucas actually had trouble reading her father's handwriting as he had done so for many years when tutoring here. It wasn't until Lady Alexandra had begun to take over her father's role and presence in the museum that Mr. Lucas needed the added assistance.

She suspected it was in part due to a growing affection he had to her. Though Lady Alexandra found Mr. Lucas to be a very kind and generous man, she simply didn't have the time to think of matrimony for herself when she had three younger sisters to think of.

That was the excuse she told herself everytime moments like this came up between them. It was, in Mr. Lucas's mind, opportunities for them to grow closer so that Lady Alexandra might realize her affection for him. For Lady Alexandra, though she never tried, she was sure that even if she had, she would never see Mr. Lucas as more than a dear friend.

She knew that marriage was a very limited possibility for her and she supposed that was the reason that she limited her decision to only marry for love. In that way, she could convince herself that it wasn't the lack of suitors that had caused her to fall into spinsterhood, but the elusive fairy tale of true love that was surely never to come.

Taking one of the notebooks that her father had instructed her to take with the creature, Lady Alexandra sat down in the chair across from the desk and began to read the first few paragraphs out loud. Mr. Lucas for his part took his seat on the other side of the specimen, studying each detail as she pointed it out and occasionally writing out his own conclusion on the notes in front of him.

"I thank you dearly for your help, Lady Alexandra," Mr. Lucas said several hours later as he walked her down the steps and out the front door of the museum.

Dusk had fallen quickly, still being the early months of spring, but luckily the heat had held on, and the chill wasn't too present in the night air.

"I am happy to help anytime, Mr. Lucas," Lady Alexandra said with a smile.

Though she didn't care for him as she was sure he would like, she still had a loving fondness for him and was proud to help him be successful in his career any way that she could.

"Do you expect you are ready for your lecture tomorrow?" She asked walking with him down the outside stone steps.

"I am sure I am ready as I will ever be. Do tell me you will come and hear it. It has been some time since you have come to one of my lectures. I do appreciate and consider your opinions of them on the highest regard."

Lady Alexandra had once attended all his lectures. It wasn't because she had a keen interest in such things as he or her father did, but simply out of support for a good friend. When she had begun to discover his feelings for her, she had oft made reasons why she couldn't come. She feared her presence, especially as the only woman present during the lectures, was encouraging something she didn't feel. For this reason, she hesitated at the thought.

"Please do say you will come," he said as they stopped at the bottom of the stairs where he would bid her goodnight.

There was another reason Lady Alexandra particularly didn't want to be present at tomorrow's lecture. The Duke of Raven had informed them both that he was interested in attending it. The only thing worse in Lady Alexandra's mind than spurring on Mr. Lucas's affections when she didn't reciprocate was the thought of seeing that man again.

She had already done irreparable damage, she was

sure, this season when it came to her sisters' chances at matches. Seeing him again was sure only to make it worse.

Lady Alexandra opened her mouth to say as much but hesitated as she looked up at the gentleman's face. Though he was gaunt, he resembled a poor lost puppy at that moment with his large blue eyes looking down at her imploringly.

"Oh, I suppose I will make a great effort to attend," she said somewhat reluctantly.

Mr. Lucas lit up like a lantern just ignited, and she couldn't help but feel joy in knowing she made her friend happy.

"Are you sure you won't have me call you a hackney, it is awful dark already," Mr. Lucas said preparing to hail one.

"No, thank you. I know the way well. Plus, I have Polly here to keep me company," Lady Alexandra said, waving to the maid who had stayed a few steps to the side for privacy's sake.

With that, Lady Alexandra gave Mr. Lucas her nightly farewell and started her long journey home. It was one that offered too little distraction having so few people to greet in passing. This left her alone to her thoughts to consider what disaster might befall her on the morrow if she were to come into the presence of the Duke of Raven again.

13

Though Raven was naught but the perfect gentleman as he saw Lady Charlotte back to his gig and to her own front door, he couldn't shake a feeling of animosity towards her. Though she had in truth done little to warrant it.

Lady Charlotte had been an amiable companion the whole afternoon through. She was also well within her right to be shocked at the scene that had played out before them. Even still with every mention she made of sharing the story of their encounter that day, he bristled.

Raven wasn't sure why, but his heart had seemed to entangle itself with Lady Alexandra on the steps of the museum, or perhaps it did from the moment of their first dance, he wasn't entirely sure. All he knew of a surety that any conversation shared among the ladies of the ton on what they had encountered that day would only increase Lady Alexandra's embarrassment.

It was something he simply couldn't bear. He was sure he felt a literal pain at the thought of it. It was a curious feeling and one he had never experienced before in his life. That wasn't entirely true; he corrected himself that night as he pondered over his feelings. He felt a similar pang every time he watched the shores of Virginia sink farther away on the horizon standing on the deck of a ship. It was the feeling of losing something so cherished and valued by him, and the fear of never seeing it again.

Though he didn't enter the museum with Lady Charlotte that day, it didn't remove his resolve to step inside it again. In fact, he was rather glad for the interaction with Mr. Thomas Lucas as it gave him a perfect excuse to return to the place on the following morning.

Raven was keenly aware of the scientific lectures that occurred there on almost a monthly basis. He had attended some as a boy. The fact of the matter was that they were a shadow in comparison of some of the universities he had also had the chance to visit.

For a person just seeking general knowledge or interest in the subject there was nothing wrong with the lectures, but in all honesty, he found them to be shallow and at times filled with misinformation. He had little interest wasting his time in such a place once he had access to the universities in his early manhood. Now he had little use for lecture halls at all as he used the world around him and magnificent scientists he encountered out in the fields as a vastly superior educator.

Even still he had the gnawing desire to set foot into the museum that had mesmerized him as a child and perhaps see how it had changed for the better since that time. It was with this excuse, and the conviction it wasn't for a chance to connect to Lady Alexandra again, that Raven made ready early in the morning and left before his aunt was even out of her room.

He took his fine carriage and studied the people he passed on the street. The sun was just rising, and a mist was creeping out of the local gardens and burning away against the cobblestone. It was in this attitude of leisurely study that he picked out a figure he recognized well.

In an instant, Raven perked up in his seat as he came closer to the form of the woman with her lady's maid at her side. He drunk in every aspect of Lady Alexandra as his carriage rode closer.

She was not in a casual walking dress as she had been the day before, but in an elegant black silk dress with matching Spencer jacket with white lace ruffles protruding from the cuffs. It was very scholarly, indeed. Her hair was pulled back again in a tight chignon with a simple black silk hat to adorn it. Though she was in the simplest of beautiful attire, he couldn't help but find her regal as he passed her by the few yards before arriving in front of the museum.

He paused in his carriage for just a moment giving her a chance to catch up to him. He wanted to exit just as Lady Alexandra arrived so that he might walk her in. After waiting a few moments, he could already hear the soft conversation the lady's maid was having with her mistress. He hoped that she had not noticed him pausing so on the street before getting out.

With a heavy breath of nerves, he grabbed his beaver hat and exited the carriage making sure to place it perfectly atop his head. He turned just as Lady Alexandra approached him. Raven couldn't help but catch his breath at the sight of her all over again.

Though her brown eyes quickly darted to the ground as he looked upon her, he still couldn't help but be mesmerized by her. Her skin was of the perfect pale color with a little rouge at her cheeks. He wondered if it was a natural state or just caused by her morning walk. He desperately searched his mind for a memory of the rose cheeks in their last meeting.

"Good Morning, Lady Alexandra," he said, tipping his hat politely at both ladies.

"Good Morning, Your Grace," she addressed him with a proper curtsy.

"I am surprised to see you here for today's lecture," Raven started hoping to make casual conversation with the lady to eradicate any embarrassment from their previous meeting at these steps. "Are you very interested in species of the American continents?"

"Not particularly no," she said with a short answer; her eyes still every direction but at him.

"Then, pray tell, what brings you to a lecture on one so early in the morning?"

"Mr. Lucas asked me to attend. He is a kind friend, and so I agreed to it," she said finally looking Raven in the eye with a thin-lipped smile.

He could easily see she was still filled with embarrassment over their last meeting. He was sure she would never look at him without shame again. How he suddenly wished to wash that moment away.

He gave her a wicked smile as a thought came to him.

"Perhaps," he said holding out his arm for the lady to take. "You won't mind if I escort you in as we are going to the same place. I am quite sure you are able to make the journey on your own, but I would hate just to stand by and watch this time around," he said with a broad smile.

She looked up at him in utter shock at his words. For a second, he thought he might have fractured her constitution. One he had thought much stronger than to be injured by teasing. Luckily, he was right as Lady Alexandra lifted her chin just slightly and folded her arms in front of her.

"I am afraid that I couldn't accept such an offer from a

man I barely know," Lady Alexandra said narrowing her honey eyes on him.

"I understand," Raven said solemnly.

Lady Alexandra nodded once, proud with her determination, and turned to take the first step alone.

"I will just have to stand here, I suppose and watch as you make your way up," he said in a low but deliberate breath.

Lady Alexandra turned with a visible gasp. She was now put in the corner that he had anticipated. She would either have to take his arm and let him escort her in, or openly agree to allowing him to examine her as she walked.

She took the short step back to him and thrust her arm through his own.

"I suppose if you insist, Your Grace, I have no choice but to accept your kind offer," she spit out with little feeling beyond anger.

Raven gave a hearty chuckle at the situation. He couldn't have imagined how much he enjoyed ruffling this lady's feathers.

"I am sure you will find me to be an amiable company," he said as they made their way up the steps.

"I am not sure I agree to that statement," she said keeping her eyes straight ahead, determined not to look at the man whose arm she was on. "You seem very contradictory to me if I was to be completely honest with you."

"I do find honesty a very vital trait," Raven encouraged. "Please do tell me, what exactly do you find contradictory?"

"For a start, your obvious abhorrence for my father's museum, yet here you are two days in a row paying homage to it."

"Well if you remember correctly, I never got past the steps yesterday," Raven said, brandishing his white teeth again in a wicked grin.

"Also, for a man of such distinguished a title and serious a mannerism you do seem to enjoy terrorizing me so," Lady Alexandra said utterly calm.

If it were not for the rose raising to her cheeks again, he would have believed her indifferent to his teasing.

"I promise you, Lady Alexandra, this is a contradiction that I can safely put to rest this moment. I may look the part of a fine duke, but I do promise you on the inside I am quite the wild adventurer," he said leaning down and speaking just above a whisper.

Lady Alexandra turned surprised at his words, and he chuckled deep in his throat again having received the reaction he desired.

"Perhaps I should reconsider my escort if he, himself, claims to be a dangerous man."

"Oh, not dangerous at all, I can promise you that, Lady Alexandra. Simply a man with an eye always to the horizon. I will play my part well here in London, but I can promise you that it is not who I am but who I must be."

"Then pray tell, Your Grace, share with me your true nature."

"I wouldn't consider such a thing with a lady I have just yet made the acquaintance of," he said again pretending offense at such a notion.

She turned and narrowed her eyes up at him again.

"Perhaps," he added as they entered the building and made their way to the row of chairs at the back of the main open room, "if you allowed me to escort you home in my carriage, I would be more willing to share my true nature with you."

"I couldn't allow such a thing, Your Grace," Lady Alexandra responded in shock. "It would be entirely inappropriate."

"How so? Your maid will be right with us," Raven said impressing that he had no ill will wished on her.

Raven wondered if he had perhaps gone too far in his teasing and the lady actually feared him to be a blackguard.

He watched as Lady Alexandra waited for a proper reason why a respectable gentleman should not give his assistance to a lady in need.

"In true honesty?" Lady Alexandra finally said as they paused before the chairs. She looked up at him with her large honey eyes and swallowed back her nervousness.

"I readily encourage any honest words you might have

to give me," Raven said looking down at her and praying that she didn't genuinely fear him as a rake.

"I don't want you to know of my residence," she said just above a whisper before turning away and releasing her arm from his.

It utterly stunned him to the core that he scarcely heard Mr. Lucas coming forward to greet his two distinguished guests. It cut Raven deep down to the core, and he would have rather liked to turn Lady Alexandra back to him and shake her.

He couldn't image how shamed she must have felt to have spoken such words to him. He was even more engaged that she would actually consider her address something he would look down upon. Perhaps it was little that the woman had disguised from him in their few encounters thus far.

As much as he wanted to be offended that Lady Alexandra would think such prideful notions of him, he couldn't fault her for it. He was after all a duke and rarely would his paths have crossed with someone such as she if it were not for that serendipitous night when he had mistaken her for another. It wasn't that he considered himself too good to socialize with an impoverished earl's daughter, just that their circles simply didn't mix regularly.

In fact, he wasn't altogether sure how his aunt would feel if she knew of his whereabouts at this very moment. There was little a duke could do to tarnish his standing with the ton. Even mixing with impoverished earls would do little to harm him. After all, did he not have a slight connection to the lady by his dear friend Lord Eagleton?

He agreed at that moment to use the connection to his advantage to show the lady there was no wrong in their association. Though they may not have naturally been in the same circles, there was no impropriety in including her in his. He was sure that though she didn't seem to want such interactions at the moment, it was only the shock of such an unorthodox suggestion.

More than all of this, Raven was hoping to prove to himself that this strange hold Lady Alexandra had taken on his mind was but a fleeting emotion. He certainly couldn't have already gathered such affection for a lady he barely knew. It was merely the interesting circumstances of their meeting that had piqued his interest. Time alone in association with the lady would help the feelings wane and prove his hypothesis that love was nothing more than fleeting passionate feelings.

14

Lady Alexandra took her seat at the front of the very familiar large room. Often, they used the large entrance as the lecture hall. Her father had some notions that it would be so crowded with guests that a small room just wouldn't do.

This had never been the case, but the routine of lectures in the large room carried on. At the least, the extra-high ceilings did wonders for the acoustics and carrying the presenter's voice.

Mr. Lucas was not a timid sort of man, so he rarely had issues with those in the back row of seats hearing him. The presenter would stand on a small platform raising him slightly off of the ground with a podium in front to hold their notes.

The wooden chairs were lined in rows with a center

aisle. Though there was room enough to sit at least fifty, not more than a few handfuls were seated. Most of these were fellow colleagues in the museum.

Mr. Lucas ushered Lady Alexandra to the front row with the duke not far behind. Lady Alexandra made a point to seat herself in the chair closest to the center aisle of the front row. In this way, she hoped the duke would not sit near her. After all, it might look a little scandalous for him to sit right next to a lady that he scarcely knew and had no family connections to.

As she hoped, the duke took the seat across the aisle from her, though right on the edge as she had done so that only the walkway put space between them.

Lady Alexandra did her best to keep her focus on the front of the small stage, and not the man across from her. There was little for her to see up there at present, however. Just the podium where Mr. Lucas shuffled through his notes once more and a small table next to him with the lump of a beast underneath a small sheet.

"I see that the conservatory is still in good working order," the duke said, motioning with his fine cane the glass dome that served as the lecture's backdrop.

"I'm sorry, your grace?" Lady Alexandra asked, having not heard him.

"I said I am rather fond of the conservatory," he amended, this time leaning in across the walkway so the lady could hear him correctly over the other conversations echoing around the room.

"You are?" Lady Alexandra asked in surprise. She would not have expected the duke to notice the room, let alone comment on his favoring of it.

"Does this surprise you?" Raven asked with a twinkle in his dark eyes.

"It does, if I am being honest. Don't get me wrong I love it dearly myself. In fact, it has been a sort of project of mine these last few years. I just never would have suspected that with all the other attractions, a garden house would be your favorite."

Lady Alexandra's eyes went automatically to the African safari room to her right.

"I suppose I could not say in all truthfulness that it is my favorite," Raven said upon further reflection. "I am sure a great many new wonders have entered this edifice since I last saw it. And of course, you know," he said with a bright smile, "I have yet to take a tour of it since my return. But I can honestly say," he added quickly before Lady Alexandra could reproach him for his teasing yet again, "as a boy, it was my favorite place."

"I suppose," he continued on seeing that his response yet surprised the notions that Lady Alexandra had about him, "it is because inside the conservatory you were completely surrounded. It made it all so real. The other exhibits are nice in their way, but just that, an exhibit. One stands there and looks in on a world that they have yet to experience. Within the conservatory, you are immersed entirely into a beautiful oasis of beautiful flowers and delicate creatures."

"Well then you must surely take a look at it after my lecture," Mr. Lucas inserted himself in the conversation. "Lady Alexandra has worked tirelessly to transform it into a tropical paradise."

The duke's gaze didn't leave Lady Alexandra as Mr. Lucas spoke.

"You are too kind in your praise, Mr. Lucas. I can assure you of that," Lady Alexandra said, stealing away from the duke's penetrating stare.

She could feel the heat physically rising up her spencer jacket collar and flushing her face.

"Do not be bashful. I know how proud you are of your endeavors," Mr. Lucas continued. "In fact, your grace, there are often times that Lady Alexandra will go missing for hours only to find her seated within its glass walls and enjoying the sounds of the tropical creatures."

"Creatures, you say?" Raven said turning his gaze upon the lecturer at this point.

He couldn't help but see the admiration in Mr. Lucas as he looked down at Lady Alexandra. It took all his self-composure not to stand and smack it off the offending gentleman's face.

"Yes," Lucas continued with a chuckle. "She rather

insisted on importing various creatures to decorate her little tropical oasis. There are several birds of paradise that enjoy making their presence known all hours of the day. It can be quite vexing when one is trying to work."

"How interesting," the duke agreed, letting his eyes float back to Lady Alexandra.

He could easily tell she didn't like to be spoken of in such manner.

"I am very fond of tropical birds. Perhaps when the lecture is over, you will give me a personal tour of the conservatory, Lady Alexandra? I am sure that there are few who would know it as well as yourself, owing to Mr. Lucas' words."

Lady Alexandra hesitated in responding for just a half a second. It was just enough for her to glean the duke's true intentions. Was he merely attempting to tease her again? In his dark eyes, she saw only legitimate interest and so agreed to the task.

Mr. Lucas, a little ruffled himself like a bird of paradise that he was not given the honor of presenting the Duke of Raven a personal tour of the museum, mumbled some agreement that such an arrangement would be an excellent choice before turning back to his podium.

It was only a few minutes more before the giant clock at the front of the museum chimed the hour, and Lucas cleared his throat to begin his dissertation on the habits and habitat of the American porcupine.

Mr. Lucas continued on without stopping for at least an hour and a half. Lady Alexandra did her part to sit reposed in her chair and to seem at least to be listening intently to his words. Twice Mr. Lucas referenced to her and her father for providing the specimen, and she smiled at him kindly as his eyes found their way to land on her.

There was, however, another set of eyes that she was keenly aware were on her almost through the entire lecture. It was the Duke of Raven. He was not abashed at all as he continually looked over to her and studied her. It was a movement that Lady Alexandra caught out of her peripherals and with each gaze he laid on her, she was sure she could feel the stoking of a fire within her.

Lady Alexandra couldn't deny that the Duke was a handsome, charming man, despite how much she wanted to. He apparently was also a man who had never been short on privilege or attention. There was, after all, his true intention at the ball of making acquaintance with Lady Charlotte, and then seeing them together not more than a day ago.

It made absolutely no sense to her why he was continuing to visit her father's museum, and undoubtedly seeking her out. The only conclusion that seemed to make any sense at all to Lady Alexandra was that he was enjoying some sort of freak-show like in the circus.

He clearly found her misfortune and embarrassments

wildly entertaining and so continued in her presence simply for the amusement of it all.

With this notion, Lady Alexandra was determined to turn that smoldering fire within her into a raging pit of hatred for the duke. She struggled to hold her composure with every glance he gave her way. She would have liked to shout at him, but certainly, that would only play into amusing him the more.

It was finally with the conclusion of Mr. Lucas' speech that she let out the breath she was holding and clapped for the scientist.

"Are there any questions for me?" Mr. Lucas called out to the small crowd. "And, of course, you are more than welcome to come to the stage and inspect the creature closer," he added when no questions were offered.

The duke stood and reached out a hand to Lady Alexandra to help her up to the podium and the stuffed porcupine.

"Thank you, your grace," Lady Alexandra said with a tight smile. "But I have seen quite enough of that beast and had no need to get closer."

"I can assure you in its present state it is quite harmless," Lucas said with a jolly laugh.

Lady Alexandra supposed the scientist thought she feared it, or perhaps his explanation of quills shooting faster than a horse could run when threatened.

"That is not what I currently fear malice from," she said

under her breath before reluctantly taking the duke's gentlemanly hand.

She watched her escort's gleaming eyes shine with surprise at her words. She realized that she had spoken her mind much louder than she should have. After all, a lady's opinion should only be given when asked for and no one had asked her thoughts on that matter.

Lady Alexandra pursed her lips closer together, hoping to control her wild tongue better. She only glanced at the thing as they stepped up on the small stage. The duke for his part studied it very intently.

Mr. Lucas stood behind the stuffed creature with his chest puffed out even farther than when the herpetological society had complimented him on his proper hibiscus placement.

"I do find the creature rather fascinating," Raven said as he studied it. "And I must commend you on such a pristine specimen."

"Perhaps you have some questions on the creature for me," Mr. Lucas said, filled with confidence.

"Not a question, no. You see, I have encountered it many times in my travels and wonder if I could correct a few misconceptions that you gave today."

Lady Alexandra watched as all the color drained from Mr. Lucas' face. For her part, she was slightly perturbed as well that the duke would have such high airs to assume he could correct the lecture notes. After all, most of those facts and information came from her father's extensive studies. It was only the information on the creature's physical form and scientific purposes that Mr. Lucas had contributed to the animal's study.

"I don't mean to offend, of course," Raven said, quickly realizing that Mr. Lucas wouldn't receive any suggestions of misinformation very well.

"No, please do tell us, your grace," Lady Alexandra chimed in. "After all, my father wanted this place to be a house of learning for all things natural. Learning cannot occur if there is no exchange of opinions. I am sure we can all learn so much from a man as worldly as you."

Though Lady Alexandra's words were dripping with keen interest and kindness, Raven was sure there was contempt behind her phrasing.

"It is only that, in my encounters that is," he said, trying to express humility to the lady, "porcupines don't shoot their quills at all. In fact, I have seen one swing around and strike at a poor creature with them."

"They clearly have muscles at each quill entrance that can be contracted," Mr. Lucas said, pushing up his glasses with a soft laugh.

"You are absolutely correct to this point," Raven agreed. "Though it doesn't eject the quills as one would imagine. Instead, they seem to perk up and are easier to remove when the barbed end opposite the animal strikes into something. Of course, this would be a simple mistake to make, and I would, of course, have come to the same conclusion if I had not seen it for myself."

"How very fascinating," Mr. Lucas said clearly agitated.

Though Lady Alexandra had hoped to put the duke in his place for contradicting her father, she also saw merits in what he was saying. It was, after all, the real intent of the museum to exchange information and to create a society better aware of the natural world around them. This couldn't be accomplished with the spread of falsehoods.

There was, after all, some shockingly good merit to having a seasoned traveler mix and mingle with the men who rarely saw outside their labs. Mr. Lucas may have seen the finer minute details of the creature's anatomy, but still, his knowledge was of little use without practical experience.

"The only other suggestions for amendments to your otherwise impeccable lecture," the duke added a little reluctantly.

"Yes, please, I am happy to hear any of your grace's suggestions," Mr. Lucas said, however, his face didn't show as such.

"Well," Raven said a little reluctantly but also happy to stick it to the scientist who had looked down so affectionately throughout his talk. "You mentioned that the porcupine secretes a poison to coat the darts in."

"Yes, it was very apparent that an oil secretion gland near the quills would also push out a liquid when the muscles were contracted," Mr. Lucas tried to explain his reasoning quickly.

"I would beg you to reconsider the oil's purpose. You see, porcupines love to climb trees. They are very slow, clumsy creatures and often fall out of them, jabbing themselves with the quills. It would seem to make little sense that they would poison themselves."

"Climb trees? That seems a little outrageous. They neither have the body shape nor footing for it," Mr. Lucas said with a little scoff.

Raven narrowed his eyes on the gentleman. He was trying to be polite about his corrections, but he didn't have to be.

"I can assure you, sir, they do. Most often in the early months of spring. The new blossom buds that tip the trees of Virginia are very enticing for the little creatures after a long winter with little food. I would also add to the fact that the tribes of native people find the oil to have many medicinal purposes. Surely they wouldn't if it was poison."

"It is hard to say. Savages do have many strange customs," Mr. Lucas responded.

"Certainly his reasoning has merit, Mr. Lucas," Lady Alexandra interjected without even realizing she was coming to her recently sworn enemy's aid. "It would not hurt to continue the study of the properties of the oil before coming to a definite conclusion."

"Of course, you are right Lady Alexandra," Lucas said

with an affectionate smile. "You are always the level-headed one, aren't you. I think what you propose is exactly what is needed. Some more time to study and experiment will most certainly divulge the truth of the matter.

I thank you, your grace, for your keen observations and knowledge. Were you not interested in seeing the conservatory?" Lucas offered by way of change of subject. "I know that you must be a very busy man and I would hate for you to miss it on account of me taking up too much of your time."

"You are correct. I would like to take a turn of the newly remodeled room, if you would excuse us," Raven said, holding out his arm to Lady Alexandra.

She considered making her own excuses and leaving him to walk the glass room alone. It wouldn't have been right in front of so many witnesses, and she had already been a side-show enough for the duke. She wouldn't make herself a spectacle any more than she had already been.

With a soft smile, she bid Mr. Lucas a good morning and slipped her gloved hand into the crook of the Duke of Raven's arm.

15

Raven walked silently alongside Lady Alexandra wondering how deep her connection was to this Mr. Lucas.

He hadn't considered she might have feelings for the man. It was clear that Mr. Lucas had intentions towards her, but he had never stopped to consider she might be feeling the same attraction to him.

If that was the case, he was sure that he only infuriated her more by calling to question Mr. Lucas' lecture facts. Though he had only done so by her inspiring words the other night at the ball, Raven had never stopped to consider that his opinions and knowledge might not actually be wanted here when it countered their own.

"I didn't mean to offend," Raven said finally as he cleared his throat.

They were at the glass door that entered the greenhouse. He reached forward to open it for the both of them.

"In what way?" Lady Alexandra responded, as if he had made it his mission to offend her on every turn.

Raven cast his eyes down at her, though she didn't meet his gaze. He was beginning to determine that Lady Alexandra was either a fierce woman who cared little for what others might think of her blatantly honest manners or had very little control over her tongue.

"I was not aware that I might have offended you in several ways this day. But I suppose, in that case, I will apologize on the whole. I do suppose I can be a sort of a tease in my words and I do apologize if my mannerisms offended you earlier. But that was not what I was referring to."

"Then, pray tell. What were you referring to?" she asked, lifting her soft doe eyes to him in complete innocence of any other offense.

Raven gave an inward sigh of relief. Certainly, she couldn't have feelings for Mr. Lucas if she didn't take offense to his challenges on Lucas' work.

Raven was about to explain that he had only meant to help and not harm or insult when the loud echoing caw of a bird caught his attention.

He lifted his eyes from the lady at his side to their surroundings. Of course, he had seen the fine greenery from the glass windows at a distance. As of yet, he hadn't taken it in since entering their encasement. For a moment, he had to admit; his surroundings entranced him.

The air was much thicker and warmer inside, if that were even possible for such an early warmth to the spring. Raven could hear the sounds of several tropical birds making their calls back and forth.

Dotting the rich green plants were bright bursts of fantastical colored buds almost ready to burst open. A simple pebble path led a winding turn around the whole circle building. Everything else was richly filled with various plants, some even springing high up into the air.

A thick coating of mist hung low to the ground and fogged the windows facing outward. Along with the birds, Raven could see several species of butterflies soaring gracefully around the room.

The sound of water made him turn in its direction. A man was busy watering the plants along the paths in a painstakingly slow pace with a jug of water.

"I am sure you can imagine they need a great deal of water," Lady Alexandra said, following Raven's gaze. "It is a full-time job at present. Most of these plants come from areas that see rain at least once a day, or so that is what I am told," she added quickly.

Raven wondered if she spoke that ending because she feared he might try to correct her too in a heavy-handed way. It returned him back to his subject at hand.

"I believe you have been correctly informed in that

respect. At least, I can say that by what I have seen thus far. Which brings me to how I may have caused offense."

He tore his eyes from the beautiful scenery that so reminded him of the great wild without the London city walls and looked down to the lady at his side.

She looked up at him with those large doe eyes and waited patiently for him to continue. For some reason having this lady's complete attention was both intoxicating and mesmerizing all at once.

"When I gave those, shall we say suggestions, to your colleague, Mr. Lucas, I never meant it in a belittling fashion, or to say that I was looking down on the museum's expertise on the whole. In fact, I myself would have scarcely known such facts if I hadn't encountered them myself."

Raven took a deep breath realizing he was going on in a very ridiculous manner. For some unknown reason, he cared deeply for Lady Alexandra's opinion of his person.

"I certainly wasn't offended," Lady Alexandra put him at ease. "Though I cannot say the same for Thomas. Mr. Lucas, I mean of course," she amended quickly.

"Well I didn't mean to upset him either, and I would be more than happy to apologize. I should have kept my opinion to myself."

"I don't think you should have at all," Lady Alexandra said as they took a leisurely stroll around the gardens. "In fact, I think what this museum needs is more outside opinions. The same minds have been running it since my father first took it on. It needs some freshening up, in my opinion, more especially if they are incorrect."

"Well, it does look that you have already done quite a bit of renewal in at least this room," Raven said, letting his eyes sweep the room.

Though he had always enjoyed these indoor gardens with their array of colorful butterflies as a boy, it took on a completely different appearance now. Lady Alexandra had truly taken the idea of a year-round green room and turned it into a spectacular oasis.

"I hoped it might bring in more spectators, honestly," Lady Alexandra replied, a little shyly.

At that very moment, they rounded a bend of lush green trees to a small opening. It was more of a widening of the path in a semi-circle that looked on one large straight stick with a bird perched on top.

The bird was a fine tropical specimen with its short black beak, rich green feather coat, and highlights of red feathers poking in its wings. He was more or less walking the length of his stick back and forth absentmindedly removing small pieces of fruit hanging from a small tin pail at one end, walking to the other side, eating it, then repeating the process.

Upon their turning of the bend, the bird immediately perked up. He held still, his black talons curled tightly around the post and the crown of lime green feathers on his crown raising slightly in anticipation.

"I can't imagine a beautiful gent such as this wouldn't bring in crowds," Raven said admiring the live creature.

"This is actually Miss Nutters."

"Pardon me," Raven said with a slight bow to the bird as they stood before it.

"Nutters?" He asked turning back to his companion. "An interesting name."

"She loves nuts. She can crack open any nut we have presented her with that strong beak of hers. You should see her with walnuts. She just cracks them open and peels back the shattered shell, picking out the meat with her tongue."

Raven studied the woman as she spoke. In all honesty, he was sure this was the first moment she had looked alive since being in the place. She truly had a shared passion for the natural world, though it seemed that, unlike the members of this museum and her father, she had a love for the living creatures in their element.

"She can talk too," Lady Alexandra added with a bit of pride.

"Really? What can she say then?"

Lady Alexandra took a step closer to Miss Nutters to catch her full attention.

"Good morning, Miss Nutters."

"Good morning," the bird replied in its high pitched tone.

"How are you today," she continued.

The bird bobbed her head up and down in anticipation of this practiced conversation.

"Very well, indeed, very well indeed," she repeated with excitement.

"Good girl," Lady Alexandra cooed smoothing down the crown feathers that had puffed out, ending the little performance.

"Very impressive," Raven said with a relaxed smile.

She turned to face him with a wide, bright smile on her face. For the first time since he met Lady Alexandra, she actually looked her youthful age unmarred by stress and worry. He had the strong desire to tell her so but thought better of it. She had no choice in her lot in life or the stress it brought upon her. He was determined, however, to at least alleviate it any way he could.

"This is all very impressive," he reiterated when he saw her lit face fall in shyness.

"Well, at least one person thinks so," she replied walking away from the bird after a final pet.

"How is it that your tropical oasis hasn't attracted more people?"

"Well, this is the first spring that we are completely ready. It took time for the plants to mature, of course, and Miss Nutters only joined us last year. It is still early in the year, of course, so I am hoping more will come as the months pass. I had the Zoological Society walk the space last fall, and they gave me some constructive tips as well as encouraging words about returning again to have their yearly banquet here."

"You plan to host events in the room," Raven said finding it to be a superb idea if done correctly.

"I do hope so. So often Father's museum only caters to families who bring small children for a leisurely trip. Really the lectures do little to bring in customers and are more just a way for an aspiring scientist to learn and grow. I feel it is necessary to add more uses. It's such a lovely building it could have so many wonderful uses."

Raven realized she was trying to explain away a relatively new idea that she assumed he thought of as odd.

"I think it's a wonderful idea. I am on the Zoological Society's board. I would be happy to bring up this option at their next meeting."

"I could never ask such a favor," Lady Alexandra waved off his offer.

"It is no favor at all. I will be returning to society after many years of not being in attendance. I will need some sort of offering to appease them over my absence."

He didn't add that he was also a principal benefactor for the society, and whether Raven showed up or not, the men of that society would happily accept any recommendation for their yearly banquet from him as he often provided the funds for it though he himself had not attended in some time.

"Show me what plans you have to hold such events?" Raven said quickly to stop her discouragement again.

They walked a little way farther. The whole pebble path seemed to wind its way around the edge of the enclosure with the center full of lush greenery. When they reached the almost halfway point of the room, a fork appeared in the path.

Lady Alexandra led him along the path that led straight into the heart of the room. He guessed that it was at least, if not bigger than the size of the museum that the greenhouse was attached to with its own overarching two-story walls.

As they walked, they seemed to become encased with the greenery on either side so that you could just make out the glass paneling above through the splits in tree leaves. Raven recognized most of these plants from the short time he spent in the West Indies and knew them to be leafing plants all year around. It created a magical tunnel-like walkway.

"I have made this path wider," Lady Alexandra explained, "so as to accommodate pedestrians as well as a row of lanterns to light the way for a night venue."

He nodded in understanding, taking it all in. Finally, the walkway opened up into a large open area. It was surrounded on all sides with just the one entrance.

Surrounding the area was a wall of vibrant greenery. The floor was made of slates of stone smoothed out to almost a completely flat surface.

"I wanted the room to be wide and open. Of course, I would make sure that it was spotless," she added, kicking a stray fallen palm leaf to the side with the tip of her shoe. "I also have a man who regularly cleans the windows, inside and out of course, so that the night sky would shine brightly should the timing allow it."

At that particular moment, beautiful rays of light reflecting from the glass encasement were streaming down in angelic beams.

"I think it looks remarkable in here," Raven commented with honesty.

The room was wholly circled by the beautiful plants already giving off the tropical perfumes of flowers just about to bloom. Raven couldn't believe she was able to keep these plants - so accustomed to the tropical climate - not only alive but flourishing in here. He even spied a palm tree with bananas growing on it. It was surely a treat most Londoners had never seen or tasted.

"I am hoping to use the space for both a dining hall as well as a ballroom so that anyone can use it for their needs."

"It seems a bit narrow of a walkway for tables and chairs to be brought in for dining," Raven said, full of interest. He did not doubt that she had some ingenious solution to that problem.

"There is a second service entrance, though it is covered, just across from us," she pointed to the area that was nearest to the door of the greenhouse. "I want the guests to walk the length first and experience the beauty of the room before coming straight into this little enclosure."

"Very sensible. And what about the food for a banquet?"

"There is actually a fully serviceable kitchen area in the main building on the first floor. It was always used as storage, but I have been working already to get it ready and acquire the necessary staff. Men have their halls and clubs; I thought there might be a use of such a thing but for anyone. Private balls could be held here, society events," she said with a nod in his direction though her mind was far from the duke.

Instead, he could see behind her irises the images that she already created for the future of this space and the museum on the whole.

"I don't think I have ever encountered a woman with such a head for business let alone with the foresight to see such a spectacular novelty never created before."

"Well, certainly there are halls for public events," she said modestly.

"Yes, that is true. But what you have here is far superior

to empty spaces. This is an entire experience in one place. In fact, I would say you have convinced me."

"Convinced you of what, your grace?" Lady Alexandra said with utter shock.

"That this will be the place of the Zoological Society's yearly banquet."

"That is a very kind thought, but..."

"No, no but's at all," Raven said waving a hand at her. "I, in truth, am completely at liberty to decide the venue as I host it, even when I am away. They will have no objection to my decision. Though it is no more than six weeks from now. I fear that is too soon."

"Not at all," Lady Alexandra said standing a little taller never willing to shy away from a challenge. "I could do it."

He wouldn't have considered any less from the lady. They may have only met on a few occasions thus far, but he already knew her to be a strong-willed, fearless, and capable woman. In that regard, she reminded him very much of his mother, or at least the memories he had of her. Raven's aunt often told him as well that his late mother was never one to sit at home while his father saw the world. Instead, she walked toe to toe with him. Raven rather suspected that Lady Alexandra had a matching personality in that respect. She wasn't the kind to sit idly or fill her time with frivolous activities as many of the ladies of the ton did.

"Wonderful, then I should like to call my solicitor today to call on you if you don't mind. Mr. Jenkins will handle the payment of the space. And if you don't mind, I would like to give you and Polly a ride to your house so that I might ask your father for permission."

"Permission ?" Lady Alexandra's face went pale.

"For the use of the building. Lord Grebs is, after all, the proprietor is he not?"

"Oh yes, of course. That really isn't necessary. I would be happy to convey your gracious offer. Father will be very pleased to hear that our first host is the Duke of Raven."

Raven was unsure why Lady Alexandra was quick to wave off his meeting with Earl Grebs. Raven had heard from his aunt that the man was a bit of a recluse. Perhaps she was just as embarrassed by him as she was her street address. Neither mattered to Raven. In fact, he had plans to call on the lord anyway later in the week, if only to discuss scientific matters, which they both clearly shared an interest in.

"I really do insist," Raven said with a broad smile knowing that under no circumstances would she be able to deny a duke when he insisted upon anything.

16

Lady Alexandra would have liked to stay behind and get right to work. As her first client of the museum's new tropical hall, she would have a lot to prepare for. Her mind was still spinning over that fact. She had slightly over exaggerated their level of preparedness. There was a kitchen, yes, but it was not quite yet in working order, and she hadn't even begun to procure a staff for such an event.

Though she would have liked to insist that the duke not send his solicitor with payment until after he was satisfied with her work, the truth was she would have no means of getting the room ready without it. She realized as they exited the building together, Polly waiting politely on one of the benches by the front door, Raven hadn't even asked her the price.

Of course, speaking of money wasn't exactly a gentlemanly thing to do, and she had no doubt that was doubly true when it came to a female proprietor. She would make a point to make sure that Mr. Jenkins was told a reasonable amount and not a penny more.

Certainly she, no, the museum, could use the bluster from a wealthy man's pockets, but she would not lower herself to that level. She would only ask for a fair price, though it wouldn't be enough to cover all the expenses of starting this endeavor. She would have to convince her father somehow to take a loan out for the remainder of the costs.

It would certainly make things much tighter in her household. It was also a nerve-racking decision when the season had only yet begun, and so many expenses would be accumulating over the course of it for her sisters. It was all the more reason she would have to keep her eyes focused on them. She would need to see at least Josephine properly wedded by the end of the year if there was any hope of surviving to the next.

Between that and the impossibility of preparations before her, Lady Alexandra scarcely could make herself breath beneath her corset as the duke's carriage was brought around. It was indeed a heavy weight that fell upon her with the loss of her mother.

Not only was it to be a mother herself to her three

younger sisters, but to also see that her father's monetary needs were seen too. If only he hadn't collapsed so into a state of despair after her mother's death.

Surely the weight of siblings to settle off and financial burdens on one child alone was much to ask of even a son. She was sure the task was that much harder because she was a woman.

If she was being entirely honest with herself, she never truly expected someone, let alone a high standing gentleman such as the Duke of Raven, would even consider the museum. She still believed the man to be quite vexing and couldn't help but have hurt pride over their first meeting, but in the end, this man who seemed to enjoy tormenting her, whether his motives were pure or not, could be her savior.

Mayhap he was only continuing this charade as a means of entertainment at her misfortune as she had suspected earlier that day. Even if that were the case, she wouldn't care. She would give the Zoological Society a banquet that they would talk of for years to come.

Even if it meant the death of her, news of her success and at the behest of an influential duke would give her idea validation and hopefully result in more of the members of society following in the duke's wake.

The duke, Lady Alexandra, and her maid, Polly, all entered the carriage at their respective places. Polly's next to the driver of the open-aired cart. The duke took the position to the back of his driver so that Lady Alexandra could take the opposing seat and have a view of where they were going.

Lady Alexandra did have a slight concern for taking the ride as all eyes would easily see her in the duke's company. Again, she wondered at the gossip it would cause and rather wished she had come with a larger hat or perhaps a parasol to at least partially give her some anonymity. Though scandal would have little effect on the duke or his reputation, it had the potential to hurt her, which damaged her sisters in turn.

Lady Alexandra was practically a spinster from the moment she stepped out into society. In fact, that wasn't even entirely accurate. To be a spinster, one must have passed their time of finding a match.

In truth, she was still in the tail end of what would be deemed a reasonable time for her. The fact was, she had never been considered a match to anyone. Instead, she was the matron of her younger sisters and nothing more.

Now here she was seated next to a rich, handsome, and very available duke. No doubt that the whole of the ton would be gossiping about the impoverished circumstance that clearly led her to be a desperate vixen attempting to turn his head.

For the first portion of the ride, they both sat in silence, choosing to watch as London and its occupants passed by them. To Lady Alexandra's relief, she recognized few and knew that they would at least not be passing by very fashionable parts of town on the way to her father's house.

She rather wished she could send on a messenger ahead to warn her sisters and prepare her father. Well, she wasn't sure such a thing was possible in either case. How would her sisters react when she introduced the Duke of Raven to their father? She was sure her younger sisters would be gushing with girlish glee.

Williamina told little Sophia about the duke's sudden appearance at Sir Hamilton's ball, and since that moment Sophia had talked on no other subject. She did everything in her power to pry every last detail of the night out of her three older sisters.

Naturally, it didn't take long for one of them to mention that Lady Alexandra had in fact danced with the duke. That had sent Sophia swirling with more questions and an added amount of melancholy that she was not yet of the age to attend such events.

Lady Alexandra never told her sisters that the dance had been a mistake. Instead, she explained that the duke was merely kind to a friend of Lord and Lady Whitehall whom he was closely associated with. None of her sisters had accepted that answer.

Josephine knew Alexandra well enough not to continue

questioning. She could see clearly it was an uncomfortable subject for her eldest sister and left it at that. Williamina for her part was either far too shy to ask or simply had no interest. Sophia, unfortunately, had continued on without hesitation or pause.

Lady Alexandra could only guess at her youngest sister's behavior when she entered their house tonight with the duke as a guest. She just hoped that the small girl could gather enough decency not to mention that dance in his presence.

Lady Alexandra didn't know what would be more embarrassing, having her sisters speak of that horrible mistake, or listening to the duke explain to them what really happened that night.

"It's a surprisingly fine day, isn't it," Raven said taking Lady Alexandra away from her thoughts.

She looked above at the blue sky not even marred by smoke today. The wind was just swift enough to brush away the chimney smog without being difficult to stand. Only occasional white puffs dotted the never-ending blue. It was one of those rare days that Lady Alexandra imagined she was getting a glimpse of the world outside this city.

"They remind me of cotton," Raven continued, following her gaze and seeming to know her thoughts.

"I've only ever seen the fabric, though I have seen pictures of the plants in some of my father's books."

"They look very soft and fluffy like the clouds, but actually when you touch it there is a bit of stiffness to them, I suppose because they are balled so tight. And then there are the thorns of the stiff outer shell, dried in the heat of the sun to irritatingly sharp points."

"Are you quite familiar with it, then?" Lady Alexandra asked turning her attention to him. She knew he had seen much of the world, and clearly knew the Americas well after this morning's conversation with Mr. Lucas.

"I have seen it quite frequently in Virginia, though I believe it is more common in the southern colonies. My estate is predominately tobacco."

"How interesting. My father insists on getting much of his tobacco from the colonies. He insists it is a better product. I detest the smell myself. He is constantly smoking it in his library, and I am sure the walls have blackened more from that than the hearth."

Lady Alexandra who had run on with her opinion without thinking realized she might have offended the duke. After all, he just announced a considerable holding in the plant and here she was openly detesting in.

"I didn't mean to offend, your grace. I am sure many people find it to be a pleasant past time, and I know it also has medicinal properties," she said, quickly feeling her cheeks flush.

Raven gave a soft chuckle, "Have no fear, Lady Alexandra, my pride was not wounded in the least by your opinion. I am not entirely fond of the product myself if I am entirely honest. I will enjoy some tobacco from time to time, but beyond that, the only use I have for the leaves is in the monetary gain it supplies me."

Lady Alexandra relaxed a little in her seat as he waved her worry away.

"You must know much about the colonies. I have always tried to imagine a place so wild and untouched by civilization."

"It is certainly beautiful. The land can be quite enchanting and surprisingly holds more variety of environment than one could imagine."

"Do you plan to make it your permanent home? I only ask because the abundance of land draws so many to take the treacherous trip across the sea."

"I did consider it at one time. I do enjoy spending time on the plantation, but no I don't think I will ever go to the colonies permanently."

Raven got a far-off glazed look to his eyes, and Lady Alexandra wished his thoughts were as easy to read as her own.

"I have my aunt here, of course," he added after a moment's pause. "I could never convince her to step on a boat, and I couldn't bring myself to leave her behind, permanently that is. Do you know my Aunt Rebecca, Lady Sinclair that is?" he added for clarification's sake.

"I know her name well, though I don't think I have ever had the pleasure of making her acquaintance."

Lady Alexandra thought to herself that there would have been few situations in life where their two paths would have crossed. Though they were both unmarried and likely to never marry, they were just as vastly different in social standing as they were in age.

"You seem very like her to me," he said musing as he studied her. "I will introduce you to her. I think you two would get on very well."

Lady Alexandra only smiled softly before turning her gaze back to the landscape around her. She recognized the streets well and knew that they were coming close to her residence. She wasn't exactly sure if Lady Sinclair would share in her nephew's interest of impoverished, ridiculous ladies as he seemed to be.

The ball of nerves that had been temporarily halted by the distraction of their conversation began to well within her again. In only a few moment's time, they would turn the last street corner and arrive at her father's London home. She didn't believe she had ever felt so scared and vulnerable ever before in her life, including that moment she promised her mother to fulfill her dying wish. But as she felt the carriage slow, and her home come closer and closer to view, she knew she would have no choice but to face what lay ahead of her.

She was happy to see that for the most part, the streets were clear of people. The sun was now starting to rise to the peak of its rotation across the sky, and the warmth would be at its peak. With this, most who could would seek the security of shaded homes or garden pathways veiled with trees.

Her sisters, she knew, would be sitting in the drawing room, perhaps with a small after breakfast meal and tea. Hopefully, Sophia would be busy with the school assignment Lady Alexandra had instructed her to complete that morning.

Williamina would no doubt be at the piano practicing as she so often did, and Josephine would either be painting, stitching, or darning as was the habit for both Lady Alexandra and her next youngest sister on most afternoons.

She could picture them easily all sitting in the drawing room in a relaxed state, perhaps even still in their morning dresses.

How she wished she could somehow enter the house and take the duke to her father in the library without having to pass right by them. In the tedium and boredom of an afternoon just like any other, she had no doubt they would jump at any opportunity for an interruption, including coming out to greet her in the hall.

It was an inevitable moment that she was regretting all its outcomes before it even happened. But as the carriage came to a halt, and the duke descended out before helping her, she knew that there would be no stopping it.

Just before turning up the cobblestone walk that intersected their small front garden, Lady Alexandra exchanged a look with Polly. She could easily tell that even the maid in her young age knew that something quite out of the ordinary for Earl Grebs and his daughters was about to take place.

17

Raven could see that Lady Alexandra was visibly nervous. She had already claimed shame over her address, though he found her father's house to be a fine townhome, well kept with a neat flower garden ornamenting the front lawn. It was a bit unorthodox for him to be following her home and presenting himself to her father, whom Raven had never met.

It wasn't entirely out of propriety, though, as he was calling on a business relation. In honesty, though, he probably should have contacted the earl by way of his solicitor as they had never been introduced as of yet.

Raven, however, had little patience for the silly formal rules of the peerage. He did find propriety in many of them, such as the maid who often accompanied Lady Alexandra for modesty's sake, or some of the societal edicts, but overall found most of them tedious and unnecessary. Being a duke, he often decided to sidestep the rules he found ridiculous knowing that few would question him.

Usually, it had worked to his advantage. Although, there was that exception when he introduced himself at Sir Hamilton's ball and found that he had confused one lady for another. Though as he walked up to Earl Grebs' home, he couldn't entirely say that the mishap had been a misfortune. In fact, he was rather enjoying the new associations the mishaps over ignored etiquette had caused.

As soon as Lady Alexandra opened the gate leading to her house, a butler pulled back the door clearly anticipating her arrival. What he was surprised to see was that she didn't come alone. His eyes widened in surprise before he straightened up to his full height trying to look as noble as possible.

Polly for her part informed the driver where a public shed was around the corner to keep the horse and carriage before she took the service entrance around the back of the building. No doubt Raven's driver would join her shortly thereafter while Raven saw to his business.

"Would you please see that a fresh pot of tea and some sandwiches be sent to Father's office," Lady Alexandra said, surprisingly coolly as she removed her hat and shawl and handed them over to the butler.

He nodded his understanding before bowing to the

duke and taking his outer effects. Once hats, outer cloak, and cane were properly stowed he hurried down the single hallway to what he guessed was the kitchen of the house.

"If you would like to wait here, I will go and see if my father is able to receive you," Lady Alexandra said, turning to Raven.

Just at that moment, a great stirring of commotion caught both their attention. Two large oak doors that came off of the foyer before the hall burst open, exposing a crowd of women.

"Alexandra, you brought a guest home with you," the youngest one said at the front of the group.

He watched as the lady physically deflated that the rest of the household had detected them. He was aware that Lord Grebs had several daughters, and that information along with facial similarities drew the conclusion that these were Lady Alexandra's sisters.

"Your Grace, may I introduce you to my younger sisters. This is Lady Josephine, Lady Williamina, and Lady Sophia."

Each girl gave a curtsey to the duke as their name was called and he promptly delivered a bow in return once introductions were finished.

"The Duke of Raven is here to discuss some business with Father pertaining to the museum," Lady Alexandra explained to her sisters, hoping that would be enough and they would leave him be, though she doubted it greatly.

"Would you join us in the drawing room for tea, Your Grace, while Alexandra goes to fetch our father," Josephine said politely.

Lady Alexandra had somewhat dreaded the invitation and gave her sister a pointed glare. She didn't fear Josephine's interactions with the duke but rather Sophia's. The young girl was already practically bursting out of her linen dress at the thought. Josephine raised a questioning golden eyebrow at her eldest sister's look. It was too late however; the invitation had been made.

"I would love to, thank you," Raven said with a dashing smile, making his way to enter the room as Lady Alexandra's sisters parted away from the door.

"Do have Polly bring us some refreshments, as well," Sophia said very importantly to her eldest sister.

She always did like to pretend an air of superiority despite her lot in life and order in the household. Lady Alexandra pressed her lips tight together to keep from responding. It was usually Josephine that would scold their youngest sister for her impropriety, but even she had the sense not to do so in front of the duke.

Raven only gave Lady Alexandra one more look with an intrigued smirk before entering the room and leaving her in the hall alone. Once gone, she let out a long sigh of frustration before turning to get her father. The sooner she saw her father ready for his guest the sooner she could remove Raven from her sisters' presence.

Raven sat comfortably in a high back winged chair in the small but comfortable drawing room. Lady Alexandra's sisters took their places, one, the youngest he believed, with a book in her hand though she didn't open it to read, another tending to the mending and the last a little unsure what to do. Raven was delighted with the idea of sitting with these ladies. He was sure he could glean more information about the Lady Alexandra that intrigued and confused him so.

"I understand you have only recently come to town after an extended holiday abroad," Lady Josephine said, with a pleasant look to her.

Though Josephine had much darker hair, almost black, where Lady Alexandra had chestnut brown, they seemed very similar in features overall. Though unlike Lady Alexandra, who seemed to always physically carry an unseen weight, none of her sisters seemed to share much in it.

"Yes. It wasn't a holiday per se. More just time to see the world, further my education, and of course see to property my family has holdings in elsewhere."

"How very fascinating. I can see why you would have an interest in meeting my father then; he is quite a lover of world travels as well."

"I hope I am not interrupting by coming on such short notice," Raven said quickly, though the fact that all three ladies were giving him their undivided attention, save for

Lady Josephine who kept her hands busy with some mending, told him that he wasn't interrupting much.

"Not at all," Lady Sophia said with a broad smile across her lips.

Raven saw that she was very young, perhaps not even of age to come out in society. Though she held herself with a high air and clearly had confidence enough to make orders of her older sister in the hall, she still had girlish youth glowing from her face.

"In fact, I was just saying how I was longing to make a new acquaintance," Sophia continued. "Josephine mentioned that you met our oldest sister at the ball though she hadn't had a chance of an introduction. Alexandra seemed to be quite tight-lipped about it though. Which of course makes me wonder all the more what really happened at Sir Hamilton's, Your Grace," Sophia urged.

"Sophia! That is not at all a proper question to ask the duke," Josephine said in a sharp, hushed tone.

Before a retort could be made on the part of the youngest sister, the doors swung open, and Polly came in, understandably a bit out of breath, with a tray of currant rolls and a fresh pot of tea. It was in that moment that Raven realized they had but the one maid.

The room was silent for the most part as the tray was set down next to Lady Josephine, and she poured out the cups only taking time to ask the duke his preferences.

Lady Sophia seemed keen on bringing up the subject of

the ball again when a moment presented itself. Raven was a little surprised that Lady Alexandra hadn't mentioned the situation surrounding their first meeting. If anything, it made him see the problem. He had been far too tired that night to wait for a proper introduction to Lady Charlotte and instead brazenly went to introduce himself. The results had been an introduction and dance with the wrong lady. Lady Alexandra had significantly been offended when the realization of the mistake came up mid-dance, and rightly so he thought.

From that moment on he had been entrenched and desperate to know more of this lady while she seemed to find him most uncouth. It was technically an accurate assumption of the duke, if he was honest with himself. He cared little for the requirements of society and often got away with less than perfect adherence to the rules solely based on his title alone.

It was surprising to Raven that Lady Alexandra didn't share her opinions of him with the rest of her sisters. Surely, in a family of four young ladies, they would be a constant pool of gossip and shared information. It made him wonder again why Lady Alexandra seemed so apart from the rest of her sisters.

Even that night at the ball while the other two were no doubt spending the time with friends and other single gents, being one of the few opportunities that singles could mingle, Lady Alexandra had stayed to the side with the matrons and already married women. She had seemed to take on the role of mother to her younger siblings though she couldn't have been much older than them herself.

"You know I often frequented your father's museum as a child," Raven said after tea was served hoping to turn the conversation to other matters.

If Lady Alexandra didn't want to tell her sisters what happened at Sir Hamilton's ball, he certainly wasn't going to.

"In fact, I could say that my passion for travel started when roaming the various exhibits."

"And have you been there since returning to London, Your Grace," Lady Josephine asked. She seemed just as happy for the change in subject.

"Yes, I attended this morning for the lecture. It was there that I met with your sister again."

"And was it how you remembered?" Lady Josephine continued.

"In many ways it was, I suppose," Raven said. "Though I can't say how recently the change was, it's been many years. I suppose you ladies would know better about rotation in exhibits than myself."

"I haven't been to the museum since childhood," Lady Sophia said with a scoff.

Raven looked around the room realizing that none of the ladies have been there in some time. It seemed curious to him since he had seen Lady Alexandra twice at its steps in two days. More than that, she seemed a constant figure and very involved in its daily running, where these three had little idea about any of that.

He came to the realization that Lady Alexandra must also carry the burden of that place on her shoulders alone as well. It was no surprise she seemed so overtaxed. This house had little help for in its running by his summations already. She appeared not only the head of the house, responsible for her sisters in a motherly fashion, but also taking on the roles of her father alone outside these walls. He couldn't believe that she had all this all on her own to see to.

"Perhaps you are aware that your sister has made many changes to the greenhouse?" Raven asked with earnest, expecting them to have no idea.

"She has told me all about it. I do wish to go and see it myself sometime," Lady Josephine said. "Though Alexandra kept telling me to wait till the flowers bloomed this spring. She has been working so hard on it the last few years."

"But you don't share in seeing to the museum's needs?"

"Even if we wanted to," Sophia said with a hint of irritation. "Alexandra is always putting us to tasks with books and such," she added, putting her own book on a side table.

Raven read the spine to see that it was a compilation of Socrates.

"Alexandra is very insistent that we see to our education. She is always finding new material for us to read, or various talents to perfect," Lady Josephine said attempting to smooth her youngest sister's harshness. "You see, our mother died when we were very young, and Alexandra has taken on much of her responsibility. I look up to her very much for her willingness to take on the house and doing it in such a magnificent way."

Raven thought it a bit unfair that Lady Alexandra did so much, but at the same time saw the true admiration Lady Josephine had for her. He had some relief in knowing that at least her sisters were grateful for all of her hard work.

He opened his mouth to speak more, but just then the doors opened again.

"Lord Grebs will be happy to receive you in the library, Your Grace," the butler said with a bow.

Raven stood, thanking his hostess before exiting the room to discuss matters with the earl, more determined than ever to see that he find a way to bring some relief to this family.

18

Lady Alexandra waited several moments after she heard the sound of the butler taking the duke to her father's study before leaving the kitchen. She spent the time busying herself over the week's menu, any shopping still in need to be done, and a pile of letters received that morning.

She always sorted the mail before giving them to her father. A few sour letters reminding him of debts, bills to be paid, or even social events that would remind him of his late wife, and often send him off in fits.

All of this was done not necessarily out of need at that very moment, but only because she instead wanted to wait in the safety of the kitchen until she was sure she wouldn't see the duke again. She was entirely sure that Sophia must have pestered him about the night at Sir Hamilton's ball. Raven would have no reason not to tell the tale, and she preferred not to meet Raven's eyes with the encounter fresh in both their minds.

She still had no idea what he was doing in her house, making acquaintance with her father. This whole situation that had started with a mistaken identity was rapidly spiraling out of control. Losing control was not something Lady Alexandra experienced often, and she was sure she didn't like the feeling of it.

After all, her whole life and the livelihood of her family relied entirely on the tight leash that she had kept all these years since her mother's passing and her father's resulting poor health.

After sifting the mail, and reading the menu twice, she had no more use to stand in the kitchen. Also, she could feel the staff, Polly and the driver at the table and the cook tending to some vegetables on a cutting board, were not as comfortable with her presence in their part of the house. So, with a heavy sigh, and the courage that the door to the library was tightly shut, she left the kitchen to make her way to the drawing room.

In her hand, she carried several letters that she would have to respond to which would no doubt keep her busy for the rest of the afternoon. She could hear the muffled sound of male voices behind the library door, and even what seemed to be laughter, something she hadn't heard within those doors for some time. She hurried her steps past the doors and straight into the drawing room with her three sisters.

Of course, the moment she entered they all looked up expectantly. She didn't say a word, however. Instead, she walked over to the small cupboard and removed her writing desk and seated herself in the high back chair. She could feel her sisters waiting expectantly for her to say something but instead, she did her best to act as if all was normal.

"Sophia did you finish your reading for today," Lady Alexandra asked, not looking up from the parchment and ink she had placed before her.

"Really Alexandra, you're not even going to say anything?" Sophia shot back aghast.

"Say anything about what?" Alexandra countered with a surprised look at her younger sister.

"Perhaps something about the dashingly handsome duke that followed you home," Sophia said in her heavy-handed way. "Why is he here? What does he want with Father? Did he go to the museum to see you?" Sophia continued to rattle off question after question with no pause for an answer.

"Sophia, it might do well to take breaths between sentences, your face is turning blue," Josephine teased, pulling another stocking from the basket of mending.

"He is speaking with Father about the Zoological Society Banquet that he would like hosted in the museum," Alexandra said, giving a little information.

"Oh how wonderful," Josephine said putting her darning down for just a second. "Will he be utilizing your new greenhouse? I knew your idea was going to be a wonderful success," Josephine continued with excitement.

"He is considering it, yes, but I don't believe anything is final," Lady Alexandra said. "He said himself that though he is a member of the society he hasn't attended for some time. I am not sure that he will have much say in the matter," Alexandra played down, though the duke had been quite clear in the fact that he would have the final decision.

"Who cares about the stupid museum," Sophia said with a roll of her eyes. "Tell us, did he plan to meet you this morning? Does he have an interest in you? He must. I mean, dancing at the ball and now this," she said with an obvious tone of jealousy.

"He went for Mr. Lucas' lecture. I am sure he didn't expect me there at all," Alexandra retorted.

"You're a terrible liar," Sophia shot back.

"And you are terrible at minding your manners," Josephine added, becoming quite tired with her younger sister's behavior.

Josephine and Sophia always seemed to be at odds, so this was nothing new between them. Still, Alexandra wanted to calm the situation quickly before voices rose and carried through the house.

"I can assure you the Duke of Raven has no interest in me," Alexandra said softly, as if her soft-spoken words might encourage the others to do the same.

"Then why did he dance with you?"

"For goodness sake, Sophia," Alexandra said, now losing her own nerve. "It was a mistake. He thought I was Lady Charlotte Wiederhold. And I can assure you that his interest is in her and not me as I saw them in Kensington Gardens yesterday."

"Lady Charlotte is charming to look at," Williamina chimed in for the first time that afternoon. "It would make sense that he would take a liking to her from the start."

The room took a very sullen tone with the declaration.

"But he is here now, that must say something?" Sophia asked hopefully.

"It says that he and father have similar interests and nothing more. I don't want you making more out of this than there is," Alexandra scolded. "In fact, I think we should be very cautious in his presence.

"Whatever for," Sophia asked with a wrinkle to her nose, not liking the thought that a duke in her home could ever be bad. "Perhaps he has no interest in you but..."

"Oh for goodness sake, Sophia," Josephine echoed her older sister's earlier words.

"His person in our company might stir up some very questionable gossip," Alexandra tried to explain. "It will matter little that he has no interest in our family outside of Father and that none of us are attempting to pursue him. You know people will talk. It won't look well that a family with three single ladies with questionable funds are putting themselves in the company of a single duke. It will not sit well for any of your chances. I've told you time and time again," Alexandra continued in a lecturing mother's tone.

"Yes, we know," Sophia interrupted, slouching slightly in her seat, "Our only hope is marriage. If we spoil our chances, we will all end up living under a bridge or something," she mumbled.

"I am very serious about this, Sophia," Alexandra said narrowing her eyes and setting down the quill held in her hand.

"You forget, though," Josephine added. "We have four eligible ladies, not three. Perhaps the duke has found an interest in you. He may not have meant to dance with you at the ball, as you say, but he has clearly found some enjoyment in your company. I can see no other reason why he would be here, why he would use your facilities for a society you, yourself, said he hasn't attended in years."

"I don't count myself because I have the three of you to see to first. And I can assure you that I am no temptation to the duke, even if I wanted to be, which I don't. No doubt he is just finding entertainment in tormenting me, or some sort of twisted charity project," Alexandra said resolutely.

"There was no cause for his actions outside of a friendly gesture. I saw no malice in his countenance when he sat with us today either. I can see no other reasoning beyond pure intent. Can you not at least agree to that fact," Josephine continued.

"You only see the good in people," Alexandra said with admiration of her dear sister. "I, however, see the dire consequences his actions may cause. Good intentions or no, we still need to keep as much distance from the Duke of Raven as we can."

"I only focus on the good because you ever fear the worst possible outcomes. It would do you some good to see the goodness in a situation for once," Josephine said softly.

It wasn't the first time that her sister encouraged Alexandra to release some of the tension, stress, and maternal guilt that she seemed to carry always with her. In some ways, she knew that Josephine was right. She did carry far too much on herself. After all, Josephine and Williamina were both older now and quite capable of taking on some of the tasks that she had shouldered and kept from them since their childhood.

Perhaps it was just out of habit that she continued to do everything and anything so that her sisters could lead the normal life of a lady. She knew any thought of giving up even the slightest control she had on things gave her great anxiety that the delicate balance she had created would all come toppling down.

It was not something she was willing to reconfigure today, however. Instead, the room fell in contented silence as Alexandra went through her letters and made responses, having no more to say on the subject.

Josephine finished her mending, Sophia turned to a portrait of herself she was working on, and Williamina returned to her piano practice. With the tinkering of the keys, none of them heard when the duke exited the home, and Alexandra was glad of it. They spent the remainder of the afternoon as they so often did and with a sigh of relief Alexandra hoped that she could now finally put the whole upheaval of their predictable life behind her.

That, however, was not the case she found as the family sat to dinner that night. For the first time since Lady Alexandra could remember, her father joined them in the dining room. Though the sudden appearance left all four girls speechless, it didn't inhibit their father's tongue in the least.

He spent the whole of the meal speaking incessantly about his visitor. It was more words than Lady Alexandra had ever heard come out of their father's mouth at one time.

"I had no idea that they could climb trees," her father jabbered on with more energy than he had shown in years, "but the duke said he saw it with his own eyes. How curious for such a large creature, don't you think? And the duke is also a member of the Zoological Society, did you know that?"

"Yes, Father, I did," Lady Alexandra replied in the first pause since he sat down to dinner.

"He wants to use the museum. How wonderful. Though I am not sure we will have time enough to prepare, and I, of course, told him my reservations on the matter."

Lady Alexandra suddenly stilled. Did her father refuse the duke use of the facilities? She hoped not. As much as she would have rathered the man be removed from her presence permanently, it was the compensation he would provide that made him a necessity in her life. She hoped her father hadn't spoiled that.

"I hope you didn't refuse him," Lady Alexandra said in a strangled voice, hoping to keep her calm.

"I tried to, but the man quite insisted. Said he would be sending over a solicitor on the morrow to pay in full. Much more than I would ask but he quite insisted and who am I to argue. With the extra funds I may finally get my wish," he added, rubbing his hands together gleefully.

"There are a great many more uses for the funds than a giraffe," Lady Alexandra said stiffly.

Though she had almost complete control over all aspects of business, in the end, it was her father's, and he would always have the final say. She was relieved that the duke wasn't put off by Lord Grebs' insistence that they wouldn't have time to prepare for the banquet, even though he had no idea how right he was on that fact. Even still, she didn't need this inkling of hope of a better financial future wasted on yet another stuffed carcass.

19

"Raven, I feel like I haven't seen you at all these last few weeks," Aunt Rebecca said, meeting him in the hall as he exited the breakfast room.

He had planned to take his morning meal extra early that day to join the men of the Zoological Society for the second time since returning home. Lady Rebecca, for her part, was just descending the staircase in her morning dress. He did have a pang of guilt at not spending much time with her since returning home.

"Are you leaving again?" She asked with disappointment seeing that he was fully dressed for the day and early morning calls.

"I was," Raven said, pulling out a watch from his pocket and studying the time.

"What have you been doing? It's far too early to be calling on Lady Charlotte. That isn't where you are off to, is it?"

"No, I was actually on my way to the Society."

"Well stay and have some breakfast with me before you go," she urged with her big, pleading eyes.

"I just ate," Raven hesitated.

He really didn't have the time, but he was sure the men could last at least the first half hour of the meeting on other matters without him. They were planning to discuss the menu for the banquet to be handed over to the museum's cook.

"I could spare a few moments to sit with you, however, while you break your fast if you would like."

"I would like that very much," Lady Rebecca responded, lighting up with satisfaction.

Raven turned and entered again the room he just left. Sitting down, he watched as the servants set the place for his aunt.

"Do humor me and tell me what things you have been up to these past days. I suppose social engagements are keeping you very busy?" she added with a hint of intrigue.

Raven didn't want to admit that beyond their first walk in the park, Raven hadn't called on Lady Charlotte once. They had met at a few social gatherings at night and exchanged polite conversations from time to time, but beyond the norm of being in similar circles, he had done little to pursue her.

It wasn't that Lady Charlotte wasn't a charming, proper young lady. In fact, one might consider her behavior that of an adequate duchess already. Raven hadn't expected anything less in his aunt's chosen partner, and Lady Charlotte hadn't disappointed either.

Her parents, as well, were most charming, and he could see them both easily getting along with his aunt. In fact, if he were to make the choice of wife based on familial comfort, he knew that Lady Charlotte was it.

However, he was still slightly rubbed indifferently to the lady after that walk in Kensington Gardens and the way she spoke of Lady Alexandra on their return ride in his gig to her house. It was indeed an unusual sight they had encountered, and Lady Charlotte was well within her right to be shocked and even speculate over it.

None the less, from the very moment he met Lady Alexandra, he felt an unearthly connection to her. One she no doubt didn't feel towards him, if her attitude and opinions were any judge of her affections. Still, he seemed to be drawn in her direction continually.

Lady Charlotte's comments on the event and Lord Grebs' family after their encounter only seemed to rub Raven in a most uncomfortable way on his opinion of the lady through no actual fault of her own.

He barely understood this strange distance from Lady

Charlotte and could by no means express it to his aunt. Not only was she very invested in this connection, but she was also very openly contrary to his association with Lord Grebs' family.

It wasn't that Lady Rebecca thought her family and circles far too superior of status to rub elbows with an impoverished, titled family. Raven had never seen his aunt take such a judgmental opinion of anyone, no matter their situation in life. It was her deep passion for Lady Charlotte and him matching that was at stake.

Raven wasn't entirely sure why this particular match was so crucial to his aunt. He asked on several occasions why she cared so profoundly now of all times. Every time the conversation arose, Lady Rebecca gave the same vague answer of her passing of age and matronly duty to uphold in the name of his mother.

Though he didn't consider her lying in her reasoning, he also knew that those simple excuses couldn't be the entire truth of the matter. Still, his aunt had given him much privacy in his own life and the freedom to do his will, he wasn't about to go prying into his aunt's life, and motives, now.

"You could say that, yes," Raven answered his aunt vaguely. "I told you that I am also heading up the banquet for the Zoological Society, didn't I?" he added as an afterthought.

"I knew you were taking more interest in the meetings while you are in town, but I don't believe you told me that."

"Well, I went to the London Museum of Natural Wonders. Apparently, they have turned their greenhouse room into more than an indoor garden. I believe it is the museum's hope to extend its services to utilizing the large area for public and private events."

"You mean that glass monstrosity that towers over the surrounding buildings? I've always considered it to be a bit of an eyesore if I am being honest," Lady Rebecca said, buttering a muffin.

"It may not be much to look at on the outside, but I can assure you, dear Aunt, that within its casing it is most breathtaking. Instead of the usual walking garden with a few varieties of butterflies, it has been completely transformed over the last few years. They have turned it into something of a tropical paradise. It even has a few exotic creatures within to entertain, including a rather talented parrot."

"And what does any of this have to do with your Society?" Lady Rebecca said with slight agitation.

"Well, naturally I thought it a perfect location for the Society banquet. It would be the first use of the venue for an event. I think it might help spread the word a bit about the opportunity there."

"And the other men of the Society agree to this? It seems a bit unorthodox if you ask me."

"I can't see how. It's a society based on the study of animals. Certainly, a place such as the Museum of Natural Wonders would be an obvious venue."

"I'm sure you know much better on the matter than I," his aunt said, resigned. "I only hope it doesn't preoccupy too much of your time, Raven," she added more in warning.

"I promise it won't," Raven placated his aunt.

"Good. Then I would like to go over a few engagements for the upcoming week. Naturally, you know most of these. Lord and Lady Jocasta invited us to a private dinner. I know I've already mentioned it to you once," she added quickly, seeing her nephew sigh at the mention. "I am only reminding you again, so you have no excuse for getting out of it. Lady Jocasta is a very kindly lady. Her health doesn't allow her out much, and I just know she would be glad to see the man you have grown into."

"Of course, Aunt. I will go then," Raven said, though he had no desire to spend an evening sitting around with the rather aged couple.

Lord Jocasta couldn't hear a word one said to him even when shouting. Conversations with him were often a cross of a shouting match and his answers still being completely different than the question asked. And that was, of course, years ago the last time Raven saw them. He couldn't image how much his hearing had deteriorated since then.

Lady Jocasta had a great fondness for cats. Raven supposed it was to give her someone to talk to besides her husband, as the lady rather treated the various animals as members of the household. Lady Jocasta had been somewhat of a mentor to his mother and aunt in their younger years, and his aunt had always made sure to keep in touch with the lady.

As a lad, he was often dragged to the Jocasta home where he sat amid cats and listened to the women chatter on. It wouldn't be what he would consider a worthwhile evening, but none the less he would go for his aunt.

"It is on Thursday, a week from tomorrow. Please do make sure you will be there," Lady Rebecca added for good measure.

"Of course."

"Also, since we are on the subject of Thursday. Tomorrow is a showing of Carlotta at the opera house. I have it on good authority that Lord and Lady Derber plan to attend. Naturally, Lady Charlotte will be there with her parents. You will be a dear and come along with me, won't you?"

"You know how much I detest the theater. Lady Jocasta's cats are torture enough for one season."

"Theodore Hendricks, Lady Jocasta is not torture," Lady Rebecca said, dropping her half-eaten muffin to the plate in shock.

"Her cats certainly are," Raven mumbled under his breath. He knew better than to counter his aunt at a volume she would hear when she used his Christian name.

"I am not asking you to enjoy the opera, just to attend it. It is vital not just for a chance to mingle again with Lady Charlotte, but also to show her parents that I bred you to be a well- mannered and sophisticated gentleman."

Raven could have guessed that this was the tactic his aunt would use. Anytime she asked him to do something he really didn't want to, she always found a way of making it a way to show she had done her duty right. He could never refuse her with this. It would be as if he was saying she had failed him in some way.

"Fine, I will go, but I promise you I will be very sour the whole night through."

"Fine," Lady Rebecca echoed. "Just mind you keep your disposition to yourself."

"I will try my very hardest," he replied with a forced smile.

"Good. We have also been invited to a small dinner party at Lord Eagleton's house. The day after the Jocasta's. I fear it might be too much, but I do know you are close friends with Lord Bembury and suppose you will want to attend."

"Young Charles stayed in the country with his wife this year," Raven informed his aunt. "She is great with child again, I believe."

"How many children is that now?" Lady Rebecca asked, a little scandalized by the idea.

"Number four," Raven replied, though he was beaming with the good fortune of his closest friend.

"So we won't attend then? I may send my condolences?"

"Actually, I would still like to attend. I am sure you are more within your rights to excuse yourself from the evening, but I will plan to go."

Lady Rebecca shrugged this off, and they finished the rest of the meal talking on the rest of the upcoming engagements and various events that Lady Rebecca had planned for her day.

Raven was glad she didn't think to consider why he was so adamant about attending a dinner party of a close friend's family when he wouldn't even be present. From the moment his aunt brought up the dinner arrangements only one thought had entered his mind. There was the possibility of seeing Lady Alexandra again.

He knew well enough now that Lady Alexandra was a close friend of Lord Eagleton's young new wife. It would only make sense that Lord Grebs and his daughters also be invited to a small dinner party of close friends. At least that was what Raven hoped for.

He hadn't spoken to or even seen Lady Alexandra since the day of the museum lecture despite the fact that he always found himself scanning rooms for her. He had no excuse to call on her at present either without it raising more alarm with his aunt that he was doing so.

After meeting with Lord Grebs, who had seemed a very

withdrawn recluse but not an altogether terrible man to converse with, he had no occasion to return to the townhome. His solicitor had done his duty the following day calling on Grebs and settling the account in full before the banquet and with a sum vastly more considerable than was asked of by the earl, all on Raven's orders.

He knew it was a blatant act of giving to a family that certainly needed it. As much as he had done it out of a great desire to help alleviate some of Lady Alexandra's troubles, he also had a sinking feeling that she might be quite furious at him because of it.

Though he had meant it in goodwill, he also couldn't help but anticipate when he saw the lady again, even if it was with her honey brown eyes narrowed in disdain, chest puffed out in prideful hatred of his kind act. She didn't seem the type to ever ask for help or accept it when it was given. Part of Raven actually relished the fact that despite her stubborn nature he had found a way around her walls, to provide her with a small portion of relief that she so desperately needed.

20

Lady Alexandra had scarcely taken a second to eat or sleep over the last few weeks. Her days were filled with task after task preparing for the Zoological Society banquet. Usually with no time for rest between, she would go straight from her daily errands to social gatherings with her sisters.

Much to her great relief, Josephine had taken on the task of seeing herself and younger sister Williamina ready for the nights' events when Lady Alexandra finally arrived home.

Josephine was also doing as much as she could to see that Sophia was tending to her lessons during the day and not causing trouble before their events.

Lady Alexandra knew that she was getting grossly behind in her regular household duties, and only had the knowledge that once the banquet was over, she could get back to them and put life back into order for the Woodley household.

Tonight was the first night that she was actually looking forward to going to a social gathering after a long day of work. She would be attending a private dinner party at Lord and Lady Eagleton's house.

Lady Alexandra was looking forward to seeing her dear friend again as she had spoken less than a hand full of words to her since Sir Hamilton's ball. She had so much stress and anxiety over the upcoming banquet, not to mention the guilt of the duties she was leaving undone, welling up inside of her, it was beginning to cause a physical toll on Alexandra.

As much as Lady Alexandra would have liked to unburden her mind of these things over the last few weeks, she didn't feel comfortable doing so, not even to Josephine. It was only with Regina that Lady Alexandra felt comfortable enough to share all of her feelings.

Lady Alexandra was walking with a spring in her step, after changing for the evening, to the carriage waiting outside. Her sisters were not far behind. Tonight was just what she would be needing to rejuvenate herself to get through the final stretch of preparations.

For the most part, the excitement level was low for the rest of the Woodley girls. Even Sophia would be attending tonight as it was a close friend's private dinner. In fact, the three younger girls had seen little excitement since the duke's sudden arrival in their home and expected no different from tonight's meal.

"Ah, Lady Alexandra Woodley," Lord Eagleton greeted upon their arrival to their home.

Already the Eagleton's drawing room was filled with half a dozen guests with sherries in hand.

"Good evening, Lord Eagleton," Lady Alexandra said with a curious tone and a curtsy to their host.

She knew little about Lord Eagleton beyond what Regina had shared with her. From that information and her few interactions with him, she found him to be a most amiable host, kind husband, and loving father to his two boys.

"I am so glad you have arrived tonight. Lady Eagleton has been most lonely without your visits these past weeks. She tells me you are very busy with a project of some sort," Lord Eagleton continued, walking with her towards the direction of his wife.

Lady Alexandra spotted her dear friend the moment she entered the ornate room recently redecorated in the French style. Lady Eagleton was busy talking to a tall gentleman with his back turned to Lady Alexandra's approaching party.

"I have been very busy as of late, but I wouldn't call it a sort of project. I have been seeing to the needs of my father's museum."

"Really? I've been meaning to stop by and call on your father again. I am sure it has been ages since I saw him last. Why does he never leave his house?"

Lord Eagleton, though probably her father's age, had never been in similar circles. It was only with the connection made between her and Regina that the Earl of Eagleton even made the acquaintance of him.

"Sadly his nerves were greatly damaged by my mother's death. He hasn't felt in good enough health since then."

"Not even enough to join us tonight?" Lord Eagleton said with a hint of doubt.

In all honestly, Lady Alexandra hadn't even told her father where they were going for dinner or thought to include him in the invitation. She was so used to him denying any outing that she no longer asked.

"I suppose that is what leaves you so busy with the museum business this year?"

"Well, I have been seeing to the needs of the museum for some time," Lady Alexandra said with a low voice. She feared it was too prideful to announce such information as they came upon Regina and her current company. "This year has just included an added challenge. Don't get me wrong, one that I am most excited to execute, but very time-consuming none the less."

"Well, I do hope it won't keep you away for too long," Lord Eagleton said, concluding their conversation since they arrived at their target. "Lady Eagleton is quite lonely without you. I fear she has made few friends outside your connection."

"I suppose we are very similar in that respect," Lady Alexandra said, smiling at her friend now having reached their side. "I can assure you I will finish with added tasks at the museum within a fortnight and, hopefully, after this first go at it, the regularity of the task will smooth out the cost of time."

"Or at the very least get some help with your tasks," Lord Eagleton said with concern in his eyes. "It does little good for a lady to be at the helm of a business, especially all alone. Certainly, there must be a gentleman who can see to your father's work."

"I couldn't agree more, though I am sure that no task, a man's work or not, would be much of a challenge for Lady Alexandra," the gentleman said, turning around to face them.

Lady Alexandra didn't have to see his face to know it was the Duke of Raven speaking. She looked down, feeling the heat of embarrassment rising to her cheeks. She didn't want him of all people to hear that conversation. What if he was to take his banquet commission away from her now because he thought her no longer up to the task?

"Ah, Raven, I thought I heard you earlier but didn't realize you had arrived," Eagleton said, slapping the duke on his shoulder with a friendly gesture. "Leave it to you to sneak away with my wife instead of one of the many eligible ladies here tonight."

Lady Alexandra snuck a peek at the duke and was surprised to see that he was a little flushed by the comment.

"I was just getting to know Lady Eagleton a little better. We had barely spoken two words when you came upon us."

"If you say, Your Grace. I warn you, however," he added with a gleam in his eye and a finger to his nose, "with both my sons gone or married I am making your future my personal mission."

Eagleton gave Raven a wink and a final pat on the shoulder before turning to greet the next party of guests entering the room.

She hoped that Raven would also excuse himself, leaving Regina and Alexandra alone to talk, but he apparently had no desire to remove himself from the small party.

"My dear, it's been too long," Regina said taking Alexandra's hand in hers and squeezing it softly for encouragement.

"Is it true then? You have been worked to the bone on my account?" Raven said pointing his dark, narrow eyes at her.

"I wouldn't say that, no," Lady Alexandra said, though she couldn't meet his gaze. "In fact, Your Grace, I am very grateful to you. This banquet will inspire many more uses of the facilities, I am sure of it."

"Even so, it isn't a task that should be taken on by one woman on her own," Raven said, not listening to her deflection. He wrinkled his brow as he thought.

Lady Alexandra was sure he was going to remove the commission altogether. She had no idea what she would do in that instance, as she had already spent a good portion of the fee given to her for hiring staff and getting the kitchen in working order.

"I suppose there is only one thing to do about it," Raven said with a heavy sigh.

Both women looked toward the duke, anticipating his next words.

"I will come to call on you in the morning to see how we can lighten your load."

Lady Alexandra's mouth dropped to the floor for just a second. It was not at all what she expected him to say when he started that sentence.

"I'm sorry, Your Grace, but I don't think it would be wise for you to assist in the preparations of a banquet you have employed me, I mean my father's museum, to plan."

"I think it's a spectacular idea," Lady Eagleton said clapping her hands together with joy.

"How could you possibly?" Lady Alexandra said turning on her friend.

Of all the people in the world, Regina was the only one to know the embarrassment she was dealt at the duke's hand. Of course, Lady Alexandra hadn't the moment to tell

Lady Eagleton of all the other nefarious deeds the duke had done.

She needed to explain that the duke tried to seem a courteous gentleman outwardly but had his own motives. Raven was only using her as a type of sideshow entertainment in what would otherwise be considered a dull season spent in London. The duke had made it clear he detested the city when he could be otherwise enjoying the adventures the world had to offer outside its suffocating confines.

None of this information had been passed to her dear friend, which was sure to change her opinion on the present matter. Even still, the one shameful act at Sir Hamilton's ball should have been enough for her friend to sense that any excuse to bring the two of them together for any amount of time was unwanted on Lady Alexandra's part.

"Well, the duke opinions on things such as the menu would matter greatly would it not? I believe he is just as invested in the success of this banquet as you are, though for different reasons naturally. It would only seem fitting."

The duke, satisfied with the lady's explanation, nodded his approval. He was beaming at the notion, and Lady Alexandra could only guess the teasing and merriment he was already planning at her expense.

Of course, she couldn't refuse him such an offer. It was, after all, his banquet. Not to mention the fact that he was a duke. He could have any part in just about anything he wanted, with few who could refuse him.

"But surely you are far too pressed for time. I wouldn't dream of asking such a thing from you when you would otherwise be occupied with more vital appointments that you no doubt have," Lady Alexandra said in a ramble of words.

She was panicking and desperate to find any way to refuse him the chance of torturing her for the foreseeable future, and at that moment she was rambling quite ridiculously.

"Nonsense. Nothing is more important than seeing I do this dinner right. I have been a silent figure in the Society these last several years. Though they are grateful for my contributions, that doesn't mean they are altogether welcoming to my physical presence. This is just the ticket to get in the gentlemen's good graces again. Something that I particularly desire at this time."

Lady Alexandra opened her mouth to find another objection, but Lady Eagleton spoke first before she could.

"And what is it that you are looking forward to from the Society, Your Grace?"

"An African exposition."

"Surely you can and have done that without their support," Lady Alexandra interjected.

"True, but this one has significant importance. The Prince Regent has called for increased involvement in the

Cape colony of South Africa. He has asked the Zoological Society to send out an expedition of the surrounding areas to find the safest lands for settlements."

"How very interesting," Lady Eagleton encouraged. "And what will your purpose be? Mapping of the area I suppose?"

"A little of that, yes. Mostly, however, we have been asked to survey the area for wildlife. I am sure you can guess how dangerous the creatures can be," he added with a charming smile. "It is our job to catalog the creatures that frequent or inhabit the area. We will also be making land treaties with local tribes that might be in the vicinity to produce areas of settlement for the men to come shortly thereafter."

"It does seem a rather dangerous task," Lady Eagleton said with true worry for her new acquaintance. "Surely your aunt can't be fond of the idea of you going to the wilds of South Africa?"

"In truth, I haven't told anyone yet, besides the two of you. I suppose I am just waiting to see if I have enough say with the Society to put my name in the hat for the job. It is highly desirable by many of the Society's members."

"Well, then this will clearly be a good match for the both of you," Lady Eagleton said, smiling between the duke and Lady Alexandra.

There was little Alexandra could do at this point to stop

the duke from the course he was heading down. She merely smiled as sweetly as she could muster in return.

She had little doubt by the gleam in Lady Eagleton's eyes that her dear friend thought she was doing her some grand match making favor by encouraging the continued connection between the two. If Regina only knew the duke's true intentions as Lady Alexandra did, she was sure her friend would have never helped to encourage such a thing.

21

Raven took his place at Lord Eagleton's fine table and surveyed the room. He would have rather wished he could have found himself seated closer to Lady Alexandra, but he knew such a thing wouldn't be possible.

He was sure from the moment he heard her voice floating towards him that night his entire outlook on the evening had elevated.

It wasn't that he had expected it to be a miserable evening. Whether the lady came, as he was hoping she would, or not he knew that the night would be a pleasant reprieve from his engagements thus far.

First, there was the opera that he was forced to sit through for the sake of a brief conversation with Lord and Lady Derber and their daughter, Lady Charlotte, afterward.

If the opera itself hadn't done the job of boring Raven to death, then Lady Charlotte's lengthy explanation of how much she adored it, with several retellings for example, certainly did. Why the woman insisted on repeating portions of it, and then even translating the opera's French into English, was beyond him.

Clearly, they all knew the language well enough not to need her guidance as to each dialogue's meanings. Despite Raven's irritation of the action, it seemed everyone else in their conversation thoroughly enjoyed it.

No, not enjoyed it, but encouraged it. It was as if Lady Charlotte's parents and his aunt were quite insistent on Lady Charlotte showing him every single one of her exquisite qualities and talents to win Raven over.

The night had brought him to one single conclusion, however. It would matter little what merits or talents a lady had. He wanted someone he could truly share a life with. Amiable qualities would do little good in a union if they had no common interest in it.

Raven couldn't honestly say if Lady Charlotte had a passion for the opera, or French for that matter, as everything she seemed to do was for the simple purpose of exposing all her good qualities and nothing more.

He considered this more irritating than finding a person who had opposing views than one's own. At least, in that case, one could agree to disagree on the matter. Lady

Charlotte didn't seem to have a genuine desire, opinion, or passion for anything save showing the best front possible to the world.

Surprisingly it was on that very night that Raven realized that he could never find Lady Charlotte a good match for him, no matter how much his aunt wanted it, or how right it looked on the surface.

That was also another matter that Raven had yet to bring up with his aunt. He was beginning to feel more distance from his dear boyhood caretaker than he had ever before, even with oceans between them.

There was still this unknown drive that was pushing his aunt to promote Lady Charlotte to him. He was sure until he found out the reasoning, and a way to rectify it, he would have little chance of convincing his aunt that she was not the right choice for him.

He looked down the table amid the candlelight, steaming dishes and chatter of the guests to find Lady Alexandra at the far end. She was sitting next to her friend Lady Eagleton with her sisters at her side. The table really wasn't that full as this was an intimate party and certainly, no more than three people separated the seats between Raven and Lady Alexandra. Still, he wished her closer so he could hear what she was discreetly telling Lady Eagleton.

It was after the opera that Raven decided to give up

fighting his fascination with Lady Alexandra. The realization had been as if a fog had cleared to reveal a bright, sunny day.

Lady Charlotte had been shallow and bland. She certainly hit all the marks of a proper lady, but beyond that, he saw nothing more than an empty shell.

Lady Alexandra on the other hand, was fierce in her determination to thrive despite the cards life had dealt her. More than that she had very decidedly become the person she wanted to be. He found it a most admirable trait.

One he couldn't help but be a little jealous of. Raven had traveled the world over partly because he had his father's love for adventure and desire to see just beyond the ever-stretching horizon. It was not only this that drove him to move and seek the new continually.

He knew part of him was also searching for that place he felt was right. The place where he could let his own shields down and be the true self he was within. He was searching for his home.

As of yet, he hadn't found it in a place. These intoxicating encounters with Lady Alexandra had shown him that a place he had once despised and hated returning to could now be a joy he anticipated every morning. It was all thanks to the person who had entered his life and not the place he found himself in.

It was a curious thought brewing in him. If nothing came of these feelings he was developing for Lady

Alexandra he would at the very least have an admiration for the lady and this new feeling she planted within his heart. No longer did he consider that peaceful, safe sanctuary of one's home as a physical place meant just for you, but instead a sensation brought on by the people one chose to surround themselves with.

As he enjoyed the meal and conversation provided, Raven couldn't help but feel for the first time that these people were the ones he belonged to. He only wished that his aunt had joined them and then he was sure the night would have felt complete.

The dinner party the night before, however, with her elderly friend had quite tired her out. Not only that, but she had left the house with what she called the coming of a cold. Raven wondered if it was instead a reaction to the cats. Especially since two more had been added to the household since last his aunt visited her friend.

Once the meal was done, Eagleton had coaxed his new wife into performing a song for their guests, though she was quite insistent that no one would want to hear such a thing.

From jeers and cheers around the table, Lady Eagleton finally agreed to the task. The whole party expectantly returned to the drawing room to find the small pianoforte brought out and chairs set in preparations for all the guests to listen.

"Lady Williamina, would you be a dear and play for me.

I couldn't bear to sing without accompaniment, and your sister talks incessantly of your fine talent."

Lady Williamina blushed at the prospect. Unable to speak, she merely nodded her head in approval and took her seat at the piano. It took the two a few moments to decide on a song while the rest of the guests took their seats.

Raven did his best to find a way closer to Lady Alexandra than he had at dinner. He would have liked to share a more intimate conversation with her before he called tomorrow morning.

However, he found himself seated between Lord Eagleton on one side with Lady Alexandra's youngest sister, Sophia, on his other with the lady herself next to the girl.

Raven did his best to keep his focus on Regina and her beautifully delicate voice, but often he found his gaze drifting back in Lady Alexandra's direction. He was entranced by her face. She had the look of a beaming mother as she watched her sister play on the piano and even got visibly nervous as the piece took her through a particularly tricky part. She relaxed again, breaking out in a pearl-white smile when Lady Williamina got through it without any mishap.

Once the piece was over, Raven gave hearty applause with the rest of the audience and stood to turn to face Lady Alexandra. Quite unexpectedly Lady Sophia stayed in his path.

"Your Grace, my sister, Williamina, and I were going to start a small game of cards, and wondered if you might like to join us," she said, looking up at him with batting lashes.

Raven smiled down at the girl. She did have beauty even in her young age, there was no denying that fact. He was sure that when her time came to join society in earnest, she would be swarming with young suitors begging for her attention.

She seemed to know that fact as well. Lady Sophia had chosen a soft blue silk dress for the evening, and though it had a slightly low cut at the bodice for someone of her age, she decided to go without a fichu to cover it. More than this she had also accessorized her dress with a royal blue ribbon at her empire waist and weaved within her dark locks of hair.

Lady Sophia was undoubtedly there to get noticed that night by someone. Lady Alexandra, in contrast, was in a simple silk of rose gold with lace trim. There was nothing to adorn her appearance or accentuate her features. Yet it was she that seemed to steal the room for Raven.

"I would be happy to join you," Raven replied. "Though I suppose we will be needing a fourth," he added, hoping to rope Lady Alexandra in.

She seemed to pay little notice to him however, and started to walk the opposite direction to meet her friend and congratulate Lady Eagleton on such an excellent concert for the evening.

"Mr. Jamison would be happy to oblige, I am sure," Lady Sophia said, standing on her toes and saying the name loud enough to get the gentleman's attention.

He had been standing quite awkwardly waiting for a moment for the other guests to dissipate from their seats a row in front of the duke.

Raven had not spoken to Mr. Jamison beyond the initial introductions of the night. He knew that Jamison was the son of the Earl of Hawthorne and planning to enter employment as a clergyman. His older brother had already assumed their father's title upon his death two winters back.

"I would be more than happy to join your party, Lady Sophia," Mr. Jamison said with another awkward bow and darting glance at Lady Williamina who was coming to join her sister's side.

Though Williamina was older than Sophia, it seemed to Raven that she took most of her moves from her youngest and vastly more outspoken sister.

"I must confess," Mr. Jamison continued with a snort of a joke no one else understood, "I am not the best at such things. Perhaps it is why I am destined for the cloth."

"Do not fear Mr. Jamison, Williamina is not at all very well at it herself. I suppose it will be up to you and me, Your Grace, to keep the game lively," Lady Sophia said with a flirtatious tone.

Raven did his best to smile politely back to her slightly racy comments for a girl of her age. Together the four of them sat at a small table where cards were already stacked anticipating such an occurrence.

It had been some time since Raven sat down to a game of cards and it took him a minute to remember the games that Lady Sophia was proposing they play. Quickly it all came back to him, perhaps with the aid of being in a familiar place repeating actions from his youth. He had sat at this very table many years before playing card games with Charles Jr. and even Lord Eagleton's youngest son, Fredrick. From time to time they had also bet money on such games, though his aunt frowned on the act gravely.

It was no surprise to any at the table when Lady Sophia won the first match. She was turning out to have quite a competitive streak within her. As the excitement mounted with the end of the game, she forgot herself and let her passion of winning run free.

Though it was nothing like Lady Alexandra's disposition, he couldn't help but see some of her in the young girl. It was that same attitude of forgetting oneself and letting all walls slide away to expose the delicate insides.

After the third game of Lady Sophia's winning, and commenting on Lady Williamina's mistakes all the while, the game was beginning to lose any sort of fun.

During the third match, Mr. Jamison brought up a

particular novel of sermons he found quite intriguing. Either Williamina agreed in interest or was just desperate to leave the game with her condescending younger sister. Either way, with the completion of the game, Mr. Jamison offered to show Williamina some passages as he had brought his copy with him. In case a reading was asked for, as the gentleman explained to the small group.

Williamina eagerly agreed, and the two were up from the table faster than Lady Sophia could protest. She looked at the duke somewhat expectant that he might stay for this moment of private interloping between the two.

"If you will excuse me," Raven said, quickly coming to stand. "I have been meaning to try some of Lord Eagleton's port he recently acquired. Thank you for the lovely game Lady Sophia," he added quickly, though little heart was felt in the words.

Lady Sophia stammered for just a moment, not sure, for once, what to say. She was disappointed to see him go as she was sure they were making a great connection. None the less, she gave a flash of her most charming smile and bade the duke farewell.

Raven had no intention of finding Lord Eagleton or sampling his port. Not only was Eagleton still serving the same beverages since his childhood, Raven had never actually acquired much of a taste for the after-dinner drink.

Instead Raven quickly scanned the room with one

target in mind. He had spent these last days thinking of no one else but Lady Alexandra, and he was determined not to leave this night until he found a moment to speak with her.

To Raven's surprise, when his eyes fell on the lady, she was already looking back at him. She was standing in the far corner of the room having a chat with Lady Eagleton and Lady Hawthorne.

He found it a bit strange that Lady Alexandra always found her way to sit with the married women of the parties and not with the other single ladies like herself. Though it was a small party, he could already see two such groups of single ladies gathered together and mingling.

Instead, Lady Alexandra always seemed to find her place with the matrons. He wondered what value she could see in their conversations. Surely, they must spend all their time talking about keeping house and the arduous duties of a married woman.

It was in that moment that Raven realized that, of course, Lady Alexandra would gravitate to those types of friends. It was, after all, the life she already led in her own home.

Raven had never really had a desire to go on the South African excursion he used earlier as an excuse to help the lady out. It would have been a fantastic adventure he was sure of that fact.

Perhaps before he would have been too enticed by the

novelty and the danger to let such an opportunity pass him by. Now he saw that his greatest adventure was lying ahead of him; not to tame the wild beasts of Africa but instead to master the willful and determined spirit of Lady Alexandra Woodley into allowing him to be in her life.

22

Lady Alexandra had a fitful night of rest despite her exhaustion. All she could think about was the Duke of Raven. The way he always seemed to draw her in, even from the other side of the room.

She would have liked to think him rude for continually staring at her through the night's dinner at the Eagleton's. She couldn't, however, as she found herself doing the very same thing.

It was almost as if without her realizing it, her body was in heightened awareness with his presence. She seemed to be always in need of knowing where he was just as he was for her that night.

It was making her feelings tangle up within her. Clearly, Raven's fascination had little to do with the feelings she was experiencing and more to do with morbid entertainment. To make matters worse, her sisters certainly didn't disappoint that night.

At first, Lady Alexandra had been so proud of Lady Williamina as she exercised her piano abilities. Lady Alexandra knew that was something that Williamina had endeavored to improve almost incessantly.

Then there was that wretched card game right after. If it had been at all in her power, she would have kept Lady Sophia as far away from the duke as was possible that night. Sophia was the biggest wild card of them all.

She still had the vigor of her youth without the weight of dignity that comes when a young woman is of marriageable age. Worse than that she seemed to share Lady Alexandra's loose tongue.

Perhaps Lady Alexandra should have been stricter with her younger sister in that regard. It was more than just the fact that Sophia was the baby, and also the one who lived almost her whole life without their mother, that kept Lady Alexandra from reprimanding Sophia's wild declarations without consideration for the consequences. Lady Alexandra was just the same.

Of course, she had tempered that, or at least endeavored to temper that less desirable trait. It was impossible for Lady Alexandra to scold her sister for something she, herself, wasn't able to control.

None the less, Lady Alexandra had wished she had done a better job as the night at the Eagleton's unfolded.

Lady Sophia had been more than just loose in her lips; she had been a spectacle. Twice she had cheered so loudly at winning that it interrupted the whole room's conversation.

More than that, the way she freely scolded Williamina for any poor choice she made in the game lead several of the older ladies to consider that respect for one's elders was not instilled in the Woodley household.

She had caused a scene for the whole group to behold not just the duke at Sophia's side. Though she hadn't spared him any flirtatious glances, Lady Alexandra had to gather all her strength not to go to that card table and remove Sophia. What a spectacle that would have been.

By the time light started to enter the room that the four sisters had shared, Lady Alexandra surmised that she would not be getting any rest that night and quietly got out of bed without disturbing Josephine.

She dressed quickly into a cream-colored morning dress before slipping downstairs to the drawing room.

The house was entirely quiet at this hour, as the servants hadn't even begun their work for the day. Luckily some hot coals could still be found in the drawing room fireplace, and she stoked them for just a bit of heat to stave off the night's chill.

Her first order of business was to search the shelves to find the book she was hoping for. Finding her target, she pulled down the overly used and heavily tattered volume of

The Mirror of Grace, Etiquette for Fine Young Ladies by Sir George Tutor.

She would be having Lady Sophia reread this volume today for her school work. She hoped the girl would take notice of the chapters of proper dining etiquette.

Next Lady Alexandra got out her writing desk to begin the day's work. Her first order of business would be to make a list of all the remainder of preparations that would still need to be made before the banquet. She was sure if she got the task down on parchment it would finally give her mind a moment's rest.

She was so hard at her work, making several lists of items to purchase, the menu created, and orders to be made that she didn't even realize when her one candlelight was replaced with the full sunrise.

The house took on its usual noise of the cook preparing the morning meal and the maid going about her task while the butler saw to the one horse in the common use stable.

It wasn't until Polly entered the room with a cup of hot chocolate, toast, and marmalade that Lady Alexandra looked up from her work and realized how long she had been at it.

"Thank you, Polly. I hope I'm not in your way," Lady Alexandra added as an afterthought. It was a rare thing for a member of the household to be downstairs so early, let alone taking up the drawing room. Perhaps Polly used it for some purpose or saw to it in some way, and Lady Alexandra was preventing that.

"You're fine where you are m'lady. Your sisters will be down by the hour if you would like to join them in the dining room for a larger breakfast?"

"No, this will suit me fine, thank you," Lady Alexandra said with a smile of gratitude for the servant's kindness in bringing it to her.

Polly curtsied and prepared to leave the room.

"Polly," Lady Alexandra called after the young girl. "I am almost finished here, and then I have quite a list of errands to run. I will need to go to the fabric shop and pick out something suitable for the tablecloths. Then, of course, they will all need to be hemmed. It would be best to do that by hand to save the cost. But before the hemming and after the fabric I need to go to the museum and talk the menu over with the newly hired cook. It is his first day today I believe," Lady Alexandra said, shuffling through her papers for the proper documentation.

It did still seem all befuddled in her head despite the transcription.

"No matter, on that," she said, placing a hand on all the papers with a long sigh. "Would you be able to accompany me to the store and museum? I can assure you it won't take long."

"Of course, ma'am. I will just see to the ladies' hair and

dressing, and then I am free to go with you," Polly responded.

"Thank you, Polly. I know I am putting more responsibilities on you than should be for a girl of your position. I do hope with the new use of the museum we will be able to hire some relief," Lady Alexandra said.

Even if they could find the way to pay for a second servant, Lady Alexandra knew the truth was they had nowhere to house one. Polly and the cook shared one room in the attic, and the butler had the only other one.

Lady Alexandra was confident that a new member of the staff, as well as a larger house to accommodate one, would be next to impossible.

Polly hesitated for just a moment before leaving the room.

"Is there something else, Polly?"

"Well, it's only that," she fidgeted with her hands in front of her white apron. "Today is the second Monday of the month, ma'am."

Lady Alexandra's eyes went wide with realization. The second and fourth Sunday of every month the servants were meant to get their wages. Lady Alexandra had forgotten entirely.

"I am so sorry, Polly," Lady Alexandra said, setting her writing desk to the side and coming to stand.

"I wasn't planning on saying a word, and cook told me not to, it's only that...You see my pa is bad, really sick that is. He can't work much anymore. My wages go to him to take care of the small ones. Going one cycle without my wages is fine enough, but two is such a burden on them. You see I wouldn't ask if it wasn't for them," Polly tried to explain desperately.

"Are you saying I have forgotten twice in a row? You should have come to me sooner, Polly. I feel a wretch. I promise you I will fix the situation right this moment.

Polly curtseyed her thanks though she couldn't look Lady Alexandra in the eye. Lady Alexandra could only wonder the embarrassment that girl had suffered just to come up to her and ask for her wages. She felt a horrible person to put her employees in such a situation.

Quickly, Lady Alexandra went into her father's study where the bank book was kept as well as the chest of bank notes.

It didn't take her long to look over the books, record the wages and separate out the bank notes for each member of the staff. By the time she was done, however, she could already hear the sounds of her sisters coming down the stairs and into the dining room. She knew her father would not be far behind them.

As much as the man would have liked to sleep longer, and Lady Alexandra dared say his nerves could use the added rest, there was no sleeping once all four of the house's ladies arose for the day.

Lady Alexandra wanted to finish her task quickly

before her father entered the study. The last thing she wanted to do right now was explain to her father why she was giving the servants a double portion of wages a day past its usual day of dispersion.

Lady Alexandra found the butler last and paid him the dues owed with many apologies. She had left the servants' section of the house with several more tasks at hand. Firstly, the pantry was running desperately low on supplies as she hadn't been to the market in weeks. Upon inspection, Lady Alexandra also found that the family was down to their last box of a dozen candlesticks. She would have to go that very day to order more, or they would be eating their meals in darkness.

With the added tasks to do, Lady Alexandra entered the central part of the house heavy with guilt. She had left so much undone over these last weeks and as a result, put such a burden on the staff.

"Are you coming to the drawing room with us this morning," Josephine asked as Lady Alexandra converged with her in the hall. "With all these extra social gatherings of the season, the mending pile has doubled. I am stitching as fast as I can, but fear I am unable to keep up."

Before Lady Alexandra could answer, there was a knock at the door. Lady Alexandra looked at the watch pinned to her bodice. It was still quite early in the day for someone to call.

"Who could that be?" She heard her father say from behind the wall of girls exiting the dining room.

The last thing Lady Alexandra needed right now was a guest putting her father into one of his fits.

Before she could say otherwise, however, the butler came and opened the door. The Duke of Raven almost took up the whole of the doorframe with rays of morning sunshine peeking out around his silhouette.

All the girls craned their necks to see their early visitor. The sight of him wasn't disappointing in the least for any of the Woodley girls.

He stepped into the house dressed in fine tan pantaloons, high leather boots shining to reflect the morning light, a light cream morning jacket with contrasting navy vest, and a black velvet hat.

"I apologize for the early hour," he said to the butler, "but I wonder if I might leave my card for Lady Alexandra Woodley," he said most smoothly.

The butler hesitated for a moment before his eyes darted to the small crowd at the end of the hall. Raven followed his gaze.

Lady Alexandra couldn't help but feel her breath catch as his eyes fell on her. It was as if his whole countenance, which seemed so stern and long, softened just a bit as their eyes met.

"I see," he said to the man at his side. "Please pardon me if I have bothered you at too early of an hour," Raven said with a bow. “I did promise to call on you and help with the preparations.”

Lady Alexandra was stunned speechless. It was her father, pushing through the girls blocking his way and coming to stand at Alexandra’s side, who spoke first.

“Your Grace, what a pleasant surprise,” he said brightening up instantly. “You are always welcome in our home no matter the hour. Come in, and we can talk in my library. Is there something you were needing?” He said all at once.

Lady Alexandra thought that for a man who had little nerves for socialization he certainly was warm and welcoming to the duke.

“I actually came to call on your daughter, Lord Grebs. It was my understanding that she was in the mind of getting some assistance on the upcoming banquet. I have come to offer my services.”

“Help?” Lord Grebs said turning to his daughter. “Help with what? You have said nothing to me about this. What could there possibly be to do anyway? Just tell the museum to get it ready.”

Lord Grebs waved his hands off like the notion of being overtaxed with obligations was something made up in Lady Alexandra’s head. She would have liked to tell her father that all the times he waved his hand in like manner and encouraged her to 'tell the museum' it meant that she was to do it all on her own.

“I think Lady Alexandra is far too modest to ask for

help when she is in need of it. I only know because I had the fortune of discussing the present state of plans last night at Lord Eagleton's house."

Lady Alexandra really didn't like the two men discussing her as if she was a small child.

"Perhaps you would be more comfortable, Your Grace, if we took the conversation into the drawing room?" Lady Josephine asked, hoping to alleviate this awkward situation. "What do you think father? I am sure the duke hasn't had his breakfast yet. We could have the cook bring something in from the kitchen?" she continued, so it seemed Lord Grebs had the idea.

"Yes, you are quite right. Let us all take a seat and perhaps we can unravel the mess Alexandra has found herself in."

Lady Alexandra balled her fist at her side and did her best to push back the tears that were beginning to sting. After all, she had done thus far to keep this family afloat for all these years, her father was suddenly waking from his trance and calling her a failure.

Her gaze met Raven's, and she was almost sure he took a step towards her sensing the distress. Quickly she looked away and followed behind her father as they all made their way into the drawing room.

23

Raven followed along with the Woodley family as they all entered the lone drawing room of the house. Each girl seemed to take her spot immediately out of habit.

In contrast, Lord Grebs seemed to flounder around a bit not exactly sure where he was meant to go. Along with this, he appeared to stare around the room and even commented on some portraits on the wall. When asked who made it, he was told the various child.

It was clear by then that Lord Grebs had not stepped foot inside the room for some years. Finally, he took a place in a wooden seat he pulled forward from along the wall as he invited Raven to take the high back he had used the time before.

Lady Alexandra, though clearly upset by her father's

words, had composure enough to call the maid forth to produce some beverages and cakes for their guest.

Raven wanted to tell Lady Alexandra not to trouble herself on his account. From the moment he walked into the room and laid eyes on her, all he wanted to do was come to her side and release even a small portion of her burden. As of yet, he had only seemed to make it worse.

Perhaps it was because he had finally come to the realization that the feelings he had for the lady were far greater than he had initially thought, but Raven felt a desperate need to make things right for Lady Alexandra Woodley.

She seemed even more worn down today than she did the night before. That and the shuffling of papers on a small writing desk as they entered the room told Raven that she had already been up for some time now working.

"Now, my dear," Lord Grebs said in a placating way. "What have you found the need to concern the duke with?"

"I can assure you, she didn't bother me in the least with the matters," Raven jumped in before she could speak. "In fact, I suppose it was my own desires and curiosity over the process that made me intercede into Lady Alexandra's work. If it is a problem, I will be happy to rescind my offer."

"Nonsense. You are of course welcome to be as involved as you would wish. It is only I don't want you to feel the necessity. I can assure you my museum is quite able to handle everything."

Alexandra pursed her lips at the use of his phrasing

again. Twice now the earl had said "his museum" as if there was a significant entity within its walls that did all the biding. Did the man have no idea that it was Lady Alexandra that was doing the hard work on the grounds while he sat back in his house?

"None the less, what is it, child, that troubles you?" Lord Grebs asked his daughter.

She stared at him for a few moments, almost in shock that he would even consider asking such a question of any of his daughters.

"It is just some tasks needed to be accomplished today I assure you and nothing more, Father. I promise I have everything well at hand."

"Then it won't be hard for you to tell me what they are?" he continued his probing.

"Well, I am to go to the fabric store this afternoon and pick the linens for the tables. I also need to meet with the onsite cook to go over the menu plan. He is to give me a mock sampling in a week's time. Then the tables themselves are to be delivered later this afternoon to the museum and must be stored properly."

"Well that doesn't seem to be much at all," Lord Grebs said with a chuckle, facing the duke.

"I believe that is just for today, sir," Raven corrected the man's thinking that once these tasks were accomplished all would be complete.

"Ah, is that true?"

"Yes, Father. The tablecloths will need hemming. I also plan to use our lecture hall chairs, but plan to cover them to make them more pleasing to the eyes. Linings and sewing will be needed for that. Then there are the floral arrangements, lighting that is still awaiting orders, a few more footmen to hire..." Lady Alexandra rattled off with a far-off look that told Raven she was grasping to remember it all.

"Much of that is simply woman's work. Certainly, you can tend to that on your own," Lord Grebs chuckled again.

Raven could almost feel the tension in the room experienced by every single one of the Woodley daughters and entirely unseen by their father.

"How about," he said taking his daughter's hand with fondness, "The Duke and I will go to the museum today. We will oversee the menu choices, I am sure that is something Your Grace would have the most interest in," he added in Raven's direction. "Then we will oversee the table delivery. It might be nice for you to make the rounds of the upper rooms as well," Grebs said turning back to Raven. "I think you might find some of the experiments and studies quite interesting."

"I don't understand," Lady Alexandra said. "You, Father? You want to go to the museum?"

Her eyes darted to Raven, remembering there was an outsider among them.

"Are you sure you are feeling up to it?" she asked in a

softer tone. “I know your nervous attacks can happen quite suddenly.”

“Oh, I am more than fine. In fact, it has been far too long since I have visited the place. It is high time I go and see that my expectations are being met.”

Raven saw the nervousness that rained down on all the ladies’ faces. He wasn’t exactly sure what Lady Alexandra meant by sudden nervous attacks, but apparently, it was something she didn’t want him to experience outside their home.

Raven also knew from information from his Aunt Rebecca and just general observation that Lord Grebs had not left his house for some time. He couldn’t understand what was drawing the man to do so, now of all times.

“I wouldn’t want to trouble you,” Raven said to the lord.

In truth, he had actually been looking forward to spending the whole day, and hopefully many after, with Lady Alexandra today.

Yes, he still wanted to help her, even if it meant with Lord Grebs at his side instead of the enchanting lady. None the less, the prospect still had its disappointments.

“No trouble at all,” Lord Grebs said rubbing his hands together in anticipation. “I had nothing else planned for the day. I am still waiting on my next specimen to arrive. I am still hoping for a South American jungle creature from the Spaniards. But of course, it is hard to trust those kinds,” he went on in a conversational tone.

"I am sure that Alexandra will be happy for the help too, won't you, my dear. The cook mentioned only yesterday that we needed more candlesticks if I was going to stay up so late with my studies. I fear you have neglected a great many duties of the house as of late."

Lady Alexandra visibly deflated even more if that were possible. Raven could feel his muscles tightening with the desire to stand up and protect her.

"Why not take Josephine with you, dear," he said in a manner which told the girls they were excused to leave now.

Josephine's eyes shot up at the mention of her name. Unlike the youngest two Woodley girls who had sat with hands folded in their laps as the conversation had transpired, Josephine had been quietly set to work on a rather full basket of mending and shirts.

Raven came to the realization that where the two younger girls seemed to do little to support the house the weight was put on the elder two girls.

Josephine hesitated for a moment. She would never refuse her father, and certainly not in front of a guest, but at the same time, she eyed the massive pile that awaited her.

"I would be happy to accompany Alexandra," she said after only a moment's pause.

"Oh and do go and get me some fresh ribbon while you are out," Sophia said quite suddenly. "The Derber ball is only a few weeks away. I must have some new ribbon for my dress."

"Sophia," Lady Josephine started in a severe tone but was interrupted.

"I think we should start off right now, if we are to make it to all the shops, don't you think Josephine," Lady Alexandra said coming to a stand.

"Sophia, let us discuss the matter at a later date," she added for good measure.

"Oh, but you wouldn't deny me going to Lord and Lady Derber's ball. I am sure the duke wouldn't hear of such a thing," Sophia said pulling her face into a pout.

Lady Alexandra forced a smile on her lips. "As I said, that is something to be discussed at another time. I bid you good morning, Your Grace," Lady Alexandra said, face rosy with embarrassment.

Raven yearned for her to look him in the eye. She would not, however. No doubt she was feeling embarrassed for the less than acceptable manners of her youngest sister.

"If you will just give me a moment to ready myself," Lord Grebs said standing as well, "We can be off as well. I shall call Thomas to bring the carriage around," he added, motioning to the door where the butler was to be found.

"If you would like, I already have mine ready and waiting outside," Raven offered.

"Oh, yes. That will do nicely. Girls, please be kind to our guest. I will be but a moment."

The earl left, leaving Raven alone with the youngest two Woodley sisters. Williamina didn't seem to have much care at all for the company, and instead, her eyes kept flittering over to a small piano against the wall.

Lady Sophia Woodley, for her part, was all too happy to have the company of the Duke without the nagging of her older sisters.

"Is it not true that you are good friends with Lord and Lady Derber," she started on the instant her father left.

It was clear that Lady Sophia had a one track mind. Her single goal was to secure a place for coming out in society.

"I don't know if I would say good friends. I have only made their acquaintance recently."

"I suppose that must be true, as you have been away for so long," she continued with a polite smile. "It does make sense that they were one of the first families for you to connect with. After all, Lady Rebecca has such close ties to them."

Lady Sophia talked with an air of confidence. He was confident that she wanted to show him that she clearly was wise enough to be included in social events as she was already well versed in them.

"In what way do you mean?" Raven asked interestedly.

"Well, Lady Derber is the chairwoman for the Woman's Society for Orphaned Children. It is said that Lady Rebecca Sinclair, your aunt, of course, has been a candidate for the society's board. A very prestigious position."

Suddenly things were starting to clear in Raven's mind. That was why his aunt had been so insistent on the choice of Lady Charlotte. She had insisted that Lady Charlotte was the most suitable choice for his wife and future Duchess of Raven.

The truth of the matter was, she was just the most suitable choice to get Aunt Rebecca a distinguished seat in a woman's group.

"You don't say," he replied, relaxing back in his chair with a devious smile curling on his lips.

He couldn't have been gladder to be left alone in the room with the younger Woodley girls. Now that he knew his aunt's real purpose for pushing Lady Charlotte to him for marriage, it would be easy for him to find fault in it.

Naturally, when it came down to the choice of his wife, he would have followed his own personal desires, in the end, no matter what his aunt thought. Now, however, he understood why Lady Rebecca was so reluctant to show any sort of excitement or encouragement at the prospect of Raven actually finding a match of his own choosing.

It would take little effort to resolve this matter of a board seat. In fact, it seemed quite comical the lengths Raven's aunt had gone to. He was sure to secure her the desires of her heart all on his own and without her way of a marriage proposal to Lady Charlotte.

With that complete, his aunt would have no reason to not look on Lady Alexandra with fondness. He was sure that once her own personal desires were removed from the equation, Lady Rebecca would open her heart to Lady Alexandra. He had already seen so much that the two shared in common, he was almost confident that his aunt would be happy to accept her into their family.

Of course, he would also have to find a way to convince Lady Alexandra of that as well. It seemed to be a far more difficult task. As much as he admired Lady Alexandra's stubborn, tenacious willpower, he also feared it was what kept her at arm's length from all around her.

Raven would make it his goal to not only help the lady in her endeavors but to show Lady Alexandra that life would be so much greater if she chose him to be at her side.

Yes, Lady Alexandra had expressed some distaste for Raven, most often when he couldn't help but tease her. None the less, he was sure that the feelings he had for her were reciprocated. He had known it, without realizing it, that first night he met her as they danced.

Every time their eyes had met since then, it had been confirmed to him. Just as he was swelling with admiration for the lady, so she was for him. He doubted she was willing to admit such a thing just as he hadn't been at first. Once he broke through that hard outer shell, he was sure he could get Lady Alexandra to see the truth within her.

Lady Sophia's little discussion with him in the drawing room while they waited for Lord Grebs to return had been aimed at her own self-satisfying needs. Little did she know that her boasting might have just solved almost all the obstacles that laid in the way of his happy future.

Had he been a different man, he might have exclaimed with delight at the prospect. He was not a different man, however. He was the Duke of Raven and stayed composed as such while the lady spewed on with all the rest of the information she was fluent in regarding societal connections.

24

Lady Josephine and Lady Alexandra went about their day's shopping with relative ease. It was an excellent day for it as the air was warm, but there was plenty of cloud coverage to protect their delicate skin from the sun.

At their father's dismissal from the drawing room, both girls had gone upstairs to change into more suitable attire for walking the shops. Lady Josephine chose a soft pearl-colored gown with a blue striped Spencer jacket. Lady Alexandra took the time to accent her sister's dark hair with a soft blue ribbon to complete her look. As for Lady Alexandra, she changed into her brown muslin walking dress. She hadn't even fixed her hair as of yet and wore it with half of her long brown curls in a tight bun at the back of her head and the rest flowing back freely.

She took a moment to pull it all back into one tight chignon with only a few short locks left framing around her face. Lady Alexandra studied her face in the mirror reflection for a few seconds. Almost every day for the last month she had spent out of the house walking to and from the museum as well as other errands. She feared that she had spent too much time out in the sun.

Already her hair was taking on natural rusty red highlights mixed in with her brown locks. Though she had seldom cared about her complexion, she couldn't' help but notice a smattering of freckles across her cheeks already warmed with a golden glow of exposure. Before she realized it, her mind went to wondering if the duke found her complexion displeasing. She knew a lemon concoction that would remedy the coloring to her cheeks and absentmindedly considered using one later today.

Shaking her head with a slight laugh, she waved off the notion. She had never once considered frilling herself up, as Lady Sophia liked to call it, for anyone. Why on earth she had considered doing so for the Duke of Raven just now was downright ridiculous.

Removing the notions from her mind, Lady Alexandra announced she was ready, and the two sisters made their way back downstairs. Lady Alexandra was surprised to find that the duke and her father had already left for the museum.

She would have liked just a moment alone with her father to ensure that he was ready to go outside the walls of their house. Her greatest fear was that he would have another episode, only this time it wouldn't be within the safety of his library with only the Woodley girls and the servants to witness it.

She couldn't even imagine what would happen if he went into a fit out in public, not to mention what the duke would think of him. If Lord Grebs did lose control of his fragile sanity, would the duke revoke his use of the greenhouse room? Any sensible gentleman would upon facing someone prone to maddening fits.

Already her family had been shameful enough when it came to the duke in Lady Alexandra's opinion. It was true that her father did seem better around the duke, but that still didn't mean he wouldn't lose his wit. If that was the case and the duke shared the information with others in the ton, it would be the kiss of death for her sisters. No one would take on a lady of little wealth with a mentally ill father.

It was bad enough that he was already well known as a recluse. It wasn't completely unheard of for a widow or widower to withdraw after the death of their spouse, and so some forgiveness could be given on the part of society for such behavior. Maddening fits, on the other hand, would only gain him a bed in Bedlam.

Lady Alexandra enjoyed the quiet solitude of the earlier hours. For most of the other classes, the day had already begun, and they were well about their work. For members of the peerage, it would be at least another hour or so before they would leave the sanctuaries of their own homes to call on others or perhaps walk the parks and shops.

Lady Alexandra preferred this time to get her errands done as she could be more relaxed as she did it. Little did she have to worry about running into another lady who might question why she was picking up the candlesticks for the household and not one of the servants, and so on.

Lady Josephine, who had traveled the shops on several occasions with some of her lady friends, had probably never ventured out so early in the morning, Lady Alexandra ventured.

"It's almost a completely different world before the fashionable hour," Lady Alexandra explained as they neared.

"Quite a bit more people in my opinion," Lady Josephine surmised as she studied the carts and passerby of Bond Street.

"I suppose it is busier. Many are getting the items for their houses before the gentlefolk emerge. I find it more peaceful, oddly enough," Lady Alexandra said with a laugh.

Lady Josephine gave her a look of surprise.

"I just mean, everyone goes about their own business. They don't stop to gossip or judge others like our kind. It's a bit relieving to know I can do my shopping and not worry about offending, saying the wrong thing, or heaven forbid buying something out of season," she added with a roll of her eyes.

Just last year she had been in Mr. Goshin's shop buying trimmings for an evening gown. Her eyes had caught on a muslin fabric in cream with periwinkle patterns of fleur de lis on it. She had almost purchased some of the material, an extravagance, to make a gown for Lady Sophia. She was sure her sister would suit the slightly bold pattern well.

Just as she was holding it in her hands, however, waiting for assistance, she heard the voice of three other ladies chatting in hushed tones. They commented on Lady Alexandra's choice and how unpatriotic it was to pick such a thing when the crown was currently at odds with France. They continued gossiping with no pause until Lady Alexandra could bear it no longer. She promptly set down the fabric and left the shop without buying anything.

"How you always seem to think the worst of your own kind," Lady Josephine scolded, but in a soft tone. "Not everyone enjoys gossiping and judging. If you would just open yourself up from time to time, you might see that."

"I do open myself up. All the time in fact," Lady

Alexandra countered as they entered Goshin's shop for the table linens.

The room was wall to wall bolts of fabric, loosely organized by color and type of material. Hanging down from the ceiling were box chandeliers. Instead of holding candles they held spools of ribbon. The ends of the ribbons hung loosely down inviting any lady to come and take a closer look. Dotting the floor of the store were several tables with an array of buttons and brooches for sale.

"Lady Alexandra, Lady Josephine, how fine it is to see you this morning," the proprietor greeted them as they entered with a long bow.

There were only two other women in the shop, both clearly wearing the uniform of a housemaid. No doubt they were picking up orders for their household and doing a little of their own purchasing as well.

"Good morning, Mr. Goshin. I wonder if you might point me to the cream linens. I am in need of several yards of fabric for some tablecloths."

"You will want this wall here. It has the sturdier material for drapes and the like," he said, happy to help.

The ladies went to their work studying the various choices of fabric and trying their best to decide if a solid color would do well or a print. After some great debating between the girls, they finally settled on a beautiful solid ivory with gold lace trimmings along its outer edge.

By the time the order was made for Thomas their

butler to pick up later, they had gone on to acquire the items for their own house. First would be the candlesticks, then to the market for pantry items, and finally to Mr. Blots to purchase more parchment and ink for their father's use.

Every time orders were made to be received later that afternoon by Thomas and the cart. It was far too much for even the two girls to carry on their own. As they entered Mr. Blots, Lady Alexandra was relieved that their day's shopping was almost done.

Several hours had passed since their start. It wasn't the taxing work of walking from street to street, from Bond to Oxford street, but rather, she worried over her father.

Lady Josephine had insisted he would be fine, or else he wouldn't have offered to go. Lady Alexandra wasn't so sure. He often took on several of his science studies at once that often left him overwhelmed and near physically sick from the stress of it.

Lady Alexandra was ready to return home, give Thomas his instructions for procuring the orders at the various shops, and head straight away to the museum to check on Lord Grebs' well-being.

"What a pleasant surprise," a familiar voice called from around the corner of a high shelf of writing utensils.

Lady Alexandra smiled as she saw Lady Eagleton step around the large display. She was dressed in a fine cotton lemon dress with rich green trimmings and black velvet hat that made her golden ringlets shine.

The women greeted each other.

"This is a nice surprise," Lady Alexandra agreed.

Together the three women spent much longer than needed within the shop enjoying each other's conversation more than taking notice of the various items for sale. With the booming sound of the church bells ringing noon, Lady Alexandra remembered herself.

"Oh, forgive us, but I really must go check on my father," Lady Alexandra explained. "He decided to go to the Museum of Natural Wonders today."

"He did?" Regina said in surprise. If there was one woman in the world who understood Lady Alexandra's anxiety, it was Lady Eagleton.

She had only come over to Lord Grebs' house on one occasion to call on her friend. It just so happened to be a day that Lord Grebs spun out in a rather large fit of rage and distress. Lady Eagleton had not come over since.

"I am sure you are both worrying for nothing at all," Lady Josephine intervened again. "If he is distressed, I have no doubt the duke will return him home."

"The duke?" Lady Eagleton asked in surprise.

"Yes. Thanks to you," Lady Alexandra narrowed her honey eyes at her best friend. "The Duke of Raven called early this morning asking to be of assistance for his own banquet. Father was very upset, thinking I had begged the man for help. He considered me incompetent and insisted on taking the duke to the museum himself to oversee today's preparations."

"I think you are too quick to be offended by Father's words," Lady Josephine said. "I believe he was just surprised to realize how much time and preparations were necessary for such an extravagant event. I am sure he only wanted to add his own hands to help with the new-found knowledge."

Both Lady Eagleton and Lady Alexandra looked at Lady Josephine skeptically, before breaking out into giggles over the girl's constant positive outlook.

"I swear, Lady Josephine," Lady Eagleton said between giggles. "If everything in the world went wrong you would still find a way to be happy about it."

Lady Josephine blushed at the jesting though she knew that both girls only meant it as a compliment and nothing more.

"I do agree, however," Lady Eagleton added. "Raven is a very capable man. If he sees your father is agitated in the slightest, I am sure he will bring him right home. You have nothing to worry about on that matter. Won't you come back and have a small luncheon with me instead?"

Lady Alexandra considered the idea. It was relieving that at least two people thought her father would be in good hands with Raven, even if she weren't entirely sure of his character herself. There was also the fact that she had scarcely had any time to speak with her friend the night before at dinner. She rather hoped she could sit and confide in Lady Eagleton over all that had happened thus far.

It was with these desires, and the clear encouragement to do so from both other parties that stood with her in the shop, that Lady Alexandra agreed that an afternoon tea with friends was just the right thing to do.

25

CHAPTER 25

Raven was quiet on the drive over to the museum. He was well aware that the earl hadn't left his house for some time, and he worried how Lord Grebs would react to the changing scenery around them.

For the most part, Lord Grebs seemed to be thoroughly enjoying himself. He looked out his window like an expectant pup and soaked in everything around them.

"I have to say, I am so excited to get out and see the museum again," Grebs said as the museum came into view.

"Has it been quite some time since you have visited the place, then?" Raven asked though he knew the answer.

"I never really felt up for much after, well," Grebs' features went serious, "since my wife died. Everyone said it would get easier over time; I found quite the opposite to be true," he said with a shrug.

"You speak of your late wife with such love. I do admire that. Certainly, it isn't true for all relationships."

"We were brought together by our families," Lord Grebs said in honesty. "I couldn't have been happier for the match, though. She seemed to complete me in every way possible. When she took ill, well I didn't have that balance anymore. Poor Alexandra," he said with a sniff. "I feel she has taken on the brunt of the house with my wife's death. She doesn't know I know, but the night my wife died, when she said goodbye to the girls, I was there listening. Lady Grebs asked Alexandra to look after the others, see to the house. I think she just hoped to give the girl some purpose to distract her from the sadness that was to come. Alexandra took it so seriously, she is a very determined girl in nature, after all. I fear she gave up her own chances for happiness all so that she could take care of the others."

Raven knew this about Lady Alexandra, though he had never learned the reason why. Knowing her personality as he did, though, he completely understood why she had chosen to take on her mother's role in life for the sake of her younger sisters. If it was his parents' dying request, he knew he would collapse from exhaustion before he stopped working to that end. Lady Alexandra was no different. In fact, he was sure that she would drop soon from exhaustion if she didn't allow her younger sisters to take on more of the household roles and encourage her father to step up and retake his place.

"I felt like I was in darkness for some time there," Grebs continued.

"And what made you awake from it?" Raven asked a little tentatively.

It was clear that though the earl was making progress back into a functioning part of his household, it was still yet the beginning. Raven was sure that one misstep would send the earl spilling back into his mourning and seclusion, leaving Lady Alexandra again to brunt the whole household on her own.

"I don't know for sure," Lord Grebs said as he searched his own mind. "I do know, however, that you were the first person to call on me for some time. In fact, I was sure the whole world had forgotten me. It was nice to know that even if I wither away in my house, my legacy – this museum –" he nudged his gaze to the erect building they now pulled alongside. "At least this can still impart some good in the world."

Raven returned the earl's smile as the carriage came to a stop at the foot of the museum's stairs. Together they walked in, each lost in their own thoughts.

For Raven, it was the admiration of a marriage full of love, even if it was short lived. It reminded him so much of his own parents. He wondered if all matches made with pure hearts filled with love were destined to end that way.

When they entered the massive doors of the museum, several of the employees gasped in shock before welcoming the earl. It must have been an exceeding amount of time since he last visited this place.

Raven followed the newly returned proprietor as they made their way to the service areas behind the exhibit. Lord Grebs must have known this place well at one time as he walked with great confidence.

They entered a large, spacious kitchen that still smelled of fresh paint. There were already several workers inside clearing the remaining boxes and delivering cooking supplies.

They made their way back to a man who seemed to be directing the others. Mr. Brown was hired through a service without much foreknowledge of his employer. Now having arrived at the place he was greatly unnerved when he heard from the others that the said employer was a woman. His relief was all the greater when it was Lord Grebs and the duke that greeted him that morning.

"I was worried I might have to give my resignation right here on the first day," he said with the drawl of an upper-level servant.

"My daughter, Lady Alexandra, enjoys the museums and comes from time to time when I am unable. But I can assure you that nothing out of hand goes on here. I support the museum. Various departments are run by gentlemen of my choosing whom I find to be trustworthy and hard-working."

Raven did his best to bite his tongue. He knew that it was very unusual for a lady to have the type of pioneering spirit that Lady Alexandra did, let alone use those talents on such a large scale as this massive museum. All the same, he didn't like the way Mr. Brown suggested working under Lady Alexandra would be beneath him.

Raven made a note of being on alert for any other servants that might share the same reservation. They had no place finding an income here if they wouldn't show Lady Alexandra the respect she deserved.

It didn't take them long to square away the menu. Having anticipated meeting a woman that morning, the cook already had several menu options for her to choose from with all the courses detailed out.

Just as they were finishing with Mr. Brown, a man came in to inform the earl that the tables had arrived. Lord Grebs was to inspect the craftsmanship of each one before they were temporarily stored in a large holding room behind the safari exhibit.

"The design was of Lady Alexandra's making, and quite a genius one it was, if I don't mind saying," the carpenter said as he pulled the first long wood table out of the back of his cart.

Raven studied the rich walnut wood that shined in the

light of the day. Each slab of wood wasn't painted but instead showed the natural grain and knots of the original product. It was only the top of the table, however, with no legs to be seen.

"What is so genius about it," Raven asked curiously.

"You see," he said, having the servant who was hauling the table out of the back of his cart flip it over. "Each one of the four legs is stored under the table for easier storage. I've put a notch at the top of each leg which fits into the pegs at all four sides of the table. Then this part of the leg here," he said motioning to a ring of wood that surrounded the top of the leg. "It slides up and has a snap on the inside to keep it in place, sealing the two pieces together for when it is in use."

"That is very interesting."

"A whole room of men could dance on this, and not one leg would slip out of place, but breaking it down back into this compact style is so simple even her ladyship could do it."

"And you said Lady Alexandra gave you the plans for such."

"She did. She also permitted me to continue use of it should the need arise for other clients. Mighty generous, if I don't say so myself."

Raven beamed at the compliment given to the lady. Though he had as of yet to make the connection with her in the way he desired the most, he still swelled with pride over the ingenuity and tenacity of his chosen lady.

Raven watched as all six long tables, easily enough to sit over fifty people, were marched to their waiting place in the storage room.

"Now that wasn't hard at all," Lord Grebs said, rubbing his hands together after the last of the tables were put away and the carpenter left to return to his shop. "I don't know what Alexandra was so worried about."

Lord Grebs looked down at his pocket watch to see the time. It was almost noon.

"Shall we go upstairs? I would love your thoughts on all the studies we're currently performing," Lord Grebs said with excitement in his tone.

Raven was happy to follow Grebs as they made their way back through the central open room and then up a set of stairs along the far wall. All the upstairs rooms had a fabulous view of the gallery down below with doors leading to various labs at uneven intervals.

"Our first stop will have to be here," Lord Grebs said, walking up to a dark wood door and knocking on it.

He didn't wait for a reply but directly opened it and entered. Inside Raven found himself in a rather spacious room that housed both an office and an experimentation lab. Standing at a table with various instruments around him was Mr. Lucas donned in gloves, a protective black apron, and a mask.

As soon as Lucas saw them both, he straightened up and began to remove his protective layer.

"Lord Grebs! How good of you to come here and visit."

Raven realized that if they hadn't just entered without response as the earl had done, there was a good chance that the scientist wouldn't have heard them at all. He was busy at work with some sort of chemical compound.

"What is it you've been working on here, my boy," Grebs asked, giving the gentleman a hearty slap on the back in welcome.

"I have been testing the substance recreated from the porcupine," Lucas said with a sideways glance at the duke.

"Yes, Raven was just telling me the other day about his theories. I am inclined to believe him, of course. How many years did you say you lived in the Americas, Your Grace?" Lord Grebs asked, turning back to Raven.

"I'm not sure I could count them all up as it wasn't consecutively. I would guess at least two or three of the last five, however."

"Wouldn't that be the adventure," Lord Grebs said with admiration.

"Perhaps so," Lucas said rather coolly, looking the duke up and down.

"Perhaps," Lord Grebs scoffed. "I can't even fathom how much information we can glean from the duke here. We all sit in our little rooms and look at specimens on a table, this man here has gone out and seen the real live breathing things."

Raven did not doubt that Lord Grebs had the same taste of adventure that had driven his parents as well as himself to explore the farthest reaches of the world. The only exception was that Grebs lacked the funds to do so.

"Well, then we must be lucky to have you here, Your Grace," Lucas said, though there was no feeling in it. "Lady Alexandra explained to me that you had made her a sort of proposition for the Zoological Society."

Raven nodded his agreement. He hadn't liked the man much at their first meeting. The second even less when it was clear that the gentleman also shared an affection for Lady Alexandra. His opinion of Mr. Lucas had only gone downhill from there.

"She does seem very excited for your temporary contributions. How long do you plan to stay in London? I am sure that someone like you with a taste for travel doesn't stay in one place too long?" Lucas continued in friendly banter.

Though the earl took Lucas' words for their surface meaning, Raven could easily read between the lines. Lucas wanted him gone so he could get back to courting Lady Alexandra.

Strangely this gave Raven hope. For the man to be threatened by his presence had to mean that Lady

Alexandra had given some indication that she had interest in him as well.

"I'm not entirely sure. Naturally, I will stay the season through. I haven't decided if I will return to my country home after that or not. My aunt is getting on in years, and I don't feel as comfortable leaving her alone for long periods of time. Who knows, I could become quite the constant figure in this place."

Raven narrowed his black eyes on the man making sure that he got his point across. He had the means to stay as long as he wanted.

"Oh, wouldn't that just be wonderful," Lord Grebs said with excitement.

They continued the rounds of several other scientists' labs where they showcased to the duke and Lord Grebs their current projects or studies. Most of the men are middle aged if not a bit older.

"Lucas seems very young for his profession," Raven said as they took his carriage back to Grebs' house.

"He was practically a prodigy as a child. Smart as a whip that one. We had him study in the museum under the best minds once he was brought to us. He practically grew up in that building," Grebs said with a fondness for the boy.

"So, you must know him and his family very well then," Raven continued to prod as casually as possible.

"No family to speak of, I'm afraid. He had a mother

when he came to us, but she succumbed to the fever not long after that, poor lad."

"Well, then he must be very grateful to have someone like you to consider his needs and sponsor him as you did."

"Ah, well," Grebs waved off and looked out the window whimsically.

Raven could tell that the outing had already taken a toll on the man. He looked a bit pale and weakened by all the excitement of it. Raven was just glad that his spirits had held up the whole trip through.

Grebs looked down at his gold pocket watch again.

"It will be getting close to dinner by the time we return. You simply must join us for a family meal tonight," Grebs insisted. "I am sure if I tell Alexandra the work we accomplished, and how silly she has been for thinking it too arduous, she would simply wave me off. She would believe you, though."

Raven hesitated. He had no intention of belittling all of Lady Alexandra's hard work. Not to mention the fact, he wasn't entirely sure if the lady detested him or not. He hoped she was warming up to him a little, but he couldn't say for sure.

"Unfortunately, I already have plans this evening with my aunt."

"Then tomorrow, and I won't take no for an answer. You will find I am quite persistent, Your Grace. Lady Rebecca

Sinclair is, of course, welcome to join as well. The more, the merrier."

Raven wouldn't refuse the chance to be in Lady Alexandra's presence again. He merely nodded his agreement. Already he knew his aunt would never agree to such a dinner let alone be happy with him going.

A private family dinner would be a clear indication that he had plans to grow a close connection with the offering family. Adding to the fact that in this case, the family in question having four unmarried daughters, it wouldn't be hard for people to draw their own conclusions about the situation.

Of course, such a thing never even crossed Lord Grebs' mind. All he saw was another opportunity to talk with the duke about creatures, flora, and fauna he had experienced in his travels.

His aunt, however, would not be willing to condone such a connection, not with her own plans contrary to that. He would have to find a way to get his aunt to meet Lord Grebs family in a different setting. He was sure that once Aunt Rebecca met Lady Alexandra, and he fulfilled Aunt Rebecca's desire for a board seat, she would be all too happy to give him her blessing on the match.

26

Lady Alexandra settled nicely into her friend's private sitting room with her sister. She instead wished that one of them had thought to bring the mending along, even though the notion was an impossible one.

For whatever reason, Lady Alexandra had always felt that if her hands or mind was not doing something, she surely was slothful. Instead, she folded her hands neatly in her lap as the three ladies settled down from their morning of shopping for some light sandwiches and tea.

"It seems so quiet in here," Lady Josephine commented. "Not at all like home," she added for good measure to show she was enjoying the stillness.

The only other time that Lady Josephine had entered the Eagleton home was for small gatherings and dinners. Even with small numbers the rooms often rang with merriment and laughter. Today the house fell in the calm silence of emptiness.

"Yes, Lord Eagleton is out looking at some horses today. Of course, there is just him and myself now, so even when he is home it is eerily silent in here," Lady Eagleton said with a glazed look.

Though it was now clear that the chances of Lady Eagleton producing a child of her own was low, that still didn't remove the desire from her heart. Lady Alexandra pondered on this. She always found her own home so noisy it was almost a relief when she could leave to do the shopping and the like. Williamina was always practicing on the piano, Sophia hardly knew how to keep her tone down to a proper ladylike level when she was excited, and then there was her father who would yell orders from the confines of his library, not wanting to leave it.

For Lady Alexandra the thought of a quiet, peaceful house was heaven. She saw now that deafening noise wasn't always heard by the ear. In her friend's case, it was the silence that caused her great discomfort.

"Soon you will be returned to your country home where you will wish you didn't hear the happy sound of little children's laughter," Lady Alexandra said hoping to lift her friend's spirits.

"Yes, you're right," she said with a smile and squeeze of hands. "Young Charles' family has been such a blessing to me. With any luck, there will be a new babe as well for me to hold and love."

They continued talking on simple matters for quite a while as they ate small sandwiches. A plate of petit cakes quickly replaced the light meal.

It was after Lady Eagleton retold how young Charles' youngest daughter, not more than two, had crawled into a basket of laundry and fallen asleep leaving the rest of the house to search for her most frantically for several hours that all three girls had to dab their eyes from laughter.

"You know," Lady Eagleton said after catching her own breath, "I think that is the first time I have seen you laugh since returning to town."

"I know," Lady Alexandra said, stuffing her handkerchief into her sleeve. "I haven't had much cause to this year, I fear."

"You do seem very overtaxed. I know you say this prospect with Raven is a good thing, but I do hope you will reach out and ask for help if you need it. I do hate to see you wear yourself out so."

"If you mean asking for more help from Raven, the answer is absolutely not. That man is insufferable."

"I don't think so," Lady Josephine chimed in.

"Of course, you don't," Lady Alexandra said with a roll of her eyes.

"Well, your father must not either, if he has awoken

from his illness at his arrival," Lady Eagleton added. "Perhaps you are just jaded from your first meeting?"

"What happened at your first meeting? The ball, right?" Lady Josephine asked, a little surprised that there was something her sister hadn't told her.

Lady Alexandra let a long breath out preparing herself. Then she began to tell it all. From their first meeting, for her sister's benefit, to all the other things that had happened between her and the duke since that moment. Lady Eagleton sat patiently and listened while her best friend told all her woes and frustrations of the man.

"You don't blame him for what happened at the steps of the museum?" Lady Eagleton said after Lady Alexandra finished speaking.

"No, it's not that I blame him. I just despise the joy he found in the situation."

"I don't," Lady Josephine said plainly. "You must have been quite a sight. I wish you would include me more. I would have liked to help you."

"You have your own needs to focus on," Lady Alexandra countered with her usual excuses. She sighed again. She had already spilled so much information, she didn't feel much resistance to continue on. "The truth of the matter is, if you don't find a husband by the end of the season, I will have to keep Sophia at home another whole year. You know she won't take to that well. I have no choice though. The house simply can't afford it."

"Or you could find someone," Lady Eagleton suggest.

Lady Alexandra gave her friend a glance that said 'I won't even dignify that thought with a response.'

"I think you are taking this whole situation with Raven all wrong. Once you see the truth of it, I don't think you will find your own match by the end of this year so unlikely," Lady Eagleton continued.

"Well, then, dear friend, please do enlighten me."

"I should think it quite clear. Almost laughable that you don't see it yourself. The duke has taken an interest in you."

"The duke is interested in Lady Charlotte. The whole of society knows that fact. The only interest he has in me or my family is our entertainment value," Lady Alexandra responded.

"Perhaps there is talk that the duke has been considering a match with Lady Charlotte, and I am sure some of it is true. But that doesn't mean he has started to court her. It was clear from the moment Raven came to London that he was here to find a wife. If Lord Eagleton was right in his telling to me, it seems his aunt, Lady Rebecca Sinclair, is most insistent on him doing so. She is even said to have faked a severe illness to get him to return home with haste."

"I couldn't imagine anyone doing such a thing," Lady Josephine said.

Both girls gave her a look that said, 'we know you

couldn't.' It was a pause of silence that sent all three girls giggling again.

"No matter what got him here," Lady Eagleton continued once they had gained composure again. "I believe he settled on acquiring a wife, and I see no other reason why he would be showing you so much attention beyond his interest of a romantic nature."

Lady Alexandra opened her mouth to protest again, but her friend wouldn't let her.

"Now, I am not saying I know the duke well. Lord Eagleton does, however, and has spoken to me quite a bit on his character. Young Charles and Raven were great friends all through their school years. My husband described Raven as a most honorable, kind, and considerate man. I don't think someone with that nature would use other's misfortune for their own personal entertainment, no matter how boring they find London," she added with a soft smile.

Lady Alexandra pondered over her friend's words on the road in the Eagleton carriage back home. Lady Eagleton had been quite insistent that they take it. In fact, she had insisted that should the need ever arise to transport a creature resembling a large pincushion she should seek her friend out first for aid before walking the street with the said creature in a baby carriage.

Lady Alexandra thanked her friend for all her goodness and kindness. She loved Regina as if she were her own sister and adored Lord Eagleton. For that reason, she paused to consider the picture that their opinions painted of the Duke of Raven.

She still couldn't wrap her head around the notion that he might have taken an interest in her for a romantic reason. Lady Alexandra hadn't considered herself a possible candidate for marriage to anyone let alone a duke.

She was the eldest daughter of Earl Grebs and technically set to marry before her younger sisters. That was not an option, however, as from the moment her mother passed she took on the maternal role in her stead. She didn't even think her sisters had ever considered her one to spend a season looking for a proper gentleman to marry.

In fact, she was sure that in the back of their minds, her father included, they had always just assumed she would still be around to see them off right and take care of their father once they were gone to their new homes. She had done the same. At the very most she had considered marrying Mr. Lucas once she was sure all her sisters had been seen off right.

Even that notion no longer seemed possible to her. As much as she would have liked to, she just didn't see Mr. Lucas in a romantic light. Of course, romance wasn't required for marriage when you were a woman with no way to support oneself. Still, she had rather thought if she ever did marry, she would want the life that her father and mother had shared.

More than the testament of her father's grieving were the memories she had of her parents before her mother's death. She knew with all her heart that they had loved each other. In some ways, those images had somewhat jaded her. She could never see herself settling for any less than the look of pure joy and happiness she saw on her mother's face when her father would come into the room and greet her.

If she were to accept any future, it would be one like that or none at all. It wouldn't be possible with Mr. Lucas. She considered for the first time since her friend gave her the notion that it might be possible with Raven.

Her cheeks flushed as she considered all their interactions. The way he looked at her so intently that it made her skin warm from the inside out. She had to admit she even did enjoy his humor just a bit or would if it wasn't always directed at her.

She shook the notion from her head. It was silly indeed. Indeed, just the wish of a friend to make a connection between two people she found admirable qualities in. The chances that the Duke of Raven would ever have feelings for her were, in her mind, just as realistic as an opportunity for her to leave the confines of the city.

27

Lady Alexandra didn't have long to consider her friend's opinion in private. From the moment she returned home and for the following day, every second was alit with the buzz of the duke.

For the second time that month, Lord Grebs decided to join his daughters for dinner. Not only that, he informed them of the impending guest of the duke on the morrow for a private family dinner.

If Lady Alexandra didn't already have enough things to do, now she had to work with cook to prepare an elegant dinner fit for a duke.

Between her usual work, added work for the quickly approaching banquet, and now planning for a family dinner with an honored guest, Lady Alexandra had to endure more prodding from her sisters.

Either Lady Josephine had shared Lady Eagleton's ideas with her younger sisters, or they just happened to be on the same page. None the less they spent every moment questioning Lady Alexandra and trying to prove there was some affection between her and the Duke of Raven.

Well, that was the goal of all her sisters, except the youngest, Lady Sophia. For her part, she was as quiet as possible – for a girl of her nature. She spent the next twenty-four hours sulking over the idea that her eldest sister might have caught the duke's eye and not herself. An impossibility in Lady Sophia's mind after she had clearly shown the duke that she would accept any attention he might be willing to send her way.

Lord Grebs insisted that his daughter spare nothing for their quiet family dinner with the duke. In fact, she would be using more on this one meal than was typically used to fund an entire month's food bill. Though Lady Alexandra didn't agree to such things, in the end, her father was the one truly in control of the household finances. Up until this point he had taken little interest, if any at all. Now he seemed to be insisting on things go his way, despite how impossible they might be.

By the night of the dinner, Lady Alexandra was at least satisfied in the fact that their house, and the smells coming from their kitchen, were far better than anything they had experienced for some years. Her three sisters had spent almost the whole of the day up in their shared room dressing and preparing for the night.

Though it was just one guest, and at a casual family dinner, it still held significant meaning. For a single gentleman to choose such a thing with Lord Grebs and his house, meant that he was planning to continue close intimate connections to the family. With four single daughters in his home, that message went far beyond just business arrangements in the eyes of society.

Lady Josephine had pointed the fact out to Lady Alexandra when the former chose to make light of their day of preparation.

"You should be doing the same," Lady Josephine encouraged. "I am finished with my hair now, allow me to do something extra nice with yours."

"I have no reason to do so, and none of you do either. Plus, if the duke is interested in me, as you all claim, then what good is it for the rest of you to work so hard to show a perfect front?"

"Do you not see how a match with the duke will improve all of our standings?"

Lady Alexandra considered that. She hadn't up until that moment, if the truth was told. All she had considered was the duke's attention to her family being a hindrance.

"Do you know how much the ladies of society must be talking about us?" Lady Alexandra countered. "The duke has caused nothing but trouble I am sure of it. They all are gossiping, and I am sure it is with the four of us in a poor light."

"You are right, that some of that is going on. But if I am right, and I am sure I am, and the duke does fancy you, doesn't that mean this is just the next step in a natural courtship? You two could be engaged and then married by year's end. Think how wonderful that would be for all of us? No longer would we be desperate to find any match that would come our way. Now we could find a man of our choosing, for love."

"I suppose that is true," Lady Alexandra said. "Though that is with the assumption that the duke would wish to marry me, and I wish to marry him. I can promise you with absolute certainty at least one of them is untrue and the other just as likely to be false."

"Or perhaps you are as blind to your own feelings as you are to his," Lady Josephine said grabbing her sister's hand and pulling her up the stairs and into the room.

Despite Lady Alexandra's denial her sister, always the optimist, would hear none of it. Instead, she sat Lady Alexandra down in front of their one looking glass and began to re-do her eldest sister's hair in the most splendid way.

"I also thought it might be nice for you to wear this," Lady Josephine said opening the small jewelry box that the four sisters shared. Reaching into it, she lifted the false bottom to reveal their most prized possession.

It was only the two older sisters that knew it was even there. They both knew if either younger sister found out about its hiding place it would end up in Lady Sophia's hands, and no doubt treated as something light.

Of course, it wasn't exactly an expensive trinket. The value of the thin pink ribbon with its one charm hanging was not of monetary value but sentimental. It was a small rose quartz stone rubbed smooth into oval shape. On top was a delicately carved profile of a woman in ivory. The over stone encircled in a simple thin sheet of gold that had one single hoop that attached it to the ribbon.

It was the only jewelry they had that once belonged to their mother. Her father had sold or simply destroyed much in the early days of her mother's death. Lady Alexandra had never been happy with her father's actions, but the age of eight had been far too young to realize what he was doing, let alone stop it. Lord Grebs hadn't removed every item of his wife's out of spite, or even for money. Instead, he had wanted to wash away every memory that pained him.

In the process, he had also stripped all four of his daughters of a mother. If Lady Alexandra's promise hadn't been weight enough on her eight-year-old shoulders, she now had the pressure of fulfilling the memory of a woman they no longer could have any physical reminder of.

This pendant was the only thing remaining of their mother; not even a small pocket portrait had escaped their father's purging. The only reason they still had this small trinket was that it had fallen under her mother's bed. It wasn't until years later that the maid found it cleaning the room. Lady Alexandra was old enough by then to understand its importance and had promptly hidden it away.

"I'm not sure that would be a wise idea," Lady Alexandra hesitated.

"Why not," Lady Josephine said lowering the object slightly.

"What if I break it?" Lady Alexandra responded tentatively.

She had barely allowed herself to brush her fingers over the pendant all these years. It was just too precious to risk even for the possibility, however unlikely she thought it, of turning the eye of the Duke of Raven.

"You won't," Lady Josephine waved off her sister's worry and placed it delicately around her neck, tying it in the back. "Mother would want you to wear this. Perhaps it will be your good luck charm."

Lady Alexandra rolled her eyes at her sister through the looking glass but now in a more playful manner.

Lady Josephine smiled in returned before her face went solemn.

"Do you remember her?" Josephine said softly, her golden eyes off in a different place.

"A little," Lady Alexandra said just as soft. "There is just one memory in particular. She was sitting in the drawing room. In that high back chair. I think it was her favorite," Lady Alexandra said, screwing up her brows in concentration. "She was reading a book of some sort. I just stood there in the doorway and watched her for a moment. She was positioned just so that the light coming in through the one window shown down on her face. She looked so peaceful, so serene. I used to play that memory over in my head before bed."

Lady Alexandra took a long slow breath out as her sister placed the last few curls into their right place.

"I seem to forget the way she looked in that moment a little more every time I try. I used to remember the exact color of her hair as it reflected the light. The shape of her face. The color of her gown that day. Or the way she had slipped out of her shoes and tucked her feet under her.

"I can't remember any of that now, however. Instead, I see Mother sitting in that chair, the sun shining down, but her face is pale. Deep dark circles shadow her eyes and beads of sweat trickle down her forehead. She is trying to smile at me, but too weak to do so. Then the light fades in her eyes, and she is gone."

Lady Alexandra looked up at her sister who had finished her work and was just standing and listening.

"Sometimes I wish I hadn't a memory of her at all," Lady Alexandra said with a shrug. "At least then, all of them wouldn't be poisoned with the memory of her death."

"Trust me; it would be better to have something than nothing at all," Lady Josephine said with a frown.

It was a look that almost never crossed her sister's face. Though Lady Josephine was only a year younger than her eldest sister, it was clear that all her memories of their mother had long since gone.

"We should talk about her more," Lady Alexandra said with a weak smile of encouragement. "Maybe if we did, more would come back to our remembrance. And of course, that would be more for Sophia to hold on to. I do worry that she will grow up quite jaded with no memory of Mother to call her own."

"No, you are doing a fine job with her. I do agree, though," Josephine said with a sniff and the return of her usual pleasant face. "We should endeavor to talk about her more."

It was a relieving conversation for Lady Alexandra to have with her sister. In a way, she had been keeping these thoughts, feelings, and maybe even guilt, bottled up within her. She was beginning to see it was important to open up to her sisters more. Not just for their sake but for her own as well.

She had little time to ponder the notion, however, as the duke arrived just as the two finished their preparations in their shared room. Lady Josephine and Lady Alexandra descended the stairs in perfect time with the front door opening to welcome their guest.

28

Raven was already in a pleasant mood as he walked up the front steps of Lord Grebs' house. As much as he had hesitated to take the earl's offer yesterday for a family meal, he felt no reservations now.

He knew how the rest of society would take such an action. His aunt would be furious when she found out, of course. He cared little for that now. He had made up his mind that Lady Alexandra was the lady for him and nothing, not even his aunt whom he loved dearly, would deter him from this.

He had walked with an extra bounce in his step and even found himself humming after he knocked and waited for Lord Grebs' man to answer the door. He was stunned into silence by the view that met him as he crossed the earl's threshold.

Timed just at the perfect moment, Lady Alexandra descended the stairs just as he entered the foyer. It was as if the world around him melted away as he took her in.

She was beautifully dressed in a dark lavender dress that made her skin against it glow like ivory. Her hair was twisted and curled with a wide ribbon woven in to contrast her chestnut ringlets.

She had just a slight rose to her cheeks that brought her warm brown eyes to life in a way he hadn't seen for some weeks. Adorned around her neck was a simple thin ribbon with a pendant. It was the first piece of jewelry he had ever seen Lady Alexandra wear he realized for the first time.

"Good evening," Raven said with a bow once the ladies reached the bottom of the stairs.

He could feel the smile splitting across his face, and though he knew he should hide it, he couldn't seem to bring himself to do so. He noticed Lady Josephine looked quickly between him and her sister before trying to hide her own rosy-cheeked smile. He wondered if perhaps the younger sister had caught on to his attentions.

It was clear that Lady Alexandra had not. She greeted him politely and invited him in the drawing room for some sherry before dinner. Beyond that, she seemed rather cool to him. It was more than her usual distance. He was sure she was trying to make a point of keeping things polite but unfeeling between the two of them.

He worried whose benefit that was for. The obvious

answer was for himself. After all, he was making a rather bold statement coming to their house tonight for dinner. Perhaps this was Lady Alexandra's way of stating she had no interest in him.

He was sure that couldn't be the case. She had seemed wary of his attention, but there were still moments where Lady Alexandra finally allowed her walls to come down. It was in those moments he was sure she cared for him just as he did for her.

Lady Alexandra's other two sisters were already seated in the drawing room. It was clear to him that every member of the family was dressed in their finest for the evening's dinner. Lord Grebs wasn't far behind joining them in the drawing room once they learned of the arrival of their honored guest.

"So good to see you again, Your Grace," Lord Grebs said, clapping Raven on the back in a friendly way. "I have fantastic news I was just hoping I could share with you tonight," he continued.

Raven did his best to listen to the earl and seemed interested in the conversation but all the while he was looking for an opportunity to speak with Lady Alexandra.

Though he always kept her in his view as the earl and he discussed the indigenous animals of the Indies, more specifically how the Asian elephant differentiated from the African elephant, he kept a close watch of the lady.

He was satisfied to know that she did the same for him.

Of course, she tried to play it off as if she didn't notice his presence there at all tonight. First, she sat next to Lady Sophia, who was shockingly sulky this evening, to review some lessons from earlier that morning. He could tell as every time his eyes studied her, she rosied up in the cheeks. That meant she was just as aware of him as he was of her.

After going over Lady Sophia's work, she came to sit by the sister who had walked down the stairs with her: Lady Josephine. They talked quietly with each other. Raven had never considered Lady Alexandra to be close to any of her sisters as she always seemed to take on the brunt of the labor, leaving them separate from herself.

He saw tonight that this wasn't entirely accurate. He was glad that she at least had some moments of ease with her next eldest sister. It gave him another sinking feeling, however.

Lady Alexandra had talked to him about how she had never left the city of London and how she longed to see the world outside of it. He had always assumed if the chance arose, she would leave this city behind.

For the first time, he realized that her hesitation in leaving might not just be a monetary issue. Perhaps she didn't like the idea of leaving her sisters, or even her father. Even worse, maybe she was more like her father who chose to do his exploring from the seat of his library.

He had never considered Lady Alexandra to be like her father, shutting herself away and seeing the world through books. In fact, one of the traits that had drawn Raven to Lady Alexandra in the first place was their shared passion for tenacity and exploration. He was sure that she would have the gumption necessary to see everything the earth had to offer by his side.

He knew this too would need to be addressed tonight before he was ready to make his intentions known to the lady. Much to his satisfaction as they were called to dinner, he was seated at the head of the table with the earl on his right and his eldest daughter on his left.

He could see that no expenses were spared on the evening's meal. He felt honored for such a treatment from a family he was sure had little to spare.

“This all looks wonderful,” Raven finally said to Lady Alexandra. “You must tell your cook that she has done a stupendous job tonight.”

“I can assure you, Your Grace, she will be thrilled to hear that you think so. I know she was fretting yesterday and today that her cooking would be up to your standards.”

“Well, I don’t know that I have very high standards, to be honest,” Raven said, lowering his voice just slightly to keep the conversation more private. “In fact, I would have to say my favorite meal is something the cook on my Virginia plantation makes. I believe she calls it a corn pudding. It is very much like porridge here,” he added with a smile. “Something about the way Mrs. Mckenzie makes it, however,” he added, with the memory fresh in his eyes. “It’s just fabulous. She teases me relentlessly. Said it wasn't a proper dish to give a fine gentleman, but I liked it all the same," he added with a shrug.

"Well, perhaps I won't tell the cook that little truth, or she might think your compliments are not as authentic," Lady Alexandra said with a smile.

Raven relaxed in his little in his seat to see the lady jest with him.

"I have something I want to say to you, Your Grace," Lady Alexandra said, suddenly going very serious.

Perhaps she too was waiting for a moment that they could talk privately as well. Raven's heart caught in his throat at the notion.

"You can speak with me about anything," Raven said with complete honesty.

"It's about the other night. At Lord Eagleton's house," she gave out a long sigh as she prepared herself before her eyes darted around the table.

Once she was sure that none of the other family members were listening in, she continued on.

"I know that sometimes my sisters don't always act appropriately. I want you to know that I have made every effort to see that they are educated as proper young ladies, even with the absence of a governess. Sometimes my younger sisters can get, shall we say, a little over excited and forget themselves. I hope you will forgive them if they caused any situations that might have made you feel uncomfortable."

Raven stared at Lady Alexandra for a few seconds after she finished her small speech, clearly practiced. Her eyes were big pools of chocolate pleading for forgiveness. Forgiveness for an offense he had never felt. Yes, Lady Sophia had been a bit coarse that night and, if truth be told, a little forward, but still he had found no offense in her actions.

In fact, Raven had feared that Lady Alexandra was going to declare she knew his intentions this night and would wish that he remove himself from her presence for all eternity. With such a different declaration from the lady, Raven couldn't help but chuckle at the notions flying through his head.

Unable to keep the merriment in, his soft chuckle roared with the laughter of relief. It caught the attention of the rest of the part who were at present discussing something that Lord Grebs had read recently in the daily paper.

"I'm sorry," he said quickly when he realized his laughter had turned his companion white as a sheet with dread. She must have taken it the wrong way.

"I promise you I felt no offense at all," he said quickly as he tried to control his merriment.

"Then what is so funny?" she asked, a little upset that he was laughing at her.

"I just thought you were going to say an entirely

different thing. I am rather relieved is all," Raven explained.

"What has got you two rolling with laughter?" Lord Grebs asked, having stopped his own conversation with the rest of the sisters.

All eyes were looking at the two with anticipation.

"Lady Alexandra was just telling me a joke she heard," Raven said quickly to try and alleviate any questioning.

"Really?" her father said raising a brow at Lady Alexandra.

No doubt, he didn't find his eldest daughter the joking type. It just happened to be the first thing to fall out of Raven's mouth.

"Well, let us all hear it then," Lord Grebs encouraged.

Raven looked over at Lady Alexandra. He had no joke to give. The lady simply raised one of her eyebrows in response as if to say he got himself in this situation and now he would have to get back out of it.

"It was a trifle thing," Raven said quickly. "But as I have all of your attention for the moment, I wonder if I might extend an invitation.,"

"Of course, " Lord Grebs said, already forgetting the prospect of a joke.

"You have all been so kind and welcoming to me. My family has a small estate just on the outskirts of London. I am gathering a small party together to join me there. The land has a nice open field area which is particularly fine for picnicking. I thought it might be a nice reprieve just before the banquet if we could all get away from the city, the pressure, and enjoy an afternoon."

"That sounds marvelous. I heartily accept, Your Grace," Lord Grebs said, his face splitting in a smile from cheek to cheek.

"How soon before the banquet?" Lady Alexandra asked Raven in a softer tone.

"Two days prior. Is that too soon? I don't want to put more of a burden on you, but I do think you will find that getting away for the afternoon most invigorating."

"It is rather soon," Lady Alexandra said with honesty and hesitation. "But my father does seem very sure that it will be possible, and my sisters are already so excited," she added, looking around the table bubbling with anticipation. "I wouldn't dare deny them that fun."

"And you will be there as well," Raven said, narrowing his eyes on the lady. "I will move it to another time if you don't think you can come."

Lady Alexandra blushed and looked away.

"I am sure that you would rather have the company of my father," she said softly.

"I do enjoy his company, that is true," Raven said. He wanted to make his intentions clear. "But it is you, Lady Alexandra, that I hope to get to know better."

She didn't answer or meet his gaze. Instead, she pushed the remainder of her course around on her plate as she pondered his words. He didn't want to pressure her to say something just yet. At least not like this, in front of her whole family. Raven just wanted to be sure that she knew he had his intentions on her.

"Plus, my Aunt Rebecca is most anxious to meet you as well," Raven added quickly to alleviate the tension building.

"She is?" Lady Alexandra asked cocking that one brown eyebrow. It was an adorable quirk she had when she was disbelieving.

"Yes, I have told her a lot about you. I told you as well, I think you are both much alike. She is ambitious and hard-working, just as you are. I have great admirations for all the things she accomplished in her life, and not to mention doing so while dealing with me as a child," he added with a half smile.

"I am sure you were princely as a child."

He gave a soft chuckle.

"Well, I haven't stayed in one spot long as an adult, so that might give you some idea of how I was as a child."

"True. I am sure you were very vexing. Perhaps you're right," Lady Alexandra said with a pondering look. "I am sure your aunt and I will have much to discuss. How you harassed her in your youth and how you now like to harass me."

"Harass you?" Raven said with a wide smile. He knew she was teasing and was rather enjoying the relaxed conversation. "I can't imagine why you would say such a thing. I have been exercising great care in not teasing you tonight. In fact, I haven't even asked if you have taken any porcupines for a stroll recently." Raven concluded.

"Oh," Lady Alexandra exclaimed, though her face shone brightly with laughter. "You are a rotten man! I will agree to your picnic only so that I may inform your aunt that you must be sent away at once before you can terrorize someone else of far weaker character."

"I can promise you one thing, Lady Alexandra. I would not dream of vexing anyone else, besides you," Raven replied a twinkle in his dark eyes.

29

The time had flown by it seemed to Lady Alexandra. Before she knew it, the day had arrived to travel the short distance to Raven's house for an afternoon picnic. The girls in Lady Alexandra's house had spoken of nothing else since the invitation, and Lady Alexandra couldn't help but get caught up in the excitement.

It would be the first time any of them left the city. Though the house wasn't far outside of the city's parameter, it was outside none the less. The joy that notion brought to Lady Alexandra was unimaginable.

As the duke had said, the ride was a relatively short one, and after about an hour the busy city streets that rattled their single carriage with its cobblestone roads soon turned into dried dirt with the lift and dips of divots and ruts.

The air almost seemed fresher once they left the confines of London and Lady Alexandra had to admit that even though this trip was just two short days before the most significant event that could quite possibly determine her future, it was exactly what she needed at that moment.

Though they weren't entirely in the countryside, all the girls in Lady Alexandra's carriage fell silent as they watched the landscape around them. It wasn't long after they changed their paved road for a dirt one that they found the driver turning onto a private drive.

Already Lady Alexandra could see the house in the distance. Raven had done little to describe it, but the sight of it took Lady Alexandra's breath away. It was a two-story stone covered cottage. It looked quaint and absolutely beautiful in her eyes.

Along the stones, vines clung and crept their way up. A small line of smoke wafted up from the nearest chimney, a red brick contrast to the grey of the stone. She guessed by its location on the side of the house and towards the back half that the fire was from a kitchen hearth.

Surrounding the small house was a beautiful well-kept garden with a variety of bushes, flowers and small walking paths to enjoy it all. Behind the house were the most beautiful rolling hills with farmland far in the distance beyond that. Lady Alexandra was sure she could almost hear the sound the nearest hill made as the gentle breeze whispered its way through the soft green grass.

Instead of entering the house they were greeted outside by a growing party. Lady Alexandra knew they wouldn't be the only ones attending but had to admit she felt her family to be a little outside the remainder of the group.

Seated just to the right of the main door was a large white tent with small tables and chairs. Already two servers were making their way around the parties as they arrived, sat, and waited for their host to appear. In Lady Alexandra's opinion, it was a perfect day to spend the whole of outside.

Lady Sophia was of a different mind when she saw the tent. She wrinkled her nose in her pouting fashion and commented on how she should like to go inside the house until the picnic was prepared. She wasn't much for the outdoors.

Much to Lady Alexandra's surprise, it was her father that put a stop to Sophia's pouting with a few words of reprimand. It left all the girls speechless, most notably Lady Sophia herself.

They entered the tent and were introduced before taking their place among the guests. Lady Alexandra noted the odd coupling of the group. First, there was Lady Rebecca Sinclair, Raven's aunt. Next to her sat the much older couple Lord and Lady Jocasta.

Lord Jocasta seemed to pay no attention to anyone in particular and instead allowed his eyes to wander around absentmindedly. In contrast, his wife was in a deep conversation with Lady Rebecca. Sitting on Lady Jocasta's lap was Miss Whiskers, as Lady Alexandra was informed. Apparently, she was the newest member of Lady Jocasta's household, and she refused to leave the feline behind for even a day trip.

Along with Lady Rebecca and the elderly couple was Lord and Lady Derber, their oldest son Gregory, the Viscount Melbourne, and their next in age daughter Lady Charlotte. It was Lady Alexandra's understanding that the Earl of Derber had four children in all.

It was the first time that Lord Grebs' girls made the acquaintance of their eldest son, though they were all on the same level of the peerage, they certainly were not on the same level of society. Naturally, Lady Sophia's eyes lit at the new prospect making Lady Alexandra groan inwardly.

It was Lady Alexandra's greatest fear that this would be the party as a whole as she sat and listened to Lady Jocasta name and describe every animal member of her household. She was sure that today was going to be a much more strained picnic than she had once hoped if these were the guests that were to attend.

She had to admit she was slightly shocked as well to see Lord and Lady Derber with their family there. It had been true that the duke was setting his attention on Lady Charlotte at the beginning of the season, but she had thought such things had changed.

Well, to be honest, she hadn't thought that per se, it was rather that her friend and sisters had put such ideas in her head. They had all been so positive that Raven was now turning his attention elsewhere, to her in fact. How that could be the case when the other lady that he had been very public about making an association with was also present here today?

She would have liked to say she hadn't put much stock in all their words and encouragement, but that hadn't been true over the course of the last few weeks, and especially not after that dinner Raven shared at her house. His words to her had seemed to have a much deeper meaning than just casual conversation.

For so long Lady Alexandra had determined that the duke was only tormenting her for entertainment's sake. When that didn't seem the case any longer, she was sure he was merely making acquaintances with her out of politeness' sake because he was befriending her father over a common interest.

After that family dinner, however, Lady Alexandra had begun to believe his motives were as her friend had suggested. It had taken her some time to resolve her opinions to that fact, and now that they were at the picnic she wasn't as sure anymore. But it was too late now to go back on that notion. For as she had considered that the duke might have feelings for her it had naturally caused her to consider her feelings for him.

Though she was doing her best not to throw her heart out there wholly, it would be a lie for her to say that she didn't have feelings for him.

He was a dashingly handsome man, smart, not afraid to stand up to others when he knew they were wrong, even corrected in the politest manner. He shared her love for seeing the world and even got to do so. She wondered perhaps if it was just his tales of adventures that she had fallen in love with. Upon inspection, she was sure this wasn't the case. He may have been a sort of trickster in his teasing, but he was also good-humored and knew how to make her laugh, or even laugh himself.

Now Lady Alexandra was beginning to think she had been too quick to fall into her sister's suggestions. Now it seemed too late to look or think on the duke without admiration in her heart.

Much to Lady Alexandra's relief, the final portion of their party arrived. It was Lord and Lady Eagleton in their fine carriage. Lady Alexandra brightened at the prospect of spending the afternoon with her closest friend.

It wasn't long after Regina and her husband joined the party under the tent that the Duke of Raven also joined his guests on horseback. Lady Alexandra couldn't help but blush at how regal he looked riding up to the party on his chestnut steed.

He dismounted wearing high black leather boots, dark tan riding pants, and a dark blue riding jacket. Lady

Alexandra noted that he handed over the riding crop to the man waiting to take the horse. It looked almost new with little use. She decided she could never imagine the duke ever using the item and most likely kept it for the same reason he was often seen with a cane.

Raven greeted all his guests warmly, but Lady Alexandra couldn't help but feel that his eyes stayed on her the longest. It wasn't the first time of course. It seemed that every time they were in each other's company, there was a constant connection between them, even when she had wished otherwise. Now that she desired it, however, she seemed to second guess the significance of those black-eyed gazes that never seemed to give away the intentions of the possessor.

Once the whole party was joined, it was time to make their way to the site of the picnic. Lady Jocasta was very upset that it wasn't under the tent that the guests had been sitting at and was sure Miss Whiskers could not stand a long journey.

"It is not long at all, Lady Jocasta. If you will just follow me on this path here," Raven motioned, taking the lead of the party. "We are just going around the small cottage and up the side of the first hill. I would be most honored if you would allow me to escort you," he added, holding his arm out for the elderly lady.

She gave another huff insisting the cat might not make it, but still took his arm. Lady Alexandra was sure the fear was more for Lady Jocasta's own aged body and not that of the kitten. Much to her relief, however, a man came up with a basket stuffed with a soft pillow for the cat to rest on quite royally as the party made their way to the final destination.

Lady Alexandra wasn't at all perturbed that the duke had chosen to escort Lady Jocasta instead of herself. In fact, she quite preferred it. In her mind, it once again showed that though he didn't always hold to societal rules when it really mattered, he was the perfect gentleman that he was bred to be.

Instead, Lady Alexandra linked arms with her dear friend, Lady Eagleton, somewhere in the middle of the party. She vaguely heard her younger sisters commenting on the house.

"Did you hear that? Raven called it a little cottage. I think we could fit two of our townhouse inside his little cottage," Lady Williamina said.

"I don't even think this is his only home. Certainly not his country seat. Could you imagine that place?" Lady Sophia countered.

Lady Alexandra would have liked them to hush. It was not at all proper conversation to be having with so many others around. Instead, she chose to ignore her younger siblings and simply enjoy the day in her own way and let them do the same.

Raven was right to say the walk wasn't far at all. Once

they rounded the corner of the stone house, Lady Alexandra could already see a white cloth tent in the distance. In front of it was several spreads of blankets with pillows and even some benches for the older ladies to sit on.

It was a leisurely walk up the well-maintained path with vibrant green plants speckled with flowers of every kind along their way. Once they neared the picnic area, Lady Alexandra could smell the wonderful meal prepared wafting from inside the tent.

It didn't take long for her to realize that the food was kept inside from the elements and then brought out to them by several servants standing and waiting for their arrival.

Miss Whiskers was promptly placed in her basket next to one of the benches where Raven deposited his escort. Miss Whiskers had fallen asleep on the short walk and seemed to have no desire to remove herself from the basket. The rest of the party found their places among the pillows for a wonderful meal served under the glorious sun.

Lady Alexandra had to admit as the day wore on that it was one of, if not the, best day she had ever had in her entire life. They had been treated to spectacular food. Raven had prepared a few games for them to play by way of entertainment. Just when she thought the day couldn't get any better, in that relaxed atmosphere of good friends,

Lady Rebecca and Lord Eagleton decided to take it at turns divulging one mischievous act after another that Raven had gotten himself into as a boy.

Lady Alexandra hadn't realized it at first, but as the meal was over and games were done, she noticed that her father had not only sat next to Lady Rebecca but was also engaging with her in a great many conversations. He seemed to light up as he spoke with her in a way she wasn't sure she had ever seen before, for if she did, she certainly couldn't remember it.

They both seemed to bond over the struggle of raising children all on their own. As she listened to Lady Rebecca speak with her father, she had to admit that she did find the woman most enjoyable as Raven had surmised.

Though she wasn't able to sit near him or speak intimately with him over the course of the day, she was sure there was still something there between them. More often than not she would find him looking her way, not to just study her as before, but to almost gauge her satisfaction with the picnic.

"Do you believe me now, when I say Raven is quite taken with you," Lady Eagleton asked after quite a private moment seemed to pass between the two of them.

Lady Alexandra rosied up instantly and pretended to reset a locket that had been blown by the light breeze. She was not unwilling to admit her friend was right, for Regina seemed to be right in a great many things over the course of their friendship, it was only that she didn't want to confess it so openly in front of others.

Though she tried to hide it, Regina saw her reaction, and that was enough. She gave a knowing nod.

"He is a perfect match, and I would say that I didn't believe anyone could deserve you, my dear. But, of all the gentlemen in the world, I find Raven to be the worthiest."

Lady Alexandra nudged her friend in response as if to beg her to stop. Lady Alexandra had spent her life seeing to the needs of her younger sisters. She had never been the center of attention, choosing to support others instead. Having so much focus on herself was almost unbearable.

Getting the point, Regina did stop speaking on the subject, but still, both ladies couldn't help but burst out in girlish giggles at the conversation that they had just shared.

30

"I do have just one more fun game for us to play if you would all indulge me," Raven said, coming to stand before the group on the blankets.

He had been planning this point out in the day for many weeks now.

"This game does involve getting up and exploring. Something I gather you have all guessed I rather enjoy after the stories you've heard today," he added with chuckles from his audience.

"Now I don't want any of you to feel pressured to go. You are more than welcome to stay here and keep Miss Whiskers company, and perhaps out of your teacup," he added.

The feline had just recently woken up and had climbed

up on Lord Jocasta's lap, who was seemingly unaware, and quenched her own thirst with the cup still in his hand.

"But for those of you brave enough," he continued rubbing his hands together. "I have a challenge for you. Any willing to accept?"

There were several cheers of agreement from the crowd.

"Good then. I give you this challenge. I want you to search the gardens, both surrounding the cottage, and on the hills. We will each bring back one item. The one with the most unique object wins the game. Naturally, my gardens are filled with objects and plants spanning the globe, so this should be a real treat if you are able to seek out some unique items."

Everyone stood from their spot and with a few more words they were all off. Almost all decided to join in the game except for the elderly Jocastas and the Earl and Countess of Derber who found the idea not to their taste.

He was sure that Lady Alexandra's younger sisters were just as excited about this adventure as he was, and for a similar reason. Where he had spent the whole of the afternoon beholding the woman he hoped to marry, they had both been making eyes and desperately trying to engage Derber's eldest son.

Lord Melbourne seemed a nice enough fellow, only recently joining his family in town with a late start to the season. But to Lady Sophia and Lady Williamina, he could see their eyes glow alight with the prospect.

They saw this adventure as an opportunity to steal away for a moment, perhaps a romantic one, with the viscount and without a parental eye on them.

Raven was hoping for the very same thing with his Lady Alexandra. In fact, had it been up to him, he wouldn't have invited Derber and his family at all. He wanted this moment to be a chance for his aunt to get to know the lady as well as an opportunity for him to profess his feelings to her.

Aunt Rebecca had different plans when Raven informed her of his idea of a picnic at the cottage property. Without even consulting him, she had invitations sent out to Lord Derber defaulting on the assumption that there would be no reason not to. In truth, it wasn't her fault. Raven still hadn't broached the subject to his aunt.

He was still waiting to see if he could find the proper connection to secure his aunt's place on her charity board, the only reason she, in fact, was pushing Lady Derber's daughter on him as a prospect of marriage. Until he resolved that issue, he had little faith that his aunt would support his choice of Lady Alexandra over Lady Charlotte.

Still, he made the best of the afternoon. He had enjoyed the company all around. Even though he hadn't found a moment to even speak with Lady Alexandra, he was sure that something was different in her this meeting. Before when he couldn't help but keep his attention on her, she would do the same but pretend not to.

She had always struggled to keep her distance and seem aloof from him. Now there didn't seem to be any reservation in her eyes. He was sure that his moment had come. After his intentions were made at a family dinner, he had given her time to make up her own mind on the matter. He was almost confident that she had done so and had chosen him just as he had chosen her.

He would take this chance as they explored the property to find a moment with Lady Alexandra. Once he knew he had secured her heart, he would find a way to give the news to his aunt.

Much to his disappointment as the group stood up and left, Lady Alexandra did so in her friend's companionship. He skirted around the property waiting for a moment for her to go a little ways off on her own so that he might make his moment a reality.

He slowly perused the paths only half noticing the things growing around his feet. He could hear the merriment going on all around him and could distinctly make out Lady Sophia's flirtatious laughter. He smiled slightly to himself, thinking she found her mark.

"Your Grace?" A soft voice called out turning the duke's attention.

He scanned the near vicinity which was a weaving path of shoulder-high bushes. Standing on a stone bench along one of the green walls of the path was Lady Charlotte.

"I wonder if you might help me?" She said with a polite smile.

Raven hesitated. This was not the lady he wanted to be alone with in the garden. Still, his honor would not allow the lady to be left in need.

"What is it, Lady Charlotte?" he asked pleasantly, but coolly.

"I was hoping to take a peek in that nest just there to see if there was any worth object," she pointed to a tall tree just behind the shrub. Its lowest hanging branch was thick in size and just dangling over the shrubbery. In its crook was a bird's nest.

"It probably isn't wise to disturb a nest. The mother might return at any moment, and she won't take a liking to it. Not to mention you are dangling over rather unsafely yourself," Raven said, coming to stand next to the bench she was atop.

"I don't think it is in use," Lady Charlotte said, craning her neck on her tiptoes. "I haven't heard the sounds of babies to be sure, and no mother has appeared. I must confess I have been here for some time," she added with a slight giggle. "I am so glad you came upon me as I was just about to give up all hope."

Raven had a sinking suspicion that her hope had nothing to do with finding a treasure in the nest.

"If you will just step down, I will inspect the nest for you," Raven said, motioning for the lady to remove herself.

The sooner he got this over with, the sooner he could go and find Lady Alexandra. Lady Charlotte gave him a satisfied smile. This was just what she was hoping for. Reaching down with her gloved hand she took his and held it there for just a second longer than he would have liked.

He had to admit that Lady Charlotte was a beautiful woman. She was dressed in a soft cream cotton gown with a pattern of rosettes that brought out the warmth in her cheeks. She always had a pleasant face and knew the right things to say in any situation. If he hadn't already given his heart to another, he was sure she would have been a good choice. In fact, he could only say that one day he knew she would make someone a very lucky man. He was just not that man.

There was a pang of guilt at the thought. Raven had led her on in the beginning, not out of malice of course, but had none the less given the impression that he was interested in her. As of yet, Raven hadn't really made it clear that he thought otherwise now.

He determined that thought this moment was an annoyance, at least it would be a chance to set the record straight with the lady before he gave his heart away entirely to another.

In that moment's hesitation where their hands touched and the lady didn't move, he watched as her dark eyelashes fluttered upward and she looked at something beyond him. A small smile curled at the sides of her lips as she stepped forward.

It all happened so fast, Raven struggled to even replay the moments slower in his head after the fact. First, the lady's slipper must have caught on the hem of her dress.

He hadn't seen it but heard her sharp intake of breath as she began to fall forward off the bench. Instincts kicked in. He removed the hold of her hand and grasped her fully in his arms around her waist. She came tumbling down, the whole of her light frame collapsing into his chest.

He felt her hands grip tight to his jacket as her legs went weak beneath her. She looked up at him with shortness of breath and shining eyes. He heard the small breath of an "oh dear" float across the air.

It took him a second of watching Lady Charlotte and ensuring she was all right to realize the words had not passed her lips but another's. He spun his head around, still holding the lady in his arms, to see both Lady Eagleton and Lady Alexandra had come upon them at that very moment.

Lady Eagleton must have been the one to call out the exclamation as her hand was covering her mouth in shock at intruding on what looked like a very compromising moment. Lady Alexandra just merely stared at him.

For a woman who had little room for dishonesty or filtering of her thoughts, she was a pool of emptiness in that gaze. Raven looked back down at Charlotte and then again to Alexandra realizing in that second what she must be thinking behind her mask of an expression.

He swallowed hard, willing his mouth to speak but couldn't seem to find any words. Before Lady Charlotte had even gained her footing, all of this happening in a matter of seconds, Lady Alexandra turned on her slippered heels and walked determinately away from him.

Lady Eagleton stood watching them a few moments more. Lady Charlotte clamored to her own feet, at least having the dignity to look embarrassed at the audience before them.

"It's not..." Raven tried to stammer out motioning between him and the lady he was now trying to put distance between.

Lady Eagleton simple turned and followed behind her friend already out of view.

He didn't blame either lady. He wasn't sure how he would have reacted had he come upon such a similar situation. It was entirely accidental on his part, however, and not at all the moment he was hoping to share with Lady Alexandra today.

Lady Charlotte and Raven stood in silence, luckily with more distance between them as she took to making sure she was righted all around.

"You didn't hurt yourself, I hope," Raven said after several seconds of silence.

He was sure he would have much rather liked to run after Lady Alexandra and find a way to explain to her the scene she had witnessed. He was sure the conclusions currently running through her head was not at all accurate.

"Yes, I think I am fine," Lady Charlotte said slightly breathless. "Thank goodness you were there to catch me, Your Grace. I fear I would have twisted my ankle otherwise," she said with gratitude and he sensed a hint of something else.

Though the moment had all happened so fast, he was almost sure that the lady had either planned such a thing or taken an opportunity as it came upon them quite suddenly to produce the scene purposefully.

"I must go and apologize to Lady Eagleton, I am sure it was quite a shock for her to see us entangled so," Lady Charlotte said, emphasizing their intimate embrace.

"You will say it was a mistake, of course," Raven clarified, narrowing his eyes on her.

"I mean certainly it was an accident," Lady Charlotte corrected. "Would you truly call it a mistake though, Your Grace?" she asked batting her eyes at him.

"Yes, I most certainly would," Raven quickly responded.

He saw his words had offended the lady and took a steadying breath to calm his rising anger at the mischief a simple moment was already causing in his life.

"Yet, what's done is done," she said softly.

Raven didn't speak, he knew what she was talking

about. Though nothing had actually transpired between the two of them, they had just been publicly caught in a compromising situation. For all Lady Eagleton and Lady, Alexandra knew they were holding each other in a lover's embrace.

Honor would dictate that he take the woman's hand in marriage for the sake of her reputation. He rolled the thought around in his head. Obviously, it was what the lady had intended all along from the start. She must have noticed how all his attention had turned to Lady Alexandra and wanted to make her claim now.

"Lady Charlotte," Raven said slowly. "It was just a slip. I naturally couldn't just let you fall from such a height. I don't think we should make more out of it than it is?"

"But we were seen. What will people say?" she scoffed at his response.

"I suppose that will all depend on what you say when you explain to Lady Eagleton the situation that caused you to fall into my arms," he said with a huff.

Indeed, accidents like this happened. Though it wasn't proper contact that they had shared, it certainly was a scandalizing compromise of Lady Charlotte's reputation. A simple explanation should have sufficed. He knew both Lady Eagleton and Lady Alexandra would never gossip beyond what reason was given.

It was all in Lady Charlotte's hand if she wanted to make this moment more than it was. Raven was sure that if he made it clear that he had no intention of making a connection with her, she would lose inclination to spread her own version of the story. It would only hurt Lady Charlotte's own reputation in the end.

"I know that we met a few months ago at the start of the season," Raven said slowly and delicately. "I think you are a wonderful lady. I must confess to you, however, that my heart has been taken by another."

He wanted her to be completely clear on this fact with no questioning his determination to marry Lady Alexandra. He didn't need to say the lady's name for Lady Charlotte to know to whom he referred.

"But..." she hesitated.

"I know," he said interrupting her. "I gave an impression, and at the time I did mean it. But I guess the only reason I can give you for my change of mind, is that the heart has a mind of its own. I didn't decide this course of action, I must follow it or else be miserable all my days. Certainly, someone as kind and understanding as you can forgive me for this?"

Lady Charlotte stood staring blinking up at the duke for a few seconds. Perhaps she was debating if she was really willing to give up on him. Finally, he saw the resolve melt across her face, and he sighed with relief.

"Of course, I would not want to stand in the way of someone else's happiness," she said weakly.

"I thank you for that," Raven said with a smile. "I am

sure the rest are done with their scavenging. Would you like me to check the nest for you before we make our way back," he asked as a sort of recompense.

"No," she said her eyes floating back to the waiting party.

She pulled out of her skirt pocket a small blue feather.

"I found this here on the ground. It's what made me look up to the nest. I am sure it will do," she added sadly.

Raven nodded his understanding to together they walked back to the picnic in silence.

31

The following afternoon, Lady Alexandra sat in her friend's private drawing room. They hadn't spoken much as they waited for the small sandwiches and tea service.

Once it arrived, Lady Eagleton set to work serving the tea. It wasn't until both had cups in their hand with the ringing of stirring silver spoons that Lady Eagleton broke the silence.

"Lady Charlotte did approach me as we were leaving," she said without any introduction into the conversation they both had on their minds already.

"Did she?" Lady Alexandra said half-heartedly as she studied the ripples in her cup as the spoon made its rotation.

She hadn't forgotten the scene that she had beheld not

more than twenty-four hours earlier. Even now she was sure she could see it in the reflection of her tea.

They had just come around the corner on their way back to the picnic blankets. Lady Eagleton had chosen a violet flower, and Lady Alexandra picked an iridescent shell that decorated around one of the gardens.

Hearing voices up ahead they lowered their own conversation. Lady Alexandra was just confessing to Lady Eagleton, in their complete privacy for the first time that day, that her dear friend was in fact right. Lady Alexandra had no doubt that she has fallen completely for the Duke of Raven.

Of course, instead of lingering on the fact that she had known it first, Lady Eagleton clapped with joy at the notion that her friend had found happiness. Naturally, Lady Alexandra had cautioned her friend's excitement. Though she knew her affections to be true, she still wasn't one hundred percent certain of Raven's.

"I dare say, you will not believe it until you are walking down the aisle with Raven waiting at the other end," Lady Eagleton had teased just as they turned the bend.

The giggling had turned into stunned silence at the scene that was before them. Lady Charlotte was embraced in Raven's arms her hands clutching his jacket for support as he looked down at her affectionally.

She was hard of breath, which no doubt meant the girls had only been moments behind seeing their kiss. The way that Lady Charlotte was looking up at him, wholly supported by his sturdy frame, was just enough to send Lady Alexandra's heart shattering to the floor.

Raven's eyes followed the appearance of the intruders. He looked surprised at being caught and seemed to have no words to even explain himself.

Even if he had tried, Lady Alexandra would hear nothing of the sort. She promptly spun on her heels not waiting for her friend to follow. She seethed with her own stupidity as she circled back around the cottage the longer way and came back to the waiting blanket.

Lady Eagleton had caught up to her side. Wisely she had spoken nothing to her friend. It was a good choice as Lady Alexandra wasn't sure if she would go spinning in a rant of rage or melt into a puddle of sorrow.

They reached the picnic party just in time to see Lady Charlotte walking up next to Raven.

The only thing worse than seeing them together after such an intimate moment was the smug look on Lady Derber and Lady Rebecca's faces at their companionship.

Clearly, this had been the plan all along, and nothing had derailed it. Lady Alexandra hated herself for ever considering that she would take the duke's attention when compared to Lady Charlotte.

The declarations of treasured items proceeded but a very different mood could be felt by the whole party. Well, that was except for her two youngest sisters who were none the wiser.

As the party concluded and they all rose to return to waiting carriages by the cottage, Lady Josephine came to her sister's side.

"What's the matter, Alexandra? You were a ray of sun all day, and since returning from the hunt, you look as if grey clouds now cover your soul?"

Lady Alexandra couldn't convey how accurate her sister's summation was. Instead, she informed her sister she would discuss the matter in private later that night.

She had refused to even allow herself to look at either the duke or his companion. Walking back down to the cottage, she did so at a much slower pace so that she could still see the party ahead but not well enough to see the couple in all their joy.

"Lady Alexandra," a dark voice said startling her from her sorrow.

She looked up to see that the duke too had hesitated to leave. Perhaps he wanted to explain himself now to her. Part of her would have liked that. She wanted to make him say that he was leading her on, making close connections to her father and his family all for the sake of a malicious joke.

She remembered the banquet in two days' time, however. Accusing the duke and forcing him to show his true colors wouldn't do now. Certainly, after such an altercation he would remove his use of the building. She would bite her tongue for a few more days.

"Yes, Your Grace? Is there something you need? Perhaps some final requirements for your event? I would be happy to speak to you over business matters," she said trying to sound as pleasant as possible.

"Alexandra," he said again this time in a pleading voice.

He gently gripped her arm forcing her to stop her progression back to the carriage. Raven wanted her to look at him, but she wouldn't give him that satisfaction.

Instead, she stopped walking but took a step away from him and crossed her arms, eyes straight ahead. She had no desire to hear him out for she knew that the likelihood of keeping her thoughts to herself would be impossible.

He sighed heavily seeing that she would not meet his gaze. Shuffling his feet, he searched for the words.

"I didn't...It wasn't what it looked like. You must know..."

"Forgive me, Your Grace. I am not sure what you are referring to. Now if you will please excuse me. I don't want to keep my father waiting much longer."

With that, Lady Alexandra had marched away without so much as a look behind her. There was only one tear that gave her away at that moment. She quickly brushed it away as she entered her family's carriage.

That night had been an entirely different story. As she and Lady Josephine had laid awake in their shared bed,

Lady Alexandra had told her all, leaving nothing back. In her sister's warm embrace, she had let her sorrows flow from her like a rushing river.

It was a miracle that she had risen from her bed at all that morning. Though her eyes were still tinged with red from the night's cry, she came downstairs to breakfast with her family.

Naturally, the talk had all been about the picnic the day before. Her father mentioned that he would be spending the day at the museum doing the final preparations for the banquet the following evening. Lady Alexandra had cared little if her father even knew what to do. She would never set foot in that place again.

It seemed even the thought of the museum only brought her mind back to Raven. She couldn't bear such a thing as it would cause her to cringe with pain all over again.

Why had she allowed herself to fall for him? She had done such an excellent job all these weeks keeping her distance and not allowing the duke in. Why, on the day that she had finally let down the walls he was so determined to break, had she also seen his true nature?

It was an utter shock when, with the morning post, the footman brought in a note for Lady Alexandra with the duke's handwriting addressing it.

"Who is it from?" her father asked, only half interested in the note.

"Lady Eagleton," Lady Alexandra said quickly. "Please excuse me. The light is better in the drawing room, and I should like to read it there."

She walked the short distance into the drawing room and promptly dropped the letter in the hearth and lighting it on fire. She had no care for what the duke had to say to her. She would never look upon him or speak to him again. In two days' time, any and all connection to him would be done. He would marry Lady Charlotte and with any luck leave London for good this time.

"What was the note?" Lord Grebs asked as he intersected his daughter in the hallway after the meal was finished.

"She just wanted me to come to tea this afternoon. I think she is lonely."

"Ah, yes. I believe Lord Eagleton said he would be leaving this morning for a hunt in the country, was he not? Naturally, I could never participate in such an act against nature, though he was nice enough to invite me," Lord Grebs continued to ramble on none the wiser to his daughter's constitution.

She did leave that afternoon to seek out her friend. Frankly, she couldn't stand to be in that house any longer and listen to Sophia talk incessantly about the Derbers and more specifically their eldest son.

Lady Eagleton would not mind her calling without prior notice. Lady Josephine had asked to accompany her, but Lady Alexandra had politely declined. She was hollow within now and the more people around her, the more she was certain to feel. At this particular moment, she wanted to stay hollow for all feelings were nothing but aches and pains.

"She wanted to make sure that I didn't jump to any conclusions," Lady Eagleton continued when her friend said no more and instead continued to stir her tea. "Lady Charlotte was standing on the bench just behind them and reaching into a bird's nest when she fell. Raven saved her from great injury and nothing more."

Lady Alexandra simply nodded that she heard the tale.

"So you see it was all just a misunderstanding," Lady Eagleton said, hoping to brighten her friend's mood.

"Misunderstanding? Did you not see the way she was looking at him, the way that he was holding her? Not to mention the satisfaction on the face of every party member when they returned back to the picnic together?"

"I know it did seem very...well unsettling."

"It was not unsettling at all," Lady Alexandra interrupted. "In fact, if anything, it only confirmed what I already knew. Raven has never had any interest in me. I was a silly girl to ever think so, to ever allow myself...Well anyway, I feel more ashamed for my own actions yesterday than any of Raven's or Lady Charlotte's. I was more foolish a girl than Sophia."

"Now, we both know that could never be possible," Lady Eagleton tried to cheer her up with a weak smile.

Lady Alexandra looked at her friend with a thankful heart that Lady Eagleton was so kind to her.

"You are a good friend," she said with gratitude.

"And as your good friend, I want to tell you," Regina said, taking her friend's hand and squeezing it. "Don't give up on Raven. He is a good man, I am sure of that. Just please give him a chance to explain himself. You will see the truthfulness of the mistake we made."

"Mistake or not. Can you not see the dies are cast? His choice has been made. He will marry Lady Charlotte as it should be. We both knew matrimony was never in the cards for someone like me. Let's just return to the way things once were."

"Can you though? I was lucky enough to marry and find love in that match after the fact. But you have given your heart already. How could we go back now? You must give him a chance still."

"He wrote to me this morning," Lady Alexandra explained.

"And? Did he explain it all right to you?"

"I don't know. I burned it in the hearth. I couldn't bear to read it." Lady Alexandra looked to her friend with tears spilling afresh. "I don't think I could stand to even hear him try. I will surely die of embarrassment and foolishness if I must live through a denial from him."

"Then we won't speak of it again," Lady Eagleton said, patting her friend's hand while handing over a handkerchief. "I want only happiness for you, and if the mere thought brings you pain, then we will put it away from our minds forever."

Lady Eagleton said it in a very determined fashion that brought a small light of comfort back to Lady Alexandra.

"Instead let us talk of happy things," Lady Eagleton said with a soft smile, leaning back in her seat.

"Perhaps we can start with what on earth my father and Lady Rebecca were giggling about like school children yesterday," Lady Alexandra gave in a weak but helpful tone.

"Oh, I know. It was most curious wasn't it!" Lady Eagleton propped up in her seat excited for the new subject to ponder over.

32

When Lady Alexandra walked away from him at the picnic, he was desperate to get her to listen to him. When his letter went without a response the following morning, he called the next day.

Unfortunately, she was not at home. Lady Josephine made excuses saying her sister was preparing for the banquet that night. So, taking her information, Raven when straight to the museum. He knew that bugging her on a stressful day wasn't necessarily going to help his cause, but he couldn't let her go another day thinking him a rake if he could help it.

Sadly, arriving at the museum, he found only Lord Grebs. Lady Alexandra's father informed him next that she had decided to stay at home. The stress of the whole day had driven her to her bed with a headache.

It was then that Raven resolved that he would not be getting at Lady Alexandra through the traditional methods. He was determined, however, and so spent the rest of the afternoon at Lord and Lady Eagleton's.

"So you see, it was all just a horrible mistake," he explained to the two of them in their drawing room.

"I assumed it was when Lady Charlotte told me that she had fallen. We never questioned your honor for a moment," Lady Eagleton reassured him once the whole story was given.

"And you told Lady Alexandra just as much didn't you?" Raven asked desperately.

"Lady Alexandra Woodley?" Lord Eagleton asked still trying to keep track of the conversation. "Why on earth would Regina tell her?"

"My dear, because Raven loves her," Lady Eagleton told her husband patiently.

Lord Eagleton looked at Raven with his grey wire brows standing up in shock.

"Do you?"

"Well of course I do," Raven said coming to stand and pacing the room. "But the frustrating woman won't give me two minutes of her time to tell her such."

"Well, there is your event tonight. Why not tell her there," Lord Eagleton said as if he had just solved the world's problems.

"It is a private event for the Society. I doubt she will

come. Her father was the only one there this morning when I went there, besides," he added.

"Then you will just have to be patient," Lady Eagleton said, folding her hand's in her lap.

"I don't want to be," Raven said much like an errant child. "She will surely slip away from me."

"No she won't," Regina said with resolve. "She is just as sick in love with you as you are with her."

Raven turned and looked at the Countess, shock painting his face.

"I am sure she detested me before, and now only hates me the more."

"She was scared is all, but that didn't change the fact that the moment she met you she felt just as you did," Lady Eagleton said with wisdom beyond her years.

"Alexandra has spent her whole life caring for the needs of others and only thinking of her own needs as an afterthought. Every move she has made has only been in the hopes of presenting the best image of her younger sisters no matter the sacrifice it made to her own personal happiness."

"I don't want to rob her of all that. I don't want to stuff her down into the confines of a duchess if she doesn't want it. I only wish to be at her side," Raven said, melting back in his seat covering his face with his large hands.

"She knows this," Lady Eagleton assured him. "She is

just upset. Give her some time and space, and I promise you that you won't lose her."

Raven looked up from his hands still unsure of her words.

"Trust her," Lord Eagleton said, motioning to his own wife. "This one knows far more than you would think about these matters."

Raven watched as the two exchanged a loving look. Time, age, and arrangement of situation was no match for the love they shared for each other.

"I do agree. You are one lucky man," Raven said to Lord Eagleton.

"And you will be too, just wait and see," Lady Eagleton said with a bright smile.

Raven returned to his own house to ready himself for the night's banquet. He knew he wouldn't see Lady Alexandra there tonight and perhaps not for many days to come. As much as he wished to bang on her door and force her to listen, he knew that was not a possibility.

"Raven you look so fine," his aunt said as he entered the drawing room to say his farewells before leaving for the museum.

Raven was dressed in his most exceptional black jacket and pants with high boots, white shirt, and a perfectly tied white cravat. His hair he had chosen to slick back revealing the full profile of his long angular face. He was sure that he was imitating the image of a duke, something he didn't care to do very often.

"Why do you look so sullen, though?" his aunt asked, studying him closely. "I mean you must be ecstatic after the picnic. Lady Charlotte is sure to accept you," she added with an encouraging smile.

"Dear Aunt, could we speak for just a moment," Raven said with a long sigh.

"Of course. Come and sit with me before you leave. I only have the moment though as I am off to the Derbers for a private ball. I am sure you know they were disappointed to hear that you wouldn't be attending with me tonight, but no matter," she waved off as he followed behind her to take a seat.

Raven took his seat in the drawing room of a house that was more his aunt's than his own. He looked around from the exquisite paintings down to the perfectly placed ornaments. He knew that his aunt had built a world around herself based on what was socially acceptable and desirable.

He had no offering of a board seat to give her as recompense for the refusal of her choice in a wife. He was still determined to do so if it were in his power. Whether the possibility came or not, however, his mind had been made up. He was still unsure how much of an effect this would have on the perfect world that his aunt had made and planned for the both of them.

He only had slight reservations in broaching the subject. Raven was almost sure that she wouldn't be so upset as to drive him away. Not entirely sure, however. He had come to London with the sole purpose of rushing to her side.

Raven had promised himself in that last trip so far around the world, that no matter where he arrived at, he would be more attentive to his aunt. He was determined to see to her wishes, and to bring her joy through the rest of her years. Now he was about to tell Lady Rebecca Sinclair something that could bring her much upset.

"Aunt Rebecca, I know that you were very determined that I get to know Lady Charlotte better. I do commend you for your fine taste in a match. She is a woman of high character."

Lady Rebecca who had been waiting at the edge of her seat for whatever her nephew planned to tell her, seemed to scoot just a bit closer now.

"I am afraid I could not bring myself to marry such a fine lady when my heart is not in it. It would not be gentlemanly of me to do so for her sake."

"Oh, why not?" Lady Rebecca said throwing her hands into the air. "I am certain she is very keen on the match. Not all marriages can be based on the heart. Love is such a flimsy thing in the end, anyway. You just fear to settle down, Raven. You are a grown man. It is time to do your duty to the dukedom."

Raven let his aunt ramble on with huffs of indignation for several minutes.

"I am well aware that I am far past my time for finding my roots, as you would call it. I do agree to such terms, but not when the only benefit to the match is a board seat for you. I love you, dear Aunt, but I could not ask for a life of unhappiness from another or myself, and I promise you that is the case if I were to marry Lady Charlotte."

Lady Rebecca paused for just a moment and her small eyes rounded with shock.

"You know about that?" she asked in only a slightly weak voice. "But it is not only that," she waved her hands to push the matter aside. "I would be happy just to see you settled even if I don't get the board seat."

"Do you mean that?" Raven asked hiding the smile spreading on his face.

This was what he was hoping for. He had driven his aunt to this point in the conversation for one reason only, so that he could tell her that he was more than willing to marry. His only condition was that it was the girl of his choosing, the one who had stolen his heart.

"Of course I mean that. I only want you to be happy," Lady Rebecca assured him.

"Good. I do have a woman in mind. If she has me, I shall endeavor to make her happy every day of our lives."

Lady Rebecca clapped her hands joyously at the declaration before stopping suddenly.

"If she will have you? I am sure no lady on this earth would deny you, Raven. Tell me, who is she? Do I know her? I have had my mind so focused on Lady Charlotte that I hadn't even paid attention I suppose. Who is it that you have given your heart to?"

Again, Lady Rebecca spoke so much so quickly that Raven had to wait until she got it all out before attempting to answer any of her questions.

"She may not be who you might consider a choice, but I can assure you that she is the finest lady if I have ever seen one. She is strong-willed and determined. She is smart, beautiful, and infuriating all at the same time," Raven said with a chuckle.

"Yes, yes, boy. You love her, I get all that, no need to berate me with her qualities. Tell me her name!"

"Lady Alexandra Woodley."

"You mean Lord Grebs' daughter?" Lady Rebecca hesitated at the notion.

Raven swallowed hard as his aunt took in his news. He was still unsure how she would accept it. An impoverished earl with questionable mental health was certainly not a prominent family to attach oneself to.

"I am sorry if I have disappointed you, Aunt Rebecca. She is my choice, however. I could no more tell my mind to turn from her than tell the stars to remove themselves from the sky."

"No, it's not that at all," she said leaning forward and patting Raven's hand.

She still had that far off look to her eyes that made Raven wonder what she was hesitant about.

"I think she is a fine lady, I do. In fact, I am a little ashamed I had judged their family before meeting them the other day. I had always assumed based on the things I heard. I am far too old to fall in that way, and I am ashamed to admit that I did. They are a good family."

He watched as her eyes glistened over. Pulling out a handkerchief she dabbed at the corners of her eyes.

"If it is about the board seat, I know they will do little to promote you. I, however, will do all in my power to help you."

"Oh, it's not the silly seat. It's only, had I known you see, I wouldn't have encouraged Lady Charlotte at the picnic."

"Encouraged her?"

"I should have seen it. I don't know how I didn't. Of course, you got so close to Lord Grebs and his museum if only to make reasons to see her again. But I didn't see it, I didn't know."

"What did you say to encourage Lady Charlotte?" Raven asked fear welling in his heart.

"Just before the last game," his aunt sniffed. "I just said a few words before she left. That you were on the hunt for the most unique object in the garden, and I knew you were hoping to find her."

Raven sat back in his seat as he considered his aunt's words. He had a feeling that Lady Charlotte had been waiting for him to appear just as he had tried to seek out Lady Alexandra. He was sure that his aunt's words had only given her the added courage to follow her plan all the way through. After all, Lady Rebecca had practically told Lady Charlotte point blank that he wanted to marry her.

Perhaps, up until that point, the lady had thought he was torn between her and Lady Alexandra. She couldn't have been blind to the affection he had shown her the whole day through, even though they never directly spoke to one another.

Now that Raven thought about it, he was sure that Lady Charlotte had looked up just before she had tripped. Had she even tripped at all? Lady Charlotte had received encouraging words from his aunt and used her own wit to tip the scales in her favor. Because of that silly moment, he could lose Lady Alexandra.

"Then when you two came back together, well I just thought it had all worked out right," she continued to blubber on. "I was so happy about it. Oh, and so vocal about what a fine couple you made," she added in shock, replacing the handkerchief with a hand over her mouth.

"It's all right," Raven tried to calm his aunt.

"And Lady Alexandra looked so wretched when she came back. I wondered what had turned her mood so sullen all of a sudden. It was because she saw the two of you walking together wasn't it?"

"I'm afraid she saw far worse than that," Raven said with a slow breath.

Raven had told his aunt the whole of the tale. She, of course, was terribly shocked to hear of Lady Charlotte's behavior. None the less the damage had been done. Lady Alexandra wouldn't see him, no matter how many ways he tried to engage her in speaking the truth.

"Well, I will go and see her myself. I will explain it all," Lady Rebecca had offered.

Though it was a kind gesture, Raven wouldn't allow such a thing. His aunt meddling in his love life had already proven a failure once. He was sure the only way to get this done right was to do it himself.

For the first time in his life, however, he had no plan. He had no adventure to look ahead to. He had nothing on his horizon. The only light he had in front of him was Lady Alexandra, and she refused to show herself.

He pondered on this fact all through the night at the banquet. Of course, going to the museum, seeing the magnificent room prepared so perfectly, and hearing the general consensus of applause for his venue choice only made his ache worse.

Raven saw Lady Alexandra's hand in every little detail

of the Garden room. From the fine meal to the tasteful table arrangements, to the beautiful lush scenery that encased him. Even the several tropical birds that were brought into the center of the green room. Each had their stands at various points along the lush walls that encased the hall, including his new friend, Miss Nutters.

Before the meal began, the gents were able to circle the room, examine the fine specimens, and even get some of them to do a few tricks as instructed by the footmen standing next to each bird. It was highly entertaining and most impressive for the men of the Society.

All of this kept his mind full of Lady Alexandra. He did his best to put on a good face for the rest of the men. But by the time the evening was over, he couldn't wait to remove himself from the place.

Raven didn't care if he would have to call every day at Lord Grebs' house and stand outside the Museum of Natural Wonders every afternoon. He would do whatever it took to get Lady Alexandra to hear him out, and then win her over.

33

Lady Alexandra sat on the edge of her bed, white gloves in hand. In only a few moments she knew she must rise up and see that all her sisters were readied adequately for the evening. She hadn't the strength to do so.

In fact, Lady Alexandra had the strength to do little these days beyond crying. Even Lady Sophia sensed the change in her older sister and settled herself to a less irritating state. When their father announced that he too would be attending the ball tonight with them, Sophia hadn't even made a stir about being too young to go.

Naturally, Lady Alexandra had sent in her acceptance of the invitation several weeks in advance. She had rather hoped to send condolences on their absence that very night, not feeling the energy to go. With her father's announcement that would no longer be possible.

In truth, it wouldn't have been fair to her two younger sisters either. She knew she shouldn't deprive them of their time socializing all because she didn't feel up to it. So instead of staying home with Lady Sophia, Lady Alexandra had seen that Polly freshen out all their dresses, prepare their silk stockings and fine gloves.

She looked down at the gloves still in her hands. The button was still missing on one of them. She had forgotten to sew it on. With the fresh reminder of Sir Hamilton's ball tears rose in her eyes anew. Lady Alexandra wouldn't let herself cry again. She had done enough of that over the last few days.

She had thought after the first day following the picnic when she refused Raven's letter and call he would have given up. She was sure he was only trying to alleviate any disgruntlement between them before the banquet for the sake of its quality. That wasn't the case, however. For the past three days, Raven had come every day and called on her.

Twice he had tea in the drawing room with her younger sisters and father while she laid in bed with a pretend headache. The sound of his voice floated up the stairs and through the wall, tearing her heart anew.

Why he continued to torment her was nothing short of a mystery. He had apparently chosen his lady. With the banquet over, he should have left her be. Still, he was persistent for some unknown reason.

Lady Alexandra took a long slow breath, pushing against the stays of her corset. She smoothed out the moss green silk fabric of her dress before coming to stand. Walking forward she slipped into her tan slippers with golden embroidery.

She prayed with all her heart that Raven would not appear tonight at the ball but knew the possibility unlikely. He would be there and so would Lady Charlotte with her family. For the next several hours Lady Alexandra would be forced to watch them as they paraded around the ballroom as the new happy couple.

She swallowed back the emotions it was stirring in her again. Surely her knees would go weak if she thought on the idea too long.

"Alexandra?" she heard her father's voice call from the door. "Are you all right, dear? You have been looking rather pale these last few days," he commented, walking through the open door of her room.

"I'm fine. I just felt a little sickly for a moment, but I am fine now," Lady Alexandra said, desperate to hold her chin up just slightly higher.

Lord Grebs studied his daughter for a second before giving a nod like he had made up his mind.

"Come and have a seat with me, dear," he said padding to one of the mattresses.

Lord Grebs took his place and waited for his daughter to follow.

"You have been having several headaches as of late as well. Perhaps you are unwell?"

"I am all right," Alexandra said with a weak smile. "Plus I must be there for Josephine and Williamina."

Lord Grebs studied his daughter for a moment longer before taking her delicate hand in his worn one.

"You get that from your mother, you know?" he said in a soft tone.

"I do?" Lady Alexandra asked more surprised that her father was actually talking about his late wife.

"Mmm," he nodded. "She could be so fierce sometimes. I'm sure you can guess that I am not the most outgoing creature," he said with a half-smile. "Well, any time I just wanted to shut myself away, she would tell me that I just needed to tilt my chin a little higher. Even if I wasn't feeling up to it, a raised chin always makes you a might braver."

"Then when she was gone," he continued his voice falling sadly. "Well, I didn't have anyone to remind me to raise my chin, and I guess I just stopped. I left you to do far more than I should have. You were forced to be strong when I should have been for you. Other's would have shrunk away, but not someone like you, someone so like your mother," he added with a smile.

"I miss her," Lady Alexandra said softly. "I wish I could remember her better. Sometimes I think if I could, it wouldn't be so hard for me to...well you know, help out the others."

"You mean be a mother to them as you promised?" Lord Grebs corrected.

Lady Alexandra looked at her father in surprise. She had never shared that promise with anyone, not even Lady Eagleton.

"I was there when you made it. I had just walked into the room, and I heard it. But this, this is not what she wanted of you. You have given so much of yourself away, Alexandra. You gave a piece of it to each of us and left nothing for yourself. Part of that is my fault, and I'm sorry for it," he added struggling to control his emotions.

"You were mourning. I understand," Lady Alexandra said to make him feel better.

She saw his lip quiver just slightly.

"You're right," he said finally. "In fact, all of this time I was. I don't know if I will ever stop, truth be told. When she left us, well so much of me left with her."

"It's funny," he continued. "When Raven came that first day, it was like he reminded me that I did still matter to people out there. I had just figured when I shut myself up the world had forgotten me just as it had forgotten her. But he came here and told me what an impact the museum, my research, had had on his life as a boy. How he loved the place even now and was so grateful I was dedicated to it."

"I guess he reminded me that I still had a purpose

outside my little library. That it wasn't entirely wrong for me to live on, even if it was alone."

"He did give us that," Lady Alexandra said with a timid smile. "I suppose in that way we can all be grateful for his presence in our lives. I can't tell you how happy I was to see you at dinner that first night. For a long time, we lost our mother and our father. It meant so much to have you come back to us."

"But that isn't all he brought to this family, is it?" Lord Grebs asked, turning his gaze to meet hers.

"I'm not sure what you mean?"

"Well, I may not be the most attentive parental figure, but I am sure that as a scientist noting the correlation between headaches and Raven's visits means something."

"I can assure you it means nothing," Lady Alexandra said with determination.

"Hmm. Perhaps the correlation between the end of our recent picnic and the sudden onset of tears?"

Now it was Lady Alexandra's turn to hold back a quivering lip.

"Now as I said, I am only looking at this from a scientific point of view. My summation, however, is that you have feelings for the duke. Feelings I am almost positive he reciprocates."

"How can you think that at all?" Lady Alexandra asked her voice cracking.

"Because the duke has been just as much a mess with

every visit as you have been. Not to mention the fact that every time he came here, he was really only half interested in what I had to say or the museum and far more interested in you."

"It was all a misunderstanding, I can assure you. Like a stupid girl, I fell for him when I knew better."

"You are not a stupid girl at all, my dear" Lord Grebs cooed. "You are a fine young lady. A young lady that is in love. High time if you ask me."

"Why? Love is a terrible poison. Look what it did to you when mother died? Look what a fool it has made out of me?"

"It can be cruel at times, yes. But if there is one thing I can tell you, I would not trade away my sorrow if it meant never having your mother, and never having you girls. Perhaps if you give Raven a chance, you will be surprised at what you find. If that isn't the case, however, learn from me, my dear. Don't give up and shut yourself away. Just tilt your chin a bit higher, and I promise you will feel braver for the next time."

Lord Grebs took his daughter's hand that had been resting in his and raised it to his lips for a soft kiss. She smiled at her father and his kind words. Lady Alexandra couldn't even put into words how grateful she was to have him outside of his library and awake to the world again.

With her father's courage she tilted her chin just slightly higher, and together they walked down the stairs to join the others before the ball. Much to her surprise, she saw Josephine and Williamina already prepared and Sophia hard at work completing a writing lesson she had neglected earlier under Josephine's watchful eyes.

She wasn't sure she had ever seen the two of them carry on a conversation that didn't end in frustration or anger, but tonight they seemed to be working together to make sure the house was running smoothly. She wondered if it was because she had been so neglectful to everything these past few days that it had forced her sisters to wake up to all the duties of the house.

No matter the cause, she couldn't help but feel a weight lifted off her shoulders. Her father was out of his office and inserting himself back into household matters. Yesterday he had informed Lady Alexandra that he already saw positive results to the addition of the greenhouse facility.

As soon as they entered Lord Umbridge's fine house, Lady Alexandra settled to remove her broken heart from upon her sleeve and enjoy the night with her sisters and father. After all, this would be the first night that they had all gone out and attended an event together, ever.

"Ah, Lord Grebs, fine to see you up and about again. You are looking very healthy."

"Thank you, Lord Umbridge," Lord Grebs said bowing to the host and greeting his wife.

"Your daughters are as beautiful as always," Umbridge continued in greeting to the three ladies in tow. "I believe

Lady Rebecca Sinclair was asking after you lot," he added with a vague recollection of all the guests that had thus far passed over his threshold.

Lady Alexandra didn't blame him for the hesitation in words. Though they had arrived just at the right moment, the house was already resounding with the sounds of many guests.

"Lady Rebecca, you say?" Lord Grebs said with a question in his tone.

"Yes, I was unaware you were acquainted with that family, but I suppose I am mistaken."

"It is a recent meeting. I shall be sure that we seek her out and bid her a good evening," Lord Grebs concluded.

Lady Alexandra swallowed down hard in her throat. If Lady Rebecca was here, Raven was sure to be as well.

"Don't fret yourself too much," Lady Josephine said in a hushed tone squeezing her sister's hand for just the briefest of moment. "Perhaps Lady Rebecca is intent on seeing Father. They did take to each other at the picnic."

Lady Alexandra froze at the notion. She had been so wrapped up in her own sorrow, she had entirely forgotten the sudden grouping of the two the moment they made each other's acquaintance.

"You don't think?" Lady Alexandra asked a little shocked.

"I don't know," Lady Josephine answered before the

question was finished. “It would be wonderful for Father if he could find happiness again, don’t you think?”

Lady Alexandra pondered this for a moment. The idea that her father would remarry was so far removed from her mind she had never considered to think how she would feel on the matter. On the one hand, she was happy to think her father might have a chance at love again. She only wished it had been with any other woman but Lady Rebecca.

Of course, she had found the lady kind enough. More than that she had enjoyed the stories told by her at the picnic and the animated way in which she did it. If anyone was a force to reckon with the wild spirit of Raven as a young boy, it was surely she. It was only that Lady Alexandra now wished that the one lady that her father seemed to turn his eye at wouldn’t perpetually put her in the purview of the duke and his new happy life without her in it.

It was not a notion she was sure she could bear over a long-term period. In fact, she wasn’t entirely sure she could make it through the night.

34

"Don't fret yourself so," Lady Rebecca said to her nephew at her side.

Lady Rebecca Sinclair stood on her tiptoes scanning the room for any recognizable faces. Raven stood almost directly behind her and with every reach to her full height the feather embedded in her hair brushed against his chin.

"I wish you had not said such a thing," he replied softly.

He was desperately searching the crowd as well only a lot less obvious than his much shorter aunt. Whereas she was looking for an approaching party, Raven was sure the only image he would see was the retreating form of Lady Alexandra after what his aunt had done.

The moment they walked into the door and were welcomed by their host, Lady Rebecca had asked for the whereabouts of Lord Grebs' party. Lord Umbridge assured her that they had not yet arrived, but he would direct Lord Grebs to her the moment he did.

He was sure that as soon as Lady Alexandra learned that they were there and that his aunt was actively searching her out, she would turn and leave. It would be like every time he called on her yet again.

"Did you ever think that I might want to see Lord Grebs and his party tonight. It's not always about you, you know," she added while she patted her locks into place.

Raven froze to the spot seeing her action. Was she actually worried about her looks at this moment?

"And why, dear aunt, are you insistent on seeing Grebs' party?" Raven asked narrowing his dark eyes down at his aunt with his arms folded across his chest.

"I merely enjoyed their company at the picnic, is all," Lady Rebecca said quickly hoping to wave him off.

Raven recalled the day's event. His aunt and Lord Grebs had been getting along quite well that day. He was suddenly having a very protective feeling over his much older but also much smaller aunt.

"I'm not sure I like that notion," Raven responded to the words she didn't say.

"I don't believe you have much say in it," she retorted with hands on her ample hips.

He had seen that stance well. At any moment she could pull out her fan and snap him with it on the hand. It never hurt, of course, but always gave him a good shock as a boy.

"Well, I suppose you could do worse," Raven said with a half-smile. "At least I can say I am quite fond of the family as well."

Before the conversation could go any further, Lord and Lady Eagleton entered the room and made their way over to the two of them. They said their formal hellos and settled into a conversation with the small party while they waited for the rest of the guests to arrive.

"You look very well tonight, Lady Eagleton. It is good to see that your old husband isn't vexing you too much," he added jabbing at the older man.

"I can scarcely keep him at home long enough to bother me," Lady Eagleton responded with a relaxed smile. "I do wish I could say the same for you, Your Grace. But in truth you look a bit of a mess," she said in a low tone.

"What are you talking about," Lord Eagleton chimed in. "Look at the boy. He is fine. He looks just as he should."

Raven did make a quick sweep of himself though he knew that both were right in their summation. He was perfectly dressed head to toe in a dark dinner jacket, white cravat, and rich green pantaloons with high brown leather boots. At the same time, inwardly he felt like he was a crumbling mess.

Nothing but frustration had followed him over the last several days. Rarely did things not go his way, but when it came to Lady Alexandra that seemed to be the case at every turn. He was sure that he was unraveling from the inside out.

"Perhaps you are just seeing with your eyes, my dear," Lady Eagleton said in a sweet tone.

"What else am I to look with," Eagleton grumbled softly to his wife.

He wasn't irritated with her by any means. In fact, it warmed Raven's heart to see the loving banter between the two of them.

Before Lady Eagleton could respond, he knew Lady Alexandra entered the room. Though there was no change in the conversation, he was sure his whole world hushed as he sensed her presence. Looking across his small party, his eyes instantaneously met with hers. Lady Alexandra looked away quickly.

If he hadn't already been enchanted by her beauty, he was sure he was all over again in that moment. She stood slightly back from her father and Lady Williamina who stood at the head of their group. She was dressed in a moss green silk dress, her rich brown hair cascading in ringlets over one of her shoulders.

His heart quickened for the second that his dark eyes connected with her honey ones, but quickly she looked away. Though the party was walking towards him, he could already see Lady Alexandra holding back from the rest looking for any reason not to follow behind. Raven's chest tightened at the notion.

Without any reason to go to another place, she was forced to follow behind her family. They joined Raven's group, and the tension was so thick one could almost cut through it. Pleasantries were given all around after which the group fell into silence.

Raven held his gaze on Lady Alexandra willing her to look his direction.

"I hope you are feeling better now, Lady Alexandra," Raven said breaking the silence. "I know the last few times I called you were not well."

The whole party's eyes shifted from Raven to Lady Alexandra.

"Yes, thank you, Your Grace."

"I'm glad to hear it. Perhaps you would save me a dance?" Raven prodded on.

Again, the eyes swirled between the two.

"I thank you for asking, Your Grace, but I fear I couldn't possibly be up to it tonight."

Lady Alexandra smiled politely and said the words as she should, but still, she looked everywhere else but at him.

He could visibly feel the whole party sigh in disappointment. How was he ever to explain things to Lady Alexandra? He preferred not to do it right here in front of everyone but he would if he left her no other choice.

“If you will excuse me, Father. I think I am going to get a refreshment before the meal.”

Lord Grebs nodded his understanding, and Lady Alexandra turned to remove herself. In a second Lord Grebs’ eyes floated to Lady Rebecca who passed the unspoken words on to Raven. With a simple nudge of her head in Lady Alexandra’s direction, it was easy to see the woman’s meaning.

“I shall accompany you,” Raven said a little too sudden and loudly.

Lady Alexandra had just barely turned from the group, but the announcement made her swivel back around. He hadn’t asked but merely announced. She would have no choice but to allow him to do so.

He reached his arm out in offering to her. As the first time, she seemed to stare at it, untrusting of it’s meaning. Still slowly she placed her delicate hand in the crook of his arm. He sighed in relief. It was the first step in making amends.

“I want to explain what happened,” Raven said in a low voice as they weaved their way through the ever-growing crowd of the hall.

Skirting the walls of the hall were servers with various beverages to be served before the dinner was called. Raven was sure there had to be close to a hundred people already squeezed into the room.

“Please don’t,” Lady Alexandra said suddenly and

firmly causing him to halt in his tracks.

Reluctantly Lady Alexandra looked up at him. He could see the tears brimming her red eyes sore with tears already.

"I don't think I could bear to hear a moment of it. You have done wonderful things for my family. Father says the museum is flourishing thanks to you, more than that he has woken from the sorrow that engulfed him," she said, swallowing hard. "I thank you for all of this, Your Grace. Please let us not drag this moment on a second longer."

Raven turned to face the lady, "If you would just listen for a moment. I need to tell you. I never planned for you to find us like that. In fact, I was attempting to seek you out at that very moment when Lady Charlotte came upon me. I've been trying to tell you," he explained feeling frazzled now that the moment was there. He rubbed his free hand through his hair. "You see, after our dance at Sir Hamilton's I was enchanted with you. Meeting you on the steps of the museum wasn't an altogether accident. I was seeking you out, though I myself didn't understand why."

"Please stop, Raven," Lady Alexandra said taking a step forward and closing the gap between them more.

He watched her raise her arm to push him away, but she thought better of touching him, though their arms were still linked.

"I know you were enticed by my family's somewhat unorthodox and at times humorous behavior. I have no doubt that London must have been a very dull existence compared to the things you've seen. I don't feel any wrong caused me on your account. It was my own fault."

"Your fault? What on earth do you mean?"

"It is of little matter now. You will be married, and I truly wish you happiness from the bottom of my heart. It's just, it's just too painful for me right now. Soon we may be seeing each other more regularly," she added looking over Raven's shoulder.

He knew she meant whatever was going on between his aunt and her father.

"I am sure in time I will be better," she added with an intake of breath and a slight upward tilt of her chin. "I just don't have much strength for it at the moment."

Now it was Raven's turn to raise his hand. He so wanted to touch her. To brush his hand against her cheek and wash away all her worries. Suddenly he was very aware of all the people around them. Some had even started to stare at their close proximity and hushed tones.

Letting her hand fall from his arm, he grasped it with his own instead. Hand in hand, he tugged her out of the room without another word spoken between them. He knew they were making more of a scene than ever before, but Raven didn't care. He was tired of all of this. He would take Alexandra somewhere where they could finally speak in private.

She didn't pull against him, though he did have to remind himself to slow his large steps to allow her to keep up in her fine gown and slippers. They marched out of the main hall and into the foyer were straggling guest were still coming in and being greeted by the host, now more than ready to be seated for a meal.

Raven looked from side to side quickly summarizing the best place for a private conversation. He turned determinedly the opposite direction of the entering guest, none of whom paid them much attention. He could hear the clanking of dishes behind one door telling him it was the dining room filled with servants busy with the final tasks. The room next to it, however, was barely lit with the dying embers of a glowing fire and completely empty.

Raven pulled them both into the room and closed the doors tightly behind him. Turning around he didn't wait for Lady Alexandra to speak. He merely released his grip on her hand.

Before she had a moment's chance to take a step back from him, Raven cupped her delicate face within his hands' giant grasp and tilted her head upward to face him.

Without hesitation, he dipped his head low and gently pressed his lips to hers. He felt the sensation rush through him like a bolt of lightning as his lips brushed against her soft mouth. She didn't pull away, but he still felt her stiffen in her place. It took all his energy not to push the kiss to be more.

If she wouldn't let his words convince her of his feelings, then his actions would. Slowly he felt her relax into his touch. Her hands slowly went up the length of his fore-arms, and ever so slightly she raised on her toes to encourage him to kiss her more.

It was the encouragement he needed. Releasing one of his hands, he wrapped it around Lady Alexandra's waist pulling the whole of her body against him. He smiled in satisfaction against her lips. She loved him too, he knew for sure now.

Suddenly Lady Alexandra took a step back.

"Raven, why would you do that? We can't! What if someone was to come upon us? What will Lady Charlotte say?"

She held her hand to her lips as if the union was still there.

Raven relaxed and took a step forward again wrapping his arm around her waist. He would hold her there forever if she let him.

"I have little care for Lady Charlotte's opinion on the matter. I love you, Alexandra. How can you not see that?"

"But at the picnic?"

"Lady Charlotte saw you coming. She was standing on the bench and asked for my assistance. When you came into view, she tripped and fell against me. I am still not entirely sure if it was an accident or not," he added half under his breath. "I wanted to tell you then. I have loved you for some time now."

"But you are courting her?" Lady Alexandra continued still disbelieving.

"My aunt asked me to come to London because she thought us a good match. I acquainted myself with Derber's family as a favor to my aunt. I never expected that I could actually find someone I wanted to spend my life with. But I did. From the moment I saw you square your shoulders and attempt to pull that carriage up the museum steps all on your own, I knew," Raven said his black eyes twinkling with his mischievous words.

Lady Alexandra had relaxed in his touch. He knew he could tease her now. She believed him. Better than that, he knew she loved him too.

"You are a rotten man, Raven," she said smacking him lightly on the chest. "It's bad enough that you pulled me into this secluded room to ruin me. Now I must be subject to your cruel words as well?"

"My dear," Raven said with a wicked gleam to his dark eyes. She felt his fingers splayed across her back. "I have much more in mind than just ruining you in this room."

Raven leaned his forehead softly against hers, breathing in her beauty.

"I plan to marry you," he added softly.

"Perhaps I will refuse you," Lady Alexandra teased him in return.

He could already feel her raising on her toes, tipping

her head back, anticipating his kiss. He let his lips hesitate just over her own.

"Well, then I will pick you up, throw you over my shoulder, and carry you all the way to the church. You may be stubborn, Alexandra Woodley, but I can assure you that even you are no match for me. If I want something, I will have my way, and I want you."

35

"It was all so beautiful," Lady Josephine said to her sister as they sat at the Duke of Raven's fine dining table.

Lady Alexandra had eaten very little the whole day through. Now that she was sitting at the large table, with some of the most exquisite food she had ever seen, she was having a difficult time not to eat it all frantically.

She didn't want to ruin her beautiful new dress, however. It was an elegant cream color cotton gown with delicate lace overlaying from top to bottom. The top of her dress had simple cap sleeves that left her shoulders bare, with the see-through lace covering along her collarbone for modesty's sake.

More than the beautiful feel of the fabric against her

skin, was the warm touch of her new husband's hand gently resting on her lap.

Since the moment that Raven whisked Alexandra away and declared his love for her, there had been very few moments they were together without some sort of physical contact. In fact, she had rather felt like her youngest sister, Sophia, the last few weeks and she had giggled and swooned over her future husband.

They had planned the ceremony as quickly as possible having a quiet chapel service the first week of August. Only their closest friends and family were invited to attend. The service had been simple, private, and absolutely perfect in Alexandra's mind.

She had never in her life expected to marry, let alone find a match to a man she loved and who loved her in return.

"It was beautiful, wasn't it. I just wish Mother could have been here to see it," she said with a soft smile, rubbing the pendant around her neck.

It was the second time she had worn the gem in her life. As soon as the day was over, however, she would make sure it was promptly returned back to her sister's jewelry box. It had brought her so much luck in life and love, she wanted to make sure her sisters also got the same opportunity.

"She was. I am sure she is watching down on all of us from heaven and smiling with joy," Lady Josephine said in her ever-constant positive manner.

Both girls took a moment to look around the table. Lord and Lady Eagleton were talking animatedly between each other. Next to them was Lord Jocasta who looked rather bored pushing around the food on his plate. His wife across from him was very obviously sneaking morsels of fish to the cat that sat in the basket next to her feet. Next to her was Lady Rebecca who was purposefully placed by Alexandra's father.

It was easy to see that something was blossoming between the two of them. Unlike Raven and Alexandra, who couldn't wait another moment to make their love known before the ton and eyes of God, her father was going at a much slower, cautious pace.

Alexandra knew it was a good choice for him. The chance at a second love was going to be a very delicate and slow process for Lord Grebs.

Along the row of seats next to her father was Lady Alexandra's three younger sisters with Josephine directly next to her. She had feared to leave the three of them. Even with her father more active in his household role, there was still much that only a woman could do for them.

Lady Josephine had assured her sister, countless times in fact, that they would be just fine without her. For certainly whatever they couldn't manage on their own, Lady Rebecca had already taken a liking to helping them.

In fact, her new role as board member on the Society for Orphaned Children had given her the inspiration to adopt the three younger Woodley girls under her well-trained mentorship.

"How long until you leave?" Alexandra's sister asked with only a hint of sadness of her departure.

Lady Alexandra had never been more than across town from her siblings. Now she would be crossing a whole ocean.

"We leave two days from now for Liverpool. Raven says we will be spending a few days, maybe a week there. Then the ship will set sail for Virginia."

"Are you so excited? Or perhaps nervous?"

"A little of both I suppose. I don't know what to expect. This is all happening so fast, to be honest. I have never experienced anything outside of London. Raven says Virginia is so different than here in the winter."

"But you will come back home? I mean sometime, not right away of course."

Alexandra looked lovingly at her sister. She knew this separation would be just as hard on Josephine as it would be on her.

"I am sure we will be home very soon," Alexandra said reassuringly. "And perhaps in the future, you will be able to come visit us in the country for the colder months. Raven hasn't been to his country seat in some time, but he has told me about it, and it does sound quite wonderful."

"That would be nice," Lady Josephine said with a smile. "But I am sure you two will enjoy your time just the two of you for a while," she added with reddening to her cheeks. It sent both girls into fits of giggles.

As the meal began to wind down, Raven stood to stand. Removing his hand from Lady Alexandra's for the first time since they were seated, he used it to clink his glass softly.

"I just wanted to take a moment," Raven said once the rest of the conversations died down. "To say how grateful I am, and my beautiful wife as well," he added looking down at Alexandra.

It was the first time he called her his wife and Alexandra could see that he was enjoying it just as much as she was.

"We are both just so happy that we got to share this special day with the people who matter most to us. As you all know we will be leaving shortly for our plantation in Virginia. Though I know we may be far apart for a time," he said looking between Alexandra and Josephine, "no distance can ever truly separate us."

"You know," he said holding up his glass preparing to toast. "I have been far from my family for a great portion of my life," he motioned to his aunt. "In truth, I don't think I truly fit in with society here. My poor aunt can attest to the fact that I often chose mischief over propriety."

"I thought if I went away, I would find the place I belong," he said now turning serious. "I chased the sun till it set and then back again. I've seen amazing things, but still, I never found that place where I truly belong, that place I would consider my home."

"Aunt Rebecca convinced me to come home to London this year, a bit mischievously if you ask me. It was in my return to London that I found that my home had been here all along," Raven said looking down at Alexandra.

"You see, I learned that home is not a place at all. It is a person. A person whom once you have met, you soon learn that life will never again be the same without them. I have found my home now."

He reached down taking his wife's hand and kissed it softly.

"I would like to invite you all to join me in raising a toast to my beautiful bride, my true home."

All glasses were raised, and the sound of cheers and clinking of drinks resounded around the room.

Alexandra looked up lovingly into the face of her husband, the Duke of Raven.

EPILOGUE

EPILOGUE

"Raven! Raven, are you in here," the Duchess of Raven called out for her husband.

She had thought the plantation house in Virginia was large, but the country estate in the lake district seemed to be double in size. She had spent the last twenty minutes walking from room to room in search of her husband.

"Alexandra, I'm in here," she finally heard him respond back.

Raven stepped out of the library where he had been working at his desk to make his presence more known to his wife.

"I thought you were resting?"

"I don't need to sleep all day," Alexandra said with a little giggle as she waddled over to her husband.

"You need your rest," he insisted rubbing her swollen belly as she grew nearer. "It was bad enough that you insisted on coming home once we found out you were with child. Travel is so dangerous for someone in your condition."

"Well, I wasn't quite in this condition when we started," Alexandra tried to clarify motioning to her overly round belly.

"But we knew you were with child," Raven corrected his wife.

"And here I am, completely fine. We both are," Alexandra assured Raven again.

Ever since she told him the happy news, Raven had been especially protective over her. The once adventurous man who had allowed her to accompany him anywhere she wished despite its suitability for womenfolk, had now resigned to treating her like a delicate flower.

"I would like you to show me around the house. I have only met Mrs. Wilson. What about the rest of the staff? Our family will be arriving soon. I must get the house ready."

"You will do nothing of the sort. Mrs. Wilson is the housekeeper. You tell her what you want, and she will see that it gets done. Your only job," he said brushing a hair that had fallen while she rested, "is to sit down and prepare yourself for motherhood."

"What is there to prepare for, I've done it already," Alexandra said though she followed her husband's coaxing down the hall.

"Here is the morning room. In the right annex is a drawing room that you may use for your own private purposes. And then next to the library I came out of is a much larger one for after dinner and entertaining," Raven explained.

"What on earth will I do with so many drawing rooms," Alexandra said with a giggle.

"I suppose whatever suits you," Raven replied taking a seat next to his wife.

He still had several documents to go over before he would be done for the evening, but just for now he thought it best to enjoy his wife's company.

They had just arrived at the estate after a long journey across the ocean and then a week-long carriage ride to the country. It shouldn't have taken so long, but Raven had insisted the driver go at a much slower pace than was usual for Alexandra's sake.

She had hoped to return to their home long before the other guests started to arrive. The extended journey barely left her a few days, at the most, before the rest of her family and Lady Rebecca came. How was she to know the house and get it all ready if Raven would not allow her to move except from one drawing room to the next?

"How long has it been," Alexandra asked as Raven lifted her feet and set them on his lap.

"Hm?" he questioned half concentrating on the slippers he was removing one by one.

Alexandra had been a strong lady from the moment Raven met her. He had expected no less than her determination, and stubbornness, even in her pregnancy. That being said he was sure that she took far too much on herself that could be left to others. Her swollen ankles were testaments to that fact.

"How long since you have been here?" she asked before relaxing back into the couch as Raven began to massage one foot and then the other.

"I'm not sure," he said pondering the question.

In his concentration, Raven's hands paused in their motion. Alexandra wiggled her silk-stockinged toes with a smile. Giving her his mischievous grin, Raven tickled the sole of one foot before going back to his rubbing.

"I would guess I was sixteen, maybe fifteen, the last time I came."

"Is it all the same?" Alexandra asked looking around the room.

She had learned from the moment she had married Raven that his standard of living had been far superior to her own. Lavish houses dotted the British islands. Then there was the plantation in Virginia and the bungalow in the South Indies. Each one of these lavish houses had been furnished with no limitation of funds. Many of the English countryside estates, like the cottage outside of London, would be rented out from time to time to gentlemen.

"I suppose it is. I can't remember honestly. We really didn't come much, my aunt and I that is. I think she worried it would be too upsetting to come back here after my parents died."

"Is it?" Alexandra asked suddenly realizing that being here again might bring up painful memories.

"No," he said with a reassuring smile. "I don't remember much of them to be honest. But the memories I do have, they were good ones. I can't wait to make some of our own as well here," he added for good measure.

"And a wedding shall be the first one," Alexandra mused.

"Yes, a bit of a strange one, if you ask me," Raven said with a chuckle.

"It's not strange at all. If anything, they have taken far too long in my opinion," Alexandra said decidedly. "It's been over two years since our own."

"Yes, well I suppose not all men are like me. Swooping in, carrying you away, and claiming you as my own."

"If I remember right, I walked on my own accord," Alexandra corrected him.

"I suppose you are right," he smiled back at her.

Two days later the parties began to arrive. First was Lord Grebs with his three youngest daughters. It was a reunion of much laughter and tears shared between all the sisters. Alexandra was so overcome with shock at how her youngest sister had grown and matured in the last two years Raven feared that she might swoon from it.

The day after, Lady Rebecca arrived with her two companions, Lord and Lady Jocasta. Alexandra didn't want to admit it, but she was relieved that the latter decided on bringing only one cat with her.

The final members of their wedding party arrived the same night. Lord and Lady Eagleton had taken extra-long in traveling for the very same reason that Raven had insisted his driver travel slow.

Lady Eagleton was showing just as much of a swollen belly as her dear friend. After so many years without a child of her own, both she and her husband had been overjoyed when the miracle had happened.

"Won't it just be wonderful Regina," Alexandra mused the following day in the morning room. "Our children will grow up together. They could be wonderful friends as well."

"It is wonderful isn't it," Regina agreed pushing on her belly where a stubborn body part was preparing to push its way out. "Although I wonder if it is weird for Raven?"

"What do you mean?"

"Well, he was such good friends with Young Charles. Now here we are having a child, Charles's brother, and it will be the same age as Raven's baby. I wonder if that is strange to him."

"I don't think so at all," Alexandra concluded. "All I know for sure, however," she added readjusting herself in her seat, "is I am just glad he has Lord Eagleton to keep him in line. I am almost positive if it weren't for you, he would be keeping me in bed all day surrounded by pillows."

"Trust me, my Charles is no better," Regina giggled back. "I'll be lucky if I am allowed to attend the church service tomorrow. He talks of not leaving until the child is born and healthy. Says to go back home would be far too great a risk."

"Well, I do agree with him on that point. Not the risk so much as the fact that you must stay until you and the babe are both well and ready. I won't hear of anything less."

"It would be too much of a burden," Regina countered.

"Not at all. In fact, it would be a comfort to do it together, I think," Alexandra said reaching across for her friend's hand.

Both ladies were in fact allowed to attend the small church ceremony on the following day. With tears in her eyes, Alexandra watched as Lady Rebecca walked down the aisle in a soft blue dress. Standing by the altar was her father.

If he had seemed a changed man after the first few weeks of Raven's introduction into the family, it was nothing compared to the man he was now. Alexandra would have liked to think she was once again looking on the man who had lived before her mother's passing.

His skin was flushed with life, and his words echoed his happiness with everything he did and said. Alexandra, as well as all of her sisters, couldn't have been happier to see their father lucky enough to find love again in life.

As the ceremony ended and the guests filtered out of the small private church on the estate grounds, Alexandra beamed with joy at her gloriously large family before her.

"What is it, my dear," Raven said tucking Alexandra's arm in his for support.

Gentle tears were dripping down her face, and using a soft white handkerchief, she wiped them away quickly.

"I'm just happy, is all," she assured her husband.

Raven leaned over and kissed his wife on the top of her head, breathing in the scent of her chestnut brown hair.

. . .

"I wonder if this is what perf

looking up at him still glossy e

"I would imagine so, my love,'

all the way down to steal a qui

THE END

Did you enjoy ***Entangled with the Duke***? Check out the story of ***Hannah*** and ***Sebastian*** in ***A Mysterious Governess for the Reluctant Earl*** here.

If you want a Bonus Scene of this book visit the link below (or just click it): https://abbyayles.com/aa-014-exep/

A MYSTERIOUS GOVERNESS FOR THE RELUCTANT EARL

Preview

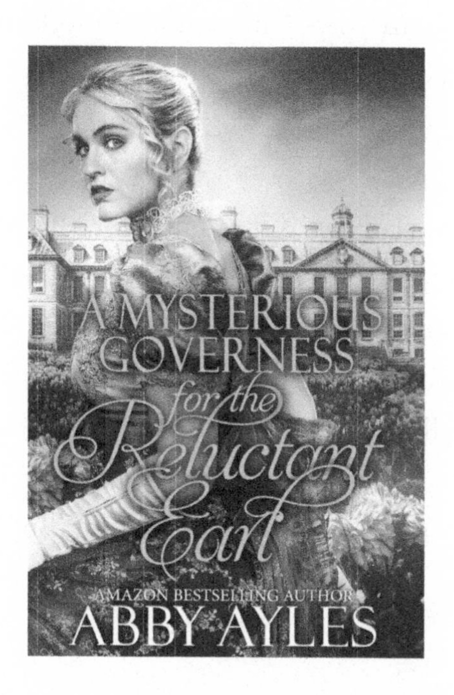

Read it now!

http://abbyayles.com/AmB11

All he wanted was a governess for his children. He never thought he would find his second chance in love.

Sebastian Blackburn Earl of Grimshaw is more the perturbed at the loss of his last governess. It would seem that she only used her employment as a means of securing a desirable match. Now he is in need of a new teacher for his two motherless girls and this time Lord Grimshaw won't be trusting a solicitor to secure the position. He's learned the hard way if he wants something done right, he'll have to do it himself.

Miss Hannah Jacobson is desperate for any employment at this. After a year harassed by Baron Edgley and then a shameful dismissal without reference when she refuses his advances, Hannah is now blackballed from any governess position in all of London. Hannah is desperate to secure not only her own living but also has her impoverished parents and many siblings dependent on her financial support.

. . .

Lord Grimshaw is exhausted by the countless young, beautiful, and sociable candidates that the solicitor provides when suddenly Hannah Jacobson walks in. She is plain, and thread barren. She wears unsightly large spectacles and a matronly cap that nearly covers most of her face. Lord Grimshaw is sure this wallflower won't be catching anyone's eye any time soon and hires her on the spot.

Hannah knows this is her last chance to secure a living and leave with an outstanding recommendation to offset her previous employment, but will she be able to suffer all those outlandish and controlling rules the Earl suggests for the sake of her family?

And what happens when she suddenly finds herself being stalked by Lord Grimshaw's footman?

Will Lord Grimshaw be able to see through his new governess and discover the secret that's been troubling her? And how will he react when though he has to a proper mother for his children, his heart draws itself to Miss Jacobson continually with a strong desire to protect her?

. . .

If you like engaging characters, heart-wrenching twists and turns, and lots of romance, then you'll love "A Mysterious Governess for the Reluctant Earl!"

Buy "A Mysterious Governess for the Reluctant Earl" and unlock the exciting story of Hannah today!

Also available with Kindle Unlimited!

Read it now!

http://abbyayles.com/AmB11

1

"Lord Grimshaw, you must understand that this is very unorthodox."

"I can't imagine how that could be," Sebastian Blackburn, the Earl of Grimshaw, stated with a huff of irritation. "I am certainly not the only one to come and seek a governess through you."

"Of course not, my lord," the solicitor replied, pushing the spectacles up his nose. "That is the main purpose of our establishment, of course. I only mean that asking various governesses here to be interviewed by you personally is very unorthodox, and quite possibly not possible on such short notice."

"Well," Grimshaw said, doing his best to keep a steady voice. "How much time would you find sufficient if you cannot procure prospects today? Would tomorrow give you a sufficient amount of time?"

"A week would be more reasonable, Lord Grimshaw."

"Well, I don't have a week!" Grimshaw said, standing up in the room.

The solicitor sat back in his chair in response to Sebastian's physical presence in the small office room.

"It is your fault I find myself here. I asked you to procure me a governess and in less than a year she goes and elopes. I obviously can't count on you to pick a proper candidate so here I am to do it myself. This trip to London has already been inconvenient enough. I want to be done with the whole thing in no more than three days' time."

The solicitor moved the glasses on his nose once more. He didn't particularly enjoy being reprimanded in his own office but nothing could be done for it. Many young ladies would take up these governess jobs only long enough to see themselves properly wed. Though a resignation in less than a year was unusually quick, it was a common occurrence for a governess to give up pupils for marriage.

"I am very sorry that Miss Watts left your service..."

"How about you tell my two girls how sorry you are? In the last two years, they have lost a mother and now their governess. Perhaps if you will not furnish me with candidates to interview myself, I will just take you with me back to Brighton Abby so that you may look into their doe eyes and explain why they have had no womanly figure to support and guide them these last four months."

"I assure you that won't be necessary, Lord Grimshaw," the solicitor said, shuffling papers on his desk. "I am sure that I will be able to find several candidates ready for your approval by tomorrow morning."

The solicitor was feeling rather terrified from the Earl's commanding presence and was willing to do whatever it took to pacify the man.

Lord Grimshaw nodded in approval with a grunt before turning to retrieve his beaver fur hat and cane.

"Then I will arrive promptly tomorrow morning at nine o'clock and I expect to have several options to choose from," he announced in a less harsh but still demanding voice.

"Of course, Lord Grimshaw. It is our passion to make sure all our clients are pleased in every way with any employment they need filling," the solicitor said, standing and reciting the business motto.

Sebastian stormed from the office and building onto the busy streets of London. He looked either direction at the various people walking along the road before donning his hat.

"Need a cab, m' lord?" a small voice called up to him.

He looked down to inspect the eyes of the dirty orphan waiting expectantly. Sebastian expected he hoped for a penny in return for his aid in procuring a carriage for hire.

"Alright, sure," Sebastian said as he studied the boy.

The small child's face brightened to finally get an affirmative answer. Sebastian had no doubt it was one of the few he had gotten all week. The child was scarcely a skeleton.

Despite his malnutrition, he donned his own ragged cap and ran out to the muddied and filth-filled street to hail a carriage.

It only took a moment for the yellow carriage pulled by a single horse to be called over by the boy. Sebastian had to admit he was quite proficient at his job.

As the carriage pulled to the side of the raised sidewalk so as to keep the Earl from soiling his leather boots in the street, the boy opened the door and removed his hat, bowing in respect.

"For you, m'lord," he said.

Sebastian reached into his pocket and pulled out a sixpence to give the child. He supposed the boy had held out his hat for the money, not expecting someone of his class would be willing to put it directly into such a dirty hand.

Instead of placing the coin in the hat, however, Sebastian knelt down to the child's level. Grabbing the boy's dirty thin hand with his own white-gloved one, he placed the coin in his palm.

"I would hate for it to fall out of the hole in your cap," Sebastian said, motioning to the worn headpiece.

"Thank you, m' lord!" The boy was so overcome with excitement at the money he could scarcely breathe.

Sebastian ruffled the boy's matted brown hair and smiled at him before raising himself back up and entering the carriage.

"Where to, guvnor?" the driver called from his high seat in front of the box.

"Grand Hotel, Covent Garden," Sebastian responded without fanfare as he settled back into the carriage seat.

He was vastly irritated to spend even one more day in London, but there seemed to be nothing to do for it.

He had trusted a solicitor once, though he wasn't entirely sure if it was that exact man he had met today as he had accused, to procure a governess for him. If there was one thing that Sebastian Blackburn, Earl of Grimshaw, had learned in life, it was that if he wanted something done properly, he was going to have to do it himself.

The following morning Sebastian walked into the employment office satisfied to see a row of ladies seated and patiently waiting.

He could easily already mark several of them off his list of candidates as they were far too handsome to look upon. He wasn't about to allow his future governess to catch the eye of a local gentleman again.

His girls had suffered enough without the loss of yet another motherly figure in their life. He would settle on a lady that would not only excel as a tutor but also one that looked so demure as to never risk leaving again.

Sebastian was shown into the same solicitor's office. He spoke rather nervously as he shuffled through his papers and made room for the Earl at the desk.

"I have a list of all qualified ladies. All are in need of employment and able to travel as far distance as is necessary. I have assured all of them that this governess position is not a temporary one and dedication is required."

Sebastian nodded his head in approval. He was aware that he could be a quite severe-looking man so he attempted to soften his look. It wasn't easy when he was in such a sour disposition already. He never liked traveling to London. There were far too many people.

"Please do send the first one in," Sebastian said, taking his seat in the solicitor's chair behind the desk.

The man only hesitated for a moment before nodding and leaving the room. A few seconds later he returned with a lady in tow. She was one of the seated misses he had singled out at once as far too beautiful for his position.

"Thank you, I am sure you are very skilled," Sebastian said before the woman even fully entered the room, "but I am looking for something else in a governess. Good morning."

He kept his thick arms on the table with his fingers interlaced. She looked up in shock between the Earl and the solicitor before the latter finally shooed her out of the room and returned with another.

"This will do fine, please have a seat, miss?" Sebastian said, taking control of the room as was his habit.

"Miss Mary Prescott, sir," she said as she took her seat.

Sebastian spent the next several hours interviewing one miss after another. Some, like the first, were dismissed right away. Others were given the opportunity to answer a few questions but quickly were found wanting.

Sebastian was just beginning to lose hope when Miss Hannah Jacobson made her way into the room. He looked her over, finding her features very satisfying to his needs.

Her dress clearly stated that she was of a lower class. Not only was it extremely plain and not of the fashion he had seen as of late, but it was also altered along the edges. He could scarcely make her face out between the large white cap she had completely covering her head and the wide brim spectacles that obscured the rest of her face.

"Miss Hannah Jacobson," the solicitor said before leaving the room.

She took her seat and, passing her information forward to the Earl, kept her eyes on the hands neatly folded in her lap. Sebastian pulled his eyes from her curious figure to the pamphlet before him.

Her dress seemed to make more sense as he read over that her schooling was at Hendrick's Preparatory School for Young Misses. He was familiar with the institution. Though it produced satisfactory educators, it was one often used by those who couldn't afford much better.

"I am in need of a lady who can both teach my two young daughters the educational lessons appropriate to their age as well as etiquette they will need in preparation for their adult lives. I trust your education at Hendrick's Preparatory was satisfactory?"

"Yes, Lord Grimshaw."

"And if you were offered the position, how soon would you be able to arrive at Brighton Abby? Of course, I would pay for your transportation," he added with a wave of his hand.

"I could leave as soon as needed, or as soon as it is convenient for you," she replied with her head still down.

He didn't rather like how dull and sullen she seemed. He wondered how that would fair with his girls who were often rambunctious and feral. Though on the other hand, he thought perhaps her demeanor might have an influence on them.

"I see here that Hendrick's first put you with the Baron Edgley. I see you spent almost a year there, but I see no reference."

"That is correct," she said as her eyes met his for the first time since entering the room.

"Could you perchance tell me why your post terminated with the baron and perhaps why there is no reference," Sebastian said, a little more severely than he had meant to.

He was just frustrated, not with the miss, but with the fact that this was yet another red flag against yet another unqualified governess.

"Perhaps you know the baron?" Hannah retorted, not yet ready to answer the question.

"No."

"Oh, well, my ward was their son, Joseph. He took ill quite suddenly and after several months without recovering they thought it best to dismiss me. Both Baron and Baroness Edgley were beside themselves with worry over Joseph, and I didn't feel it appropriate to ask for a reference in such a time."

"Why did they not supply one upon your dismissal?"

"I suppose it was just the stress they were under. I think the Baron forgot, he had so much on his mind, you see."

Sebastian thought this over and considered it to be a suitable reason for not giving a reference. Hannah Jacobson didn't seem like the type of girl who would fail in her job as an educator if her school marks were any indication.

"Well," the Earl said, standing up. Miss Jacobson did the same. "I have seen as much as I think I need to. You are hired. I will arrange a coach to collect you and your belongings first thing tomorrow morning."

"Tomorrow morning?" Hannah said, surprised to not

only get the job with such a dubious work history and suspicious explanation of it, but to also start right away.

"You said you were available, did you not?"

"Yes, yes of course. I would be happy to begin as soon as you wish. I was just surprised is all," she added with a shy smile.

She looked down from the Earl, no doubt to hide a blush behind the large ruffles of her cap. He couldn't help but wonder later that day if it was actually dimples he had also seen along with the rose on her cheeks.

Read it now!

http://abbyayles.com/AmB11

2

Hannah took a steadying breath before leaving the small rented flat that had been her home these last six months. She couldn't help but feel anxious about the new employment and one outside of London.

Hannah had told herself numerous times it would be better to acquire a post outside of the city she had been born in. She needed to get far enough away that the reputation that Baron Edgley was spreading wouldn't reach.

She grabbed her one small suitcase and locked the door behind her. More than anything she was in great need of the income this opportunity would provide. She learned to live frugally from a very young age, but it still had not prepared her for her six-month period without a job.

Of course, she could have always gone to her aunt and

uncle and asked for help if she really needed to. It was something she would not consider unless she was near death, however.

They thought they were being kind when they sent her off to Hendrick's Preparatory School. It had relieved her own parents of at least one of the seven children at that time. Now her mother's brood was boasting twelve children. Her aunt and uncle were satisfied in their charitable duty to send her, the eldest, off to receive a proper education and the promise of employment afterward.

Hannah began her education at the age of eleven. From that moment on, every waking wish for her, and every other girl at that school, was just to be freed upon their eighteenth birthday.

Unlike so many who died of malnutrition or sickness in the cramp quarters of the ill-heated school, Hannah had made it to her eighteenth year. She was promptly removed from school and placed in the baron's home.

How something so horrible as that school could have furnished her a post even more horrifying was more than Hannah would ever understand. They clearly cared little for the homes they were sending their wards to.

Hannah could only hope that her new station would be an improvement on her last, and she could again send money back to her family who needed it so desperately.

She watched the countryside pass by out the window of the public carriage. She was happy to be in the box instead of sitting outside with the cases as two other men had done for the cheaper fair.

In the carriage, she was squished tight up against the window to avoid all contact with the gentleman next to her. She would have rather not been smothered into a vehicle with five other bodies, only one of which was another woman, for the duration of the ride.

She could have no opinion on the matter, however, as it was her employer who had furnished the arraignment.

Hannah thought on the Earl of Grimshaw as dusk was beginning to set on her day-long ride. She wondered what sort of a man he was. He had seemed quite fierce at their one and only meeting. He was such an imposing figure even the solicitor had seemed to shrink away from him.

Lord Grimshaw reminded her quite a bit of the teachers from her past. Quick to strike the hand and slow to show any amount of kindness. It seemed an insufferable idea to go to a house that seemed much like her childhood upbringing.

She had no choice in the matter. She had extinguished all her reserves and had already been turned down for six different positions in London, either from lack of reference or worse from word of mouth reference from the baron himself.

At that moment while she was lost in thought, the gentleman who had fallen asleep next to her began to slouch in her direction. Hannah stiffened as his arm came in contact with hers.

Hannah did her best to lean farther out of the window. Even the mere innocent touch of a sleeping man was enough to make her wish to scream in fear.

Her nose was already freezing from the cool breeze blowing by in the darkening outside world. She didn't care if her nose fell off from the cold, she would hold herself outside the carriage as long as necessary till the man righted himself again.

Finally, just after midnight, the coach stopped at the gates of Brighton Abby. Luckily before that, her gentleman companion had woken and already removed himself at an earlier stop.

Even with the added space in the carriage, when it was her turn to dismount, she couldn't help but breathe a sigh of relief. She thanked the man who handed her chest down and began the walk through the gates to her new home.

She couldn't see much of it in the darkness. Thankfully some lights were still in the windows guiding her way. Just as she came to the front of the house a woman came around the corner.

Hannah sighed in relief to see that she would not have to sit outside and wait for the house to awaken to be let in. She smiled gratefully at the woman and followed her to the side of the house where the service entrance was.

Inside she could see the lady much clearer. She was no

doubt in her late fifties and covered her head with a large laced cap as Hannah did, though Hannah was sure for an entirely different reason.

"I am Mrs. Brennon, the housekeeper," she said as she wiped her nose against the cold. "Come inside quickly, child, and make yourself warm. I insisted that David keep the fire warm until your arrival."

"Thank you, Mrs. Brennon. That was most kind of you," Hannah replied, grateful for the warmth.

"Come and sit and I will have some tea and sandwiches brought down."

"Please don't go through such trouble on my account. If you would just show me to my quarters, I will not keep you up any longer."

"Nonsense, at my age one doesn't sleep much anyway," Mrs. Brennon said as she eased herself down into a chair in front of a warm hearth.

Hannah couldn't have been more appreciative of the light meal and warm drink brought by one of the maids. She made a mental note to repay the kindness at a later date.

"Now," Mrs. Brennon said after she finished her tea, "Lord Grimshaw will see you tomorrow in the morning room after breakfast. Nine o'clock sharp, do you hear?" she warned with a wagging finger. "He doesn't like to be kept waiting."

"Yes, ma'am."

"The earl would like to personally give you the details of your duty and the parameters of your stay at Brighton Abby. After this, I will take you to see your new pupils and a short tour of the house. It would do you no good to see it now."

"How will I find my way to the morning room," Hannah asked.

She had seen very little of the estate in the dark but what she did see was quite massive. She was sure it was an easy enough thing to get lost in its expansive halls.

"Mary will bring you your breakfast in the morning, she will be able to help you on."

"Thank you, Mrs. Brennon. This is a far better welcome than I could have ever wished for," Hannah said, grateful from the depths of her heart.

The following morning Hannah woke early in the privacy of her own room. It was nothing she had ever experienced before in the whole of her life. Whether it was sharing a bed with siblings, the massive dormitories of her school, or the servant quarters of the baron's London home, she had always had at least one companion in her room.

It all seemed very quiet to her as she got out of bed and dressed for the day. The first thing she did before even the maid could enter was replacing the hair cap and thick glasses that served no purpose but to hide her face.

As she finished this, a soft knock came at her door. Hannah wrapped herself in her shawl before cracking it open. Seeing that it was indeed the maid with her breakfast, she opened the door all the way to let her in.

"I'm Mary," she said cheerfully as she set down the tray. "You will be Miss Jacobson."

"Just Hannah, please," Hannah said as the maid turned to inspect her.

She let out a giggle.

"I've never seen someone so young wear a cap. And why do you have it on before you are even dressed?" she asked, motioning to the nightgown that Hannah was still in.

"I was just a bit chilled this morning," Hannah said by way of excuse.

"Well, I'll have the warm water coming up for you next. Can you start the fire, or do you need help?"

Hannah looked over to the small mantle with the cinders from the fire that had glowed upon her entry the night before.

Next to the hearth was a basket filled with more wood and small scraps to start the fire with. Hannah could barely contain her own joy. Having a fire to warm herself by was a treasured event.

"I can manage it on my own. I only just woke. Is there a bucket I might sweep the ashes in?"

"Don't be silly," Mary said, waving her off with another laugh, "the chambermaid will come around and take care of all of that."

Hannah wasn't used to having breakfast brought to her, or maids to clean up after her. Even in the baron's house, such things couldn't be afforded and Hannah was expected to take care of her own needs and eat her meals with the rest of the staff.

"I don't mean to make work for others," Hannah said.

After all, it was something that had been beaten into her, quite literally, growing up. Every person in this world had a God-ordained purpose. For the misses of Hendrick's Prep, it was to serve others, not to be waited upon.

"It is no more work than we are used to. This is a big house. It takes a large staff to maintain it. You will find that we are more than amply supplied to see to your comfort. In that way, you will be able to focus all your energy on Lady Caroline and Lady Rebecca. At least that is what the earl wishes."

"Well if it is Lord Grimshaw's instructions then I won't interfere," Hannah said rather reluctantly.

Mary gave her one last welcoming smile before she went on her way out of the room and to the rest of her duties.

By the time that Hannah had finished the fire, Mary was back to deliver the warm basin as promised.

"Thank you," was all Hannah could manage before Mary was on her way again.

The house may have been fully staffed but it was also a very busy place. Hannah peeked out of her room and saw the bustle of several other servants going about their daily duties.

Returning to her private room, Hannah washed, feeling most refreshed after such a long trip, and dressed in her simple grey muslin dress. She wrapped her neckline with her cotton fichu that was long enough to tuck through her bodice and double as her apron over her skirts.

She did her best to smooth out any wrinkles in both the cotton fichu and dress that had occurred in the time in her chest.

Finally feeling herself fully put together, Hannah sat down to take her breakfast. She was happy to see a steaming pot of tea, toast, and fresh marmalade.

She was feeling quite spoiled as she ate her toast and took in the sights around her. Along with her bed, there was a cabinet to place her garments in, a small table and a mirror. Additionally, she had her breakfast table and chair, and an alcove with large windows.

After finishing her breakfast, she walked over to the window to get a better idea of the grounds around her.

Hannah's breath caught in her chest as she looked out the window at the rich green forest that lay beyond the manicured gardens of Brighton Abby.

She was sure she understood why it was called such a name now. The sun seemed to touch every top of every tree, extending across the vast array of vegetation that surrounded the house.

Hannah had never seen so much green in all her life all in one place. It was a most enchanting sight to see. Reaching down, she unlatched one of the windows and let the fresh air in.

She was sure even the air smelled better than it did back in London. She closed her eyes for just a moment as she soaked in all the smells and sounds that seemed to engulf her.

Finally glancing down to the watch at her waist, she was startled out of her relaxing meditation. It was now a quarter to nine.

Panic seized her in realizing she had fifteen minutes to get her person to the morning room. Worst of all, she had forgotten to ask Mary how to get there.

If her first impressions of the earl, not to mention the housekeeper's warnings the night before, were any indication, Hannah had a feeling he would not take her tardy appearance lightly.

Read it now!

http://abbyayles.com/AmB11

3

"Please excuse me," Hannah said to a gentleman who was fortunate to be in the hall she was presently searching. "Could you be so kind as to point me to the morning room?"

She recognized the footman as the one who had stoked the fire the night before. He gave her a rather large toothy grin as he looked her over.

"So, you are the new governess, then?"

"Yes, and I am sorry to be rude, but I am a trifle late for a meeting with the earl. If you could quickly point me to the proper room I would be greatly in your debt."

He surveyed her again. Hannah could not have been more grateful for her homely appearance as his eyes drifted over her. Finally, he decided she was wanting, much to her relief.

"Well, you're going the wrong direction to start," he said, not finding much interest in her looks. "Then you will turn right at the main stair and you will find it two doors down in the east wing."

Hannah looked in the direction he was speaking and did her best to remember his words. She nodded her thanks before hurrying back the way she had come.

Luckily, she found the room just as the watch attached to her waist indicated the hour. She breathed a sigh of relief as she knocked promptly on the door.

"Come in," a deep commanding voice called from within.

Hannah opened the door, set her chin at a proper height and entered the room.

She found the earl sitting behind a small writing desk situated in a corner of the room. It was an exquisitely beautiful room with golden wallpaper and floral couches all facing some great windows to the east. It was no wonder this was called the morning room, for the light from the rising sun brought warmth to every inch of it.

"Please have a seat," the earl instructed from behind his writing desk while he continued at his work.

Hannah hesitated for a moment. There was nowhere to sit but on the couches facing the window in front of him. It didn't seem proper to put her back to him as his desk was behind the couches.

"Miss Jacobson, is there a reason why you will not sit?"

he asked rather impatiently as he put his quill down for a moment to study her.

"It is only," Hannah hesitated. "I only wonder if it would be proper for me to sit when the only available seats have my back to you."

"If you would please have a seat, Miss Jacobson, I will join you presently. I am just finishing up some business."

Hannah didn't think his sharp tone was quite necessary. Nonetheless, she seated herself and enjoyed the view out the window as best she could with the sound of his quick writing scratching the parchment behind her.

Finally, the earl finished his note and sealed it for delivery. Once finished, he rose from his seat and came to sit across from her on an opposing couch.

"I apologize for the delay," he said as he attempted to soothe his own nerves. "Have you settled yourself well in your new quarters?"

"Yes, thank you, Lord Grimshaw. They are more than I expected."

"Good. Now let us get on to the business of expectations for the girls' education and your role in the household."

"Of course," Hannah said expectantly.

"My daughters are seven and five. I am sure that you will be most adequate in seeing that they continue in their scholarly education?"

"Yes."

"I would ask that half the day be spent in scholarly learning and the other half in training as proper young ladies. You may organize the day as you wish so long as both of these standards are met."

"I would be happy to impart whatever knowledge you deem necessary."

"I am glad to hear that," Sebastian said, relieved to see the demure lady was all business as was he.

"Now, there are some rules that I must insist you follow while you are here at Brighton Abby. I assure you there is an important purpose for all of them and I would ask you to adhere to them strictly."

"Rule number one, I would ask that you do not go into the local village unless I take you myself."

Hannah's jaw dropped open.

"But, sir, I am not sure I understand the meaning of such a rule. Surely if I go along with other members of the staff that would be sufficient to see me safely there and back. What other purpose could you have for insisting I go only in your presence?"

"Please, I assure you it is for a good reason. I, perhaps, may assign another I feel would be appropriate for the task, but as of right now that is not so. We will go to town each Sunday, and then again once a week on the afternoon of your choosing. Please advise me what day would be best at your earliest convenience so that I may make my own preparations to be available at that time."

Hannah was utterly shocked at his demand as well as his delivery of it. There was no question in his mind that this was completely right to do.

"The second rule pertains to the first. I would ask that each Sunday you attend services with us in our family seat so as to watch the girls."

Hannah was growing increasingly nervous with every rule he announced. Would he insist she be in his presence at all times? Despite her fear she simply nodded in acknowledgment.

"Third, because I am alone in the house with the girls most of the time, I allow them to join me for evening meals. I would ask you to also be in attendance for dinner."

"Lastly," he continued without waiting for her to reply, "while you are here in my employment, I must insist that you do not consort with any members of the opposite sex within the town or the staff unless approved by myself."

"Consort? Opposite sex? I am not sure what you are inferring, Lord Grimshaw," Hannah said, now having heard far too much, "but I am a respectable lady."

"I am not inferring anything, Miss Jacobson. I am sure you are and I would never suggest otherwise. I am merely informing you of these rules for the benefit of my children."

"How could that possibly benefit your girls?"

"I am afraid you will just have to trust me on this one,"

the Earl of Grimshaw said with a stoic face that gave nothing away.

Hannah wasn't sure if she felt more shocked, hurt or insulted after her meeting with the Earl of Grimshaw. How could he have sanely asked such things of her?

She had hoped that this time around she would leave her employment with a promising referral. How could that ever be the case when she couldn't bring herself to agree to such rules?

Of course, she understood the necessity of grooming the girls both in their education and in preparation for their lives as proper young ladies. She also didn't mind the idea of attending to them at church and for supper although it was unorthodox.

She did, however, find herself vastly insulted to be told that she was only allowed out of the house in his presence. How dare the earl infer that she would have inappropriate interactions with members of the male staff and therefore forbid any interaction whatsoever!

It was just the same physically demanding presence of her last employer. Again and again, Hannah had told herself that the baron was just an anomaly and that her next situation would be vastly better. She was beginning to question that sound advice she gave to herself.

Standing outside the schoolroom door she smoothed her apron and took a steadying breath. She knocked first before being called in.

"Good morning, Miss Jacobson," a kind-eyed young girl said, coming to stand in front of her.

She motioned for the two small girls to stand. Hannah took the moment to look her pupils over. They both had the black hair that matched their father. In fact, everything about their demure somber faces reminded her of the earl.

She was immediately drawn to the youngest of the two who looked up at her with the largest brown eyes she had ever seen before.

"I am Abigail, their nurse. This is Lady Caroline and the little one there is Lady Rebecca," the young girl pointed out to Hannah.

Hannah was surprised that such a young girl was their nurse. She looked to be no more than sixteen. She wondered if that perhaps explained why the earl had insisted that it was Hannah who tended to the girls outside of school instead of their nurse.

"It's very nice to meet you, Abigail, as well as both of you, Lady Caroline and Lady Rebecca," Hannah said, smiling down at her wards as soothingly as possible.

"If it is alright with you, I would like to assess what your last governess has already imparted to you before we begin with our own lessons. Would that be alright?"

Both girls first looked at their nurse. Even at her young age, it was clear she was the only consistent mother figure they had had thus far in their lives.

Abigail gave them an encouraging nod and both girls turned to their new governess ready for the task.

"Our last governess would have us sit at the table over there," Lady Caroline said by way of being helpful as Abigail excused herself from the room.

"Thank you, Lady Caroline," Hannah said as she scanned the room and began to take in its layout.

There was a bookshelf amply supplied with resources for Hannah to comb over and use. A warm fireplace to be used in winter months with a comfy chair for her to sit in and read to the children. There was one desk for her use and a small table for the girls' use.

Hannah spent the remainder of the afternoon assessing her two pupils. Rebecca was very young in age, only being five, and was very new in her education. Hannah was sure her education would start at the very beginning. Caroline, on the other hand, was very knowledgeable of her numbers and letters and was even able to demonstrate some exquisite handwriting.

Both girls were very quiet, however, and much of what Hannah came to learn of them was a slow and painful process to draw out.

She did notice that Caroline's eyes also continued to float away from her task at hand. She realized that her first assignment for the child would be to focus on tasks at hand and not get lost in thought.

As the morning came to an end and a servant arrived

with a tray of light luncheon, Hannah was relieved for the break.

Her last pupil, though he truly had taken ill towards the end, had been a wild and rambunctious boy. It was a stark difference to these soft-spoken girls.

"Miss Jacobson," Caroline said after Hannah suggested they take a break for tea and a light meal, "our last governess would always read to us at the end of our lessons."

Her eyes drifted again behind Hannah, and she realized that the child's distraction had been the chair with a book already set on its arm.

"I can tell that you are very intent on having something read to you," Hannah said. "Perhaps it would be worth letting the tea stand a few moments to read just a few pages."

"The book is just there on the chair," Caroline continued encouragingly as she grabbed her sister's hand and seated them both on the carpet.

Hannah had not seen such light lit in this child's eyes thus far. She made a note of Caroline's excitement for storytelling. Perhaps it would be a way to encourage the child to open up more to her.

She followed the girls over, picked up the leather-bound novel and sat down in the chair. It was a very comfortable seat and she couldn't help but also relish the fact of many afternoons seated here reading to the children.

She had just examined the cover of the book when she felt a rustling of her skirts. Hannah felt the chills run up her spine that gave her the distinct indication that a living creature was walking around in her skirts.

Moving the book out of the way she inspected her folds and much to her dismay saw a small lump begin to move beneath the grey fabric. Grabbing the skirt and petticoat in one hand, she removed the fabric and exposed a big fat mouse with its long tail coiled around it.

For a moment Hannah froze to the spot, just watching the mouse nibble on a biscuit piece he had happily in his paws. How a mouse or the biscuit ended up on the chair she didn't care to know.

As sensation returned to her body, she promptly rose from her chair and screamed. The mouse, having been interrupted from his mid-day meal, began to scurry frantically around the seat of the chair, not sure where to go next.

Hannah screamed again. It wasn't the first mouse she had seen, certainly there were plenty in her school growing up. But she had never expected to see one in her seat. She promptly swung the book at the mouse, hoping to put them both out of her misery.

"Don't! Stop!" Caroline stood and screamed herself.

Hannah watched in utter bewilderment as the child grabbed the mouse by its tail and scooped it into her hands where it sat quite peacefully.

"Why would you try to squish Mr. Whiskers?" Lady Rebecca said with tears brimming in her saucer eyes.

Read it now!

http://abbyayles.com/AmBii

SCANDALS AND SEDUCTION IN REGENCY ENGLAND

Also in this series

Last Chance for the Charming Ladies
Redeeming Love for the Haunted Ladies
Broken Hearts and Doting Earls
The Keys to a Lockridge Heart
Regency Tales of Love and Mystery
Chronicles of Regency Love
Broken Dukes and Charming Ladies
The Ladies, The Dukes and Their Secrets
Regency Tales of Graceful Roses
The Secret to the Ladies' Hearts
The Return of the Courageous Ladies
Falling for the Hartfield Ladies
Extraordinary Tales of Regency Love
Dukes' Burning Hearts
Escaping a Scandal

Regency Loves of Secrecy and Redemption
Forbidden Loves and Dashing Lords
Fateful Romances in the Most Unexpected Places
The Mysteries of a Lady's Heart
Regency Widows Redemption
The Secrets of Their Heart
Lovely Dreams of Regency Ladies
Second Chances for Broken Hearts
Trapped Ladies
Light to the Marquesses' Hearts
Falling for the Mysterious Ladies
Tales of Secrecy and Enduring Love
Fateful Twists and Unexpected Loves
Regency Wallflowers
Regency Confessions
Ladies Laced with Grace
Journals of Regency Love
A Lady's Scarred Pride
How to Survive Love
Destined Hearts in Troubled Times
Ladies Loyal to their Hearts
The Mysteries of a Lady's Heart
Secrets and Scandals
A Lady's Secret Love
Falling for the Wrong Duke

ALSO BY ABBY AYLES

The Keys to a Lockridge Heart

Melting a Duke's Winter Heart

A Loving Duke for the Shy Duchess

Freed by the Love of an Earl

The Earl's Wager for a Lady's Heart

The Lady in the Gilded Cage

A Reluctant Bride for the Baron

A Christmas Worth Remembering

A Guiding Light for the Lost Earl

The Earl Behind the Mask

Tales of Magnificent Ladies

The Odd Mystery of the Cursed Duke

A Second Chance for the Tormented Lady

Capturing the Viscount's Heart

The Lady's Patient

A Broken Heart's Redemption

The Lady The Duke And the Gentleman

Desire and Fear

A Tale of Two Sisters

What the Governess is Hiding

Betrayal and Redemption

Inconveniently Betrothed to an Earl

A Muse for the Lonely Marquess

Reforming the Rigid Duke

Stealing Away the Governess

A Healer for the Marquess's Heart

How to Train a Duke in the Ways of Love

Betrayal and Redemption

The Secret of a Lady's Heart

The Lady's Right Option

Forbidden Loves and Dashing Lords

The Lady of the Lighthouse

A Forbidden Gamble for the Duke's Heart

A Forbidden Bid for a Lady's Heart

A Forbidden Love for the Rebellious Baron

Saving His Lady from Scandal

A Lady's Forgiveness

Viscount's Hidden Truths

A Poisonous Flower for the Lady

Marriages by Mistake

The Lady's Gamble

Engaging Love

Caught in the Storm of a Duke's Heart

Marriage by Mistake

The Language of a Lady's Heart

The Governess and the Duke

Saving the Imprisoned Earl

Portrait of Love

From Denial to Desire

The Duke's Christmas Ball

The Dukes' Ladies

Entangled with the Duke

A Mysterious Governess for the Reluctant Earl

A Cinderella for the Duke

Falling for the Governess
Saving Lady Abigail
Secret Dreams of a Fearless Governess
A Daring Captain for Her Loyal Heart
Loving A Lady
Unlocking the Secrets of a Duke’s Heart
The Duke's Rebellious Daughter
The Duke's Juliet

A MESSAGE FROM ABBY

Dear Reader,

Thank you for reading! I hope you enjoyed every page and I would love to hear your thoughts whether it be a review online or you contact me via my website. I am eternally grateful for you and none of this would be possible without our shared love of romance.

I pray that someday I will get to meet each of you and thank you in person, but in the meantime, all I can do is tell you how amazing you are.

As I prepare my next love story for you, keep believing in your dreams and know that mine would not be possible without you.

With Love, Abby Ayles

PS. Come join our Facebook Group if you want to interact with me and other authors from Starfall Publication on a daily basis, win FREE Giveaways and find out when new content is being released.

Join our Facebook Group

abbyayles.com/Facebook-Group

Join my newsletter for information on new books and deals plus a few free books!

You can get your books by clicking or visiting the link below

https://BookHip.com/JBWAHR

ABOUT STARFALL PUBLICATIONS

Starfall Publications has helped me and so many others extend my passion from writing to you.

The prime focus of this company has been – and always will be – *quality* and I am honored to be able to publish my books under their name.

Having said that, I would like to officially thank Starfall Publications for offering me the opportunity to be part of such a wonderful, hard-working team!

Thanks to them, my dreams – and your dreams — have come true!

Visit their website starfallpublications.com and download their 100% FREE books!

ABOUT ABBY AYLES

Abby Ayles was born in the northern city of Manchester, England, but currently lives in Charleston, South Carolina, with her husband and their three cats. She holds a Master's degree in History and Arts and worked as a history teacher in middle school.

Her greatest interest lies in the era of Regency and Victorian England and Abby shares her love and knowledge of these periods with many readers in her newsletter.

In addition to this, she has also written her first romantic novel, *The Duke's Secrets*, which is set in the era and is available for free on her website. As one reader commented, *"Abby's writing makes you travel back in time!"*

When she has time to herself, Abby enjoys going to the theatre, reading, and watching documentaries about Regency and Victorian England.

Social Media

- Facebook
- Facebook Group
- Goodreads
- Amazon
- BookBub